SOUND ADVICE

Matt Bardoul headed for the stable to saddle his horse.

He had thrown the hull on him and was adjusting the cinch when a voice spoke out of the darkness of a stall.

"Matt," he could not place the voice, "I'd git killed for this, if anybody knowed, but *don't go along with that wagon train!*"

"Why? What's going to happen?"

"Dunno. But somethin' . . . ain't none of 'em supposed to come back alive."

"Who's the boss?" he demanded.

There was no reply. He waited a moment, then asked the question again, but there was no answer. His unknown informant was gone.

WESTWARD THE TIDE
LOUIS L'AMOUR

BANTAM BOOKS
TORONTO · NEW YORK · LONDON

WESTWARD THE TIDE

A Bantam Book | February 1977

2nd printing .... *February 1977*	*6th printing* .... *April 1978*
3rd printing .... *March 1977*	*7th printing* .... *June 1978*
4th printing .... *June 1977*	*8th printing* .... *August 1979*
5th printing .. *November 1977*	*9th printing* .... *May 1980*
	10th printing .... *May 1981*

*Photograph of Louis L'Amour
by John Hamilton—Globe Photos, Inc.*

ISBN 0-553-20219-7

Published simultaneously in the United States and Canada

CHAPTER I

Matt Bardoul rode his long legged zebra dun down the dusty main street of Deadwood Gulch a few minutes ahead of the stage. He swung down and tied his horse to the hitching rail, then stepped up to the boardwalk, a tall young man in a black, flat crowned hat and buckskin shirt.

Instead of entering the IXL Hotel and Restaurant, he pushed his hat back on his head and leaned against one of the posts that supported the wooden awning.

In his high heeled star boots with their huge rowelled California spurs, and his ivory-handled tied-down guns, he was a handsome, dashing figure.

It was the summer of 1877 and the "Old Reliable Cheyenne & Black Hills Stage Line" boasted the Shortest Safest, and Best Service in the west. When the stage swung into Main Street Matt Bardoul turned his green, watchful eyes toward the racing six horse Concord and watched it roll to a stop in front of the IXL.

He had kept pace with the stage most of the way from Cheyenne, but aside from the mutual protection from marauding Indians, he had no interest in the stage or its passengers until he saw the girl alight from the stage at Pole Creek Ranch.

He was lifting a match to the freshly rolled cigarette when he saw her, and he looked past the flame into her eyes and something seemed to hit him in the stomach. He stood there, staring, until the flame burned his fingers. He let out a startled yelp and dropped the match, and he saw just the flicker of a smile on her lips as she turned away.

1

He swore softly, staring after her as she walked toward the ranch house, and then he turned back to his horse, but his fingers trembled as he loosened the cinch.

Discreet inquiry, laced and bolstered with a couple of shots of rye, elicited the information from stage driver Elam Brooks that her name was Jacquine Coyle, that she was bound for Deadwood to join her father Brian Coyle, and that she was a pleasant, saucy, and thoroughly attractive young woman.

"Not a kick from her the whole trip!" Brooks said with satisfaction. "Most of these durned stage ridin' females are cantankerous as all get out!"

Stepping from the stage into the dusty street of Deadwood, Jacquine looked up quickly, her alert blue eyes searching the crowd of onlookers for her father or brother. The first person she saw was the tall, narrow hipped and broad shouldered young man leaning so nonchalantly against the awning post.

Instantly she was aware of two things. That he was not at all nonchalant, and that he had been waiting to see her.

This was the man she had seen at Pole Creek Ranch. The man who had accompanied them on horseback. She remembered him very well, both from his picturesque appearance and because of what she had overheard Fred Schwartz, the owner of Pole Creek, say to Elam Brooks.

"There's one man Logan Deane will do well to leave alone!"

"Who is he?"

"Name's Mathieu Bardoul. He's a Breton Frenchman, Maine born, but raised in the west. He was in the Wagon Box Fight."

"The hell you say!" Brooks turned to stare. "Then he's the same Bardoul that killed Lefty King, over at Julesburg!"

"He's the one, all right. Nice fellow to have for a friend, and a bad one with whom to have trouble. If he's ridin' on to Deadwood you won't be surprised by any Indians. He can smell out a bad Indian a mile away!"

All that went through her eyes in the flashing instant their eyes met across the heads of the crowd. She remembered his startled stare at Pole Creek, and now when their eyes met she saw something else, something that left her startled and confused. There was no effort to mask the look in his green eyes. It was the look a man, full in the pride of his strength, gives to a woman he wants.

Her breath caught, and she turned her face quickly, yet she was conscious of a quick, stirring excitement that left her wide eyed and a little breathless.

She had seen that look in the eyes of men before but it had never affected her like this. She knew why men looked at her that way, and it was not merely because she was a young and lovely girl, it was because there was something in her shapely, rounded body that even the voluminous clothes could not quite conceal, something in the way she walked, and some of the same feeling in her eyes that she now recognized in the eyes of Matt Bardoul.

Yet this was different, too. There was something in the lazy negligence of him as he leaned there, the cigarette between his lips, his eyes upon hers, something that went beyond the handsome darkness of his face, the lean strength of his body, or the hard, strong maleness of him.

As she averted her face, her cheeks flushing and her breasts rising under a quick gasp, the crowd parted and a big man in a black beaver hat and Prince Albert coat thrust his way through. "Jackie, honey! It's good to see you again! Where's that brother of yours? Isn't he here?"

"I haven't seen him, Father." For one flickering instant her eyes wavered back to the man under the awning. This time he straightened, and he took his cigarette from his mouth in one quick, impatient gesture, and threw it down.

She had a sudden fear that he would come right

through the crowd, walk right up to her and take her in his arms. The impression was so definite that she turned abruptly away and taking her father's arm, hurried him toward the comparative safety of the IXL.

Matt Bardoul stared after her. This girl he had to have. She stirred something within him that no woman had ever touched, she awakened something in him that left him restless and excited. He liked the proud lift of her chin, liked the blue of her eyes, and liked most of all her awareness of what she was, her knowledge that she was a beautiful and desirable woman.

He had never liked women who avoided recognizing their sex, or avoided the thought of sex. Nor did he like women who so obviously were disappointed they were not men. He had the feeling this girl was alive, knowing and ready, and in her own good time would make a choice. Yet when he turned his eyes away from the door where she had vanished, the memory of the sunlight entangled in the web of her hair, and that quick, frightened look she had given him, remained in his mind.

Something had happened. The thought disturbed and irritated him. He had known many women, but none until now that he knew he had to have. Always before he could mount and ride away, and while he would often remember, he would never feel the urge to go back. Now, he knew that was over. This time he would not ride on.

His thoughts returned to Deadwood. It reminded him of Dodge, Abilene, Tascosa, Hays City or Julesburg. Here it was the lure of gold that brought them, always before in the towns he knew it had been cattle.

There were familiar faces here, faces he had seen in other towns, and some of them he knew, some of them were merely types, the faces of gamblers, bartenders, dance hall girls and their like who followed the quick money and the free spending that characterized the booming west.

This had been, only a few months ago, Indian country. Not much over two years ago Custer had made his fateful ride into the Black Hills, a ride that threw down the gauntlet to the Indians and let them know that even this treaty was to be broken, that even the hunting ground of the Great Spirit was not inviolate. And it was scarcely a year ago that Custer had made that other fateful ride, the one that took him down into the valley of the Little Big Horn and his last great gamble. He wanted one magnificent victory to win favour in the War Department and with the government and people. All he found was tragic defeat from an enemy he despised.

The Sioux had been ready for him. The greatest light cavalry the world had ever seen, and led by men knowing in the ways of war. Crazy Horse and Gall, the great battle leaders of the Sioux, had been waiting for him there. Like Fetterman, Custer had to learn his lesson and die. Like Fetterman he despised the fighting ability of the Indian, and like Fetterman he rode to his death.

The Indians were out there yet along the Big Horn Mountains, along the Powder, the Yellowstone and the Missouri, but never again would they meet the white man in full battle array. Men would be killed along the creeks and the trails, and many a month would pass before it would be safe for a white man to walk unarmed to a corral, or to a spring for water. The power of the Indian had been broken, but the spirit and the resentment lived on.

Gold and Custer had begun the opening of the Black Hills in '74, and nothing could stop the oncoming tide of the white man. Of them all, Spotted Tail was the first to understand and to act upon his knowledge. He saw clearly that the red man had reached the end of the trail and all that remained was to ease the defeat of his people and to find some way of working with the whites instead of fighting them.

Red Cloud too, understood, but for awhile longer he resisted and hated the knowing. He had won his victories. He had driven the white man off the Bozeman Trail, made him abandon his forts, but now he had come to the realization that to win a battle was not to win a war, for the white man kept coming. Now they were here. Men pushed along the dusty streets of Deadwood, the town named for the burnt-off timber along the mountain side. They were shouldering through crowds of their fellows, they were pushing up to bars, buying, selling, talking, robbing, gypping their neighbours. They streamed into the hills with picks and shovels, then days later they streamed back to buy supplies over the counters of hastily built stores or from tents, paying for their purchases in gold dust washed from the hills and creeks.

They sank shafts down to bed rock and dug the gold from the cracks and crevices where it had been accumulating for ages, and then they washed it out and sacked it up. It was gold to pay for the search for more gold, gold to make them wealthy, gold to buy women or liquor, and gold to free them from drudgery.

The moving torrent of men awakened restlessness with Matt Bardoul, and he felt the old urge to get into the drive, to join the crowd, to fight for what gold he could find and come out with wealth if he was lucky or strong. Yet as he watched the pushing and shoving in the street, as he saw their hard, bearded faces, he saw that here there was much that was grand and fine, but underneath it there was something relentless and ugly, too.

For the first time, men had found a continent lying open under their hands, untouched, undefiled. Here, for the first time, men had the opportunity to build a great future, to make a new world of their own, to build on all this natural wealth a world of democracy and freedom.

A few came with the vision, but then the others began to come and they swarmed over the land like locusts, ripping its treasures from the earth, defiling its streams with silt, tearing down the forests and then moving on to desolate new land. All of it in a wild, desperate driving greed, the urge to get while the getting was good.

Courage there was in plenty, and strength. There was rough-handed good fellowship, sympathy for the under-dog, the quick, impulsive, quixotic sympathy of the man who will fight another man for a dollar or an idea and then give the dollar to the first man who passes with a hard luck story.

In the short view there was much good in this westward trek, but in the long view it was a mad rush of greed and rapine, the lust of men who ripped the wealth from the land and then deserted it. And it was a time not soon to pass, for as the first comers moved on the more patient thieves followed them, the fat and the weak who would be content with piling up pennies rather then grabbing the dollars.

Every desire to conserve, to repair the damage to forests or grazing land, or to halt the blind looting of natural wealth would be fought bitterly as an attack upon human rights. It was an epic of strength, of heroism, and of greed.

The first comers skimmed the surface cream, then hurried on to get the cream elsewhere, and behind them came the coyotes and the buzzards to take the scraps from the bones. These slower ones took more years but left greater desolation, and neither the first comers nor the later ones had any thought for the generations that were to come that would be hungry for timber, hungry for minerals, and starving for top soil.

Matt Bardoul was a part of it. Destiny, luck, or call it as you will, decreed that he would be hurled into the seething maelstrom of a new land aborning. And he was one of the few who could see what was happening, who could look upon the scene with some bit of historical perspective.

Like a young man who inherits a fortune the people of the country were spending their birthright in a wild orgy of finance and greed, heedless of the years to come. They were spending their capital without thinking that someday there had to be an end.

Turning on his heel, Matt shoved through the doors of the IXL, and wormed his way through the sweating, laughing, cursing crowd to the bar. He had no more than won his place and called his order to the harried bartender when a bellow broke out behind him.

"Matt! Matt Bardoul! By all that's holy!"

He forced his shoulder around, recognizing the voice, and a grin broke over his sun browned face. A huge, bearded man with almost as much hair on his chest as in his beard was plunging through the crowd.

"Buffalo Murphy! What the hell are you doing in Deadwood? I'd think this was too civilized for you! Last time we were together was up on the Humboldt, and you were headed for the Snake!"

"It's been a long time! Hell, Man! Drink up an' we'll have another!" His shoulder length hair was as impressive as his beard. "I came down from the Yellowstone with Portugee Phillips."

"What's going on around? Anything interesting?" Matt tasted his rye. It was as strong and bitter as Indian whiskey and might have come from the same barrel as the last drink he had in Julesburg, "I'm on the loose," he added, "had an idea I'd ride up to Virginia City or Bannack."

Murphy leaned closer, glancing left and right. "Stick around, boy," he whispered confidentially, "there's something good in the wind. Some of the big men around camp are getting together a wagon train for the Big Horns."

"What is it?"

"Gold." Murphy downed his drink. "Gold from the grass roots down, and lots of it. Creek bottoms covered with it, or so the story goes. I never saw any gold in the Big Horns myself, but then I wasn't huntin' gold, I was after beaver. Father DeSmet always claimed there was more gold there than in Californy."

"Who's back of this? Who found the gold?"

"Man named Tate Lyon. He was prospectin' back in the Big Horns. He found gold, but his partner was killed an' he had to get out, quickest an' best way he could."

"Know him?"

"No, I don't. He's a stranger to me. I'd never seen him before, but Brian Coyle an' Herman Reutz set a lot of store by him, an' they are smart enough."

"How about the Sioux?"

"Quiet since the Custer fight. Terry an' Gibbon hunted them down an' knocked most of the fight out of them. Of course, the Sioux bein' what they are, a body better keep his shootin' iron handy when he rides into the Big Horns."

He grabbed the bottle and filled their glasses. "It ain't the Sioux that's so bad, it's some of these ornery thieves of white men. Lots of killin' goin' on in this camp, an' there's a lot of poison loose here." He looked around at Matt. "Logan Deane's in town."

"Deane?" Matt Bardoul's eyes narrowed at the thought. "The Colorado gunman? I see."

"Thought you'd better know after what happened at Julesburg." Murphy stared into his glass. "Bat Hammer's here, too, an' you'll remember him. An' you may have heard of Spinner Johns? He's a sort of crazy mean killer who came up from the cow camps."

If Logan Deane was in Deadwood it would mean trouble sooner or later. Plenty of trouble. Deane was a brother-in-law to Lefty King, a bad man who had come out on the bad end of a gunfight with Bardoul in Julesburg.

"What's the plan behind this wagon train?"

"This here Tate Lyon went to Herman Reutz with his story and Reutz liked the sound of it. He called in Brian Coyle.

"Coyle was interested, an' he's one of the biggest men in camp. He come in here with a fine outfit an' he's got the money to make more. It seems he'd been discussin' the chances of there bein' gold in the Big Horns with Clive Massey and a former Army officer, Colonel Orvis Pearson."

"I've heard of him."

"Well, the four of them got their heads together an' the plan is to head out to the Big Horns with a party of picked men, nothing but the best in wagons, stock, an' goods. They will trail into the Big Horns, set up their own town, an' file on all the best claims along those creeks."

"Coyle's going himself?"

"Sure! He's the ringleader! Him an' Massey. It's a

closed deal, an' only a few picked men will get a chance to go along. Now if you want to go, I can swing it. They need me, an' I'll refuse to go unless they count you in."

"Who's going to guide them into the mountains?"

"Lyon himself an' Portugee Phillips. Pearson's been selected as commander of the bunch because of his experience. They are plannin' on havin' plenty of fightin' men along just in case. It will be a rich wagon train when it finally pulls out!"

If Brian Coyle was going along there was a good chance his daughter might go, too. Matt reached for the bottle and poured a drink for each. He lifted his glass and looked over it at Murphy "To the Big Horns!" he said.

"That's prime!" Murphy beamed. "You an' me an' Portugee Phillips can handle any passel of Sioux that ever come down the pike!"

There were thirty men and a girl in the back room of Reutz' store at nine that night. Buffalo Murphy pushed his way through the stacks of bales and packing cases to the meeting place. The girl, Matt saw at once, was Jacquine Coyle.

Sitting beside her was a husky, handsome lad with a reckless, goodhumoured smile and a quick, impatient way of moving. His face was just enough of a combination of Brian Coyle's dark heaviness and Jacquine's beauty to prove him a brother. After a quick glance, Matt turned to look over the crowd. If these men were to be his companions on the trail he wanted to see what manner of men they were.

His first impression was good. These were obviously a chosen lot. They had confident, intelligent faces, the sort of men who had done things and could do more. Yet as his eyes strayed over the group they hesitated more than once, for there were faces here of another type of man, and they were not faces he liked.

Portugee Phillips came up to him and held out a hand. This man Bardoul had known and respected for a long time. He was a surly, dangerous ruffian. Of a brusque and quarrelsome disposition, and never believed to be overly honest, he had become on one dark night and the three subsequent days and nights, an almost legendary figure.

In a howling blizzard and bitter cold, the temperature far below zero, Portugee Phillips had made a ride no other man would attempt. He had gone for help after the Fetterman massacre, riding two hundred and thirty-six miles, killing a splendid Kentucky thoroughbred in the process, through the bitterest storm in many years. He saved the garrison, but won the undying hatred of the Sioux, who had never dreamed any human could have done what he did.

Portugee grinned at Matt. "You come along, huh? We need you." His yellowish eyes swept the room, prying, inquisitive, speculative. Matt sensed some undercurrent of feeling in the man, and in his words, and tried to catch his eye, but Phillips would not look at him again. "You come along," he insisted. "We need good men on this trip!"

His expression and manner puzzled Bardoul. Probably he was just imagining things and Phillips had meant no more than he said.

Brian Coyle stepped up behind a large barrel and rapped on the head of it with a hammer. Voices died away and heads turned toward him. Somewhere in the room a man cleared his throat. Coyle glanced around, drawing all attention to him, and then he began to speak. He spoke quickly and well in a deep, strong voice that assured you the man knew full well the method of the public meeting.

"You all understand that you have been carefully selected and called here for a meeting whose purpose is not to be discussed beyond these walls. We expect our secret to get out eventually, but by that time we hope to be well on our way, and hence to arrive far in advance of those who attempt to follow.

"However, for reasons of secrecy we five who have called this group together do not intend to divulge our exact destination. We will only say that we are go-

ing west and that we expect to be at least a month on
the trail, but all are advised to bring supplies and plan
for at least two months.

"There is gold, and plenty of it, at the end of this
trail. We have samples of that gold to show you. We
are not calling you here to do you any favours, but because we know the danger of the country into which
we go and that only a large party of competent men
can hope to survive there. Your safety is our safety,
and vice versa.

"If, after hearing our plans you do not care to join
us, you may withdraw, and we only ask that you say
nothing of our purpose until we are on the trail. Samples of the gold dust, some nuggets, and a few speci-
mens of the ore have been brought here. We had an
assay made of the ore and it runs to three thousand
dollars to the ton!"

There was a low murmur ran through the crowd,
and Matt frowned thoughtfully. That was very rich ore.
Some richer had been found in California, but in very
limited quantity. The listeners shifted their feet and
leaned forward, very interested now.

"We think so much of this project that Herman
Reutz is selling his store and I am closing out my business here. We intend to proceed to the site of the dis-
covery, scatter out and stake the best claims, then build
a town. In that town we will have a store, and each of
you will be a stockholder in that store. We intend to
sell shares here tonight, and while no man may hold
over ten shares, each man must hold at least one."

Elam Brooks arose from his barrel. "What else
does a man need to get in on this deal."

"There must be at least one wagon to every three
men. However, we hope each of you will bring a wagon.
We advocate stocking your wagons with goods the
store can handle or that can be used in trade with the
Indians. Each man must have a saddle horse and
rifle, and the stock must all be sound and in good shape.
Food and ammunition, of course."

Coyle hesitated then, waiting for questions. When

none were forthcoming he turned his head and waved a hand toward Colonel Pearson. "The Colonel here, Colonel Orvis Pearson, is a military man accustomed to command and the handling of large bodies of men. He will be in command of the entire wagon train and all personnel. After we reach the rendezvous, captains will be elected for each of the four companies into which we will divide ourselves.

"Where we are going there is good grass and plenty of water. There is timber for building, and plenty of game as well. As we will be well organized and led, there will be little to fear from the Indians. The original discoverer of this gold will be one guide, and Portugee Phillips, of whom you all know, will be the other."

Listening, Matt Bardoul could see what an attractive setup it was. Certainly, nobody knew the Big Horns better than Phillips, and few knew them as well. The talk Coyle had made was emphatic and to the point, and offered much to be preferred to the usual haphazard organization of wagon trains which were more often than not badly planned and poorly led.

A big, rawboned man got to his feet. "Name of Stark," he said clearly, thumbs hooked in his suspenders, "Aaron Stark, from Tennessee. What about the women folks?"

Brian Coyle smiled. "If you got 'em, bring 'em! I'm takin' my daughter, younder!" He waved a hand at Jacquine, who blushed at suddenly becoming the center of attention, but her chin lifted slightly and she glanced out over the room. Her eyes met Matt's, and he smiled. She lifted one eye brow very coolly, and glanced away.

Coyle faced the crowd. "If you're all agreed," he suggested, "just step over to Clive Massey there and he'll take your money for shares in the company. Then all you have to do is have your wagons at Split Rock Springs, ready to roll at daybreak Tuesday!"

Several men stepped out in a bunch and started for the barrel, and that began it. Without further ques-

tion the crowd lined up to a man, Matt Bardoul with
them. He did notice, however, that the first four or five
men who had stepped out were among those whose faces
had arrested his glance when he first looked at the crowd.

As he neared the barrel where Clive Massey was
taking names and money he got his first look at the
man. Massey was as tall as he himself and a good
twenty pounds heavier, a stalwart, handsome man with
intensely black eyes and a finely clipped black mustache. He wore one gun, low down on his right hip. It
showed slightly under the skirt of his black coat.

Matt had a haunting feeling he had seen Massey
before, but could not place him. Massey wrote rapidly
and as fast as the money was laid down and counted,
he pocketed it.

When Matt stepped up to the barrel, he put down
his money. "Mathieu Bardoul," he said.

There was a sudden movement as a man seated
behind and to the left of Massey turned suddenly to
glance up at Matt. The man was sharp featured with a
hooked nose. His slate gray eyes seemed to have no
depth, and they were disturbing eyes, long and narrow
under the straight bar of his brows and a tight skull
cap of sandcoloured hair. The man stared up at Matt,
unsmiling. "From Julesburg?" he asked.

"I've been there."

Massey looked around. "You know this man, Logan?"

Logan Deane!

Matt's expression did not change. This then, was
the killer, the man reputed to have slain twenty men in
gun battles.

The man at Dean's side was Batsell Hammer.

"Don't reckon I do," Dean said, keeping his eyes
on Matt's "only there was a Matt Bardoul in Julesburg
who was quite a hand with a six-gun."

Clive Massey looked up. Somehow, Matt had the
impression that Massey had been waiting for him, that
he was prepared for him. Why, he could not have
guessed.

Their eyes met. "Sorry," Clive said, "we don't

want any gunfighters. Too much chance of trouble, and we want this to be a peaceful trip."

The room was suddenly quiet, and men were listening. Into that silence Matt dropped his words like a stone into the utter calm of a pool. "If you'll take a renegade like Bat Hammer, you'll take anybody!"

Hammer's face whitened and he came to his feet with an oath. "I don't have to take that!" he shouted.

"That's right," Bardoul replied calmly, "you don't."

Silence hung heavy in the room, and Logan Deane, his thin, cobralike lips parted in a faint smile, watched Matt as a tomcat watches another. Matt was aware of the glance, but his eyes held Hammer's and he waited, his hands hanging loosely at his sides.

Bat's gunhand hovered over his pistol butt, and his eyes held Bardoul's, then slowly his fingers relaxed, and his hand eased cautiously to his side. Abruptly, he sat down.

Massey hesitated no longer. "Who recommended this man?"

Buffalo Murphy stepped forward beligerently. "I did, an' if he don't go, I don't. We need him bad. He knows the Sioux, an' he knows that country."

"With Phillips, yourself and Tate Lyon, I scarcely think we'll need him." Massey's voice was final.

"We'd better take him," Phillips said suddenly. "We need him."

Massey glanced up impatiently. This man, Matt decided, disliked opposition, was impatient of all restraint. Massey was irritated now, and his face showed it.

A recommendation from Phillips who enjoyed the respect of all these men for his knowledge of the country and the Sioux was not lightly to be passed over, yet Bardoul was sure that Clive Massey intended to do just that, but before he could offer further objections, Brian Coyle interrupted.

"What are we waiting for?" he boomed. "Sign him up!"

Only an instant did Clive Massey hesitate, then he wrote down the name and pocketed the money Matt had placed on the barrel head.

Matt did not move.

Massey looked up impatiently, angrily. "Next man!" he said sharply.

"Not yet." Matt Bardoul smiled down at Massey. "I want a receipt."

Clive Massey's eyes narrowed and temper flamed in his face. "Listen!" he snapped. "Do you intend to . . . !"

"This is merely business," Matt interrupted, "no offense intended."

"Give it to him!" Coyle said, waving a hand. "Why not? Come to think of it, I'll want one myself!"

Clive Massey let the air out of his lungs slowly, but anger betrayed itself in his every movement. He wrote out the receipt, and then Buffalo Murphy followed. He demanded and got his receipt. Matt's demand had set a fashion and every man who followed asked for his receipt. Even a few of those who had gone through before Matt did, returned, and asked for them.

If ever he had seen hatred in a man's eyes it had been in Massey's when he looked up at him that last time. From now on Matt knew he could expect no friendship from at least one of the leaders of the wagon train. Yet he could not escape the impression that he had been awaited and that Massey had planned to rule him out. Only he had not expected opposition.

A hand touched his arm. "Matt, don't you remember me?"

He turned, and found himself looking into the grinning face of a sun browned young cowhand. "Ban Hardy! I haven't seen you since we came over the trail from Texas together!"

Massey's eyes were on them. *He'll remember us,* Matt thought, *that's certain.*

"Gosh, Man! It'll be like old times!" Hardy exclaimed. Then he added, "In more ways than one!"

Murphy nodded. "I'm wonderin' some my ownself. But if there's a skunk up the crick, we'll smoke him out!" He shrugged. "No matter. I was aimin' to head back into the Big Horn country an' this is as good a way to go as any!"

Already, Matt reflected, they were taking sides. Clive Massey, Logan Deane and Bat Hammer. There was more than accident in their sitting together, more than accident that Massey had been so determined to weed him out.

Why?

It was a question to which he could find no answer. One thing he did know, and that was that this was only a beginning, and that more was to come between himself and Clive Massey.

And he still had to face Colonel Orvis Pearson.

CHAPTER II

Why had Pearson failed to step forward during the altercation with Massey?

Bardoul puzzled over that the following morning as he sat at breakfast. He knew Pearson hated him and the man would certainly have no desire to see Matt Bardoul accompany a wagon train where he was in command.

Without doubt if he persisted in going along he would be surrounded by men with reason to dislike or hate him. Colonel Orvis Pearson would be in command, and Clive Massey was unquestionably one of the leaders, while Logan Deane and Batsell Hammer had no cause to like him. Yet on the other side of the ledger he had such friends as Buffalo Murphy and Ban Hardy.

Why had Portugee Phillips wanted him along? The two had never been particularly friendly in the past, although each knew and respected the other's ability. Did Phillips know something unknown to the others? Or did he merely suspect something?

Regardless of enemies or danger, Matt knew he was not going to drop out. Jacquine Coyle was going along, and that was reason enough for him.

The tall girl with the red gold hair and blue eyes had upset him more than he cared to admit. Yet when he thought of her now he recalled some words he had heard once: There are in a man's life certain ultimate things, and just one ultimate woman. When a man finds that woman he does not pass on, unless he is a fool.

"And I'm not passing on!" he said aloud.

Murphy turned his head and looked at him, then

grinned understandingly. "Talkin' to yourself, huh? I do it, myself. It means you've been alone too long!"

Matt nodded thoughtfully. "Maybe you've hit it," he said, "and I think you have."

He remembered suddenly and turned to look at the burly mountain man. "Buff, didn't you have a squaw back in the Big Horns?"

"Sure did!" Murphy beamed at the memory. "Arapaho, she was an' a durned good un, too! Most ways, that is. Bought her off ol' Bear Paw Henderson! Give a dozen prime beaver for her, an' a spotted pony I took off a Crow whose aim was bad.

"Nearly killed me, he did. Shot at me an' missed. I shot at him an' didn't!"

Murphy nodded musingly. "Yessir! Quite a squaw, she was! Bear Paw, he had her from her Pa, ol' Broken Hand, the Arapaho chief?"

"What became of her?"

"Her?" Buffalo furrowed his brow. "Let's see, now. She was the one just afore the big snow . . . nigh as I can recall I sent her back to her Pa.

"Uh huh, that was it! I give her three buffalo hides an' a couple of ponies . . . that steeldust was limpin' in the off hind leg, anyway. Gettin' crabby, that squaw was. Wanted to settle down with the Injuns!"

"Only one way to handle a woman, my old man used to say," Ban suggested, "an' that was to whup 'em good with a trace chain the fust time you took 'em home. Then whup 'em good once a week for the fust three weeks, an' after that all you have to do is just rattle the chain!"

Ban Hardy drained his coffee cup and got to his feet. "Got you an outfit yet, Matt? If you ain't, I got me a German spotted who brought five wagons down from St. Cloud, up in Minnesota. He's got good teams, too."

"Let's go then," Matt said, "I'll need a wagon."

"You buyin' oxen or mules?" Ban wanted to know.

"Better git oxen," Murphy suggested. "If'n you have to, you can always eat them. I never did cultivate no taste for mule meat, though I've set up an' et it a few times, an' mighty durned glad to have it, too! Oxen are much better, an' there's more meat on 'em, an' anyway, they pull better on ground where there's no trail."

Brian Coyle was obviously a leader, and an able man. Yet when Matt considered it he was afraid that Coyle's leadership might extend only as far as the boundary of a reasonably civilized town or locality. He was a politician, an organizer, and a planner. He knew how to talk to men, but how good he would be out on the trail when the going got rough was yet to be determined. When faced with violence he might not have what was needed. And he might.

Clive Massey was a dangerous man. There was a reckless fury in him that was easily aroused, and that coupled with his driving strength and natural cunning would make him a man to be reckoned with.

Massey had seemed to sit too close to Logan Deane and Batsell Hammer to be completely honest, and while it was early to form any judgments, his actions and his tempers were unfavourable. The two men had been in Deadwood and this part of the west longer than Massey, and they might have been posted near him to render judgment on men whom Massey did not know.

Thus far there was no reason for suspicion. Nor so far had any visible opportunity for dishonesty shown itself. Nothing had been sold, nothing promised. It was all on a strictly voluntary basis. Yet his instincts and his knowledge of men warned him that something was amiss.

Of course, had he not made his own demand it was probable none of the men would have had a receipt for their money, but such things were of little importance as men seldom resorted to legal practices to make recovery of either money or property. Judge Colt usually presided at such disagreements and his decisions left no ground for appeal.

That a few of the men with the wagon train might be outlaws or the next thing to it was no cause for alarm. The west was not made up of noble, God-fearing heroes. Many of the men and women on the westward trek, and often enough the bravest of them, were criminals or worse. Portugee Phillips, of whom little good could have been said before his almost legendary ride through the blizzard, was one of these.

He had been respected for his Indian lore and knowledge of the country, but disliked for his surly temper and uncertain honesty. Yet in the pinch, when honest men had cowered in fear of the deadly cold, the blizzard and the Sioux, it had been Phillips who risked death to ride for help.

While the men of this wagon train were a chosen group, they were of a part with all those who migrated west. The United States had been settled to a great degree by the economic failures of Europe, albeit the ones with courage enough to attempt a change. The wealthy and satisfied do not migrate, they stagnate.

Even those who offered religion as a reason for migration were also those who were impoverished. Many Puritans and Quakers remained in England, but they were those who had much to lose and little to gain. It was the peasants, the lower middle class, and a few adventurers or impoverished noblemen who settled America.

The thirty men who were to form the nucleus of the new venture were like any such group that might have been chosen from a boom town. They were selected to the degree that they were better equipped physically and in a material way to face the ordeals and trials of beginning a new community in a wild and dangerous country.

Phillips, Murphy, Hardy and himself were all experienced western men. The same could be said of the former stage driver, Elam Brooks.

Aaron Stark, the hillbilly, was a lean and cold-eyed man who feared God and nothing else. He carried his squirrel rifle like an extension of his arm, as indeed it was, and he was the sort of man who would last in any venture. The juices of his hard, sinewy body had been drained away by hard living until he was one rawhide piece of toughness and durability.

Improvident in the sense that he would never ac-
cumulate much, he nevertheless possessed all the quali-
ties of the pioneer. He had courage, hardihood, and a
stubborn will that balked at no problem as too great.
In later years, in a tamed down and more civilized
world his kind would be wasted, they would become
drifting outcasts, scorned and betrayed, drifting on with
their eyes forever searching for some new, distant
horizon. They would find names for them, and call
them "Okies" and "Arkies" and they would be despised
by fatter and more adjusted men. It would be forgotten
that it was of such stuff that the pioneers were made,
the ones who always had the courage to move on.

During the growth and expansion of the nation he
was the durable body of the wagon train personnel. He
was the man who refused to remain close to forts and
so was often killed by Indians, his wife nursed her
children with a rifle across her knees, and he tilled his
fields with a gun strapped to his plough handles. He
dared off Indians, the big cattlemen, the outlaws. He
was the nester, the squatter, the man who moved west.

Eventually, thrown back upon themselves, their
horizons lopped off by the sea they would circle like
migratory birds with no place to light. Yet these were
the people who dared, the people who died for their
land, but they rarely died alone, and not always in vain.

From the source from which they sprang came an
inexhaustible supply. Fatter, weaker, home staying men
might deride them and betray them, yet when the
Aaron Starks had opened up the land, they would
follow on and buy up their land in tax sales or mort-
gages to grow fatter and weaker on the land these others
had fought to win.

Wherever there was a frontier there were men like
Aaron Stark, strong, silent, ignorant men who knew
only the longing for home and land. The others came
to loot, but the Aaron Starks brought their families
along, and of all who came west they alone came to
build, to remain, not to loot.

Railroads came west on government subsidy and
gifts of government land. They never advanced a foot

without government land to sell, government money to spend, and the protection of the Army. The Aaron Starks asked no protection from anybody, or if so, not for long, but moved out ahead of the Army wherever their path was not blocked by too tight a line, and where they stopped they put down roots.

Remembering the faces of the men in the store's back room, Matt Bardoul considered this. He had travelled and read enough to possess some historical perspective. He could in a sense see what was coming. He had seen the beaver dwindle away on the streams, and he had witnessed the slaughter of the buffalo under the get-rich-quick rifles of the hide hunters.

This was only secondarily a colonization, it was a huge rat race after wealth, a fierce, dog-eat-dog struggle to get yours before the others did. It was a fantastic, grandiose, brutal fight for wealth, the fiercest tide of greed that ever swept across the continent, and the end was not yet. There could be no end until the land was left a desert, raped and looted by a people who too often built only for now and never for tomorrow.

Nobody had come to the Black Hills because they were beautiful. They came only because there was gold, and they came to get the gold and get out. One of them, writing in his diary in that same year of 1877, expressed the feelings of all. "My intention was to make money, to get rich; at that time no one was there for pleasure."

Elam Brooks and Aaron Stark were good men, substantial men. Neither of them would ever grow wealthy. Their type is always engaged in a heartbreaking struggle to make a living and to rear their families, and they always have big families, but they are families with staying power. They were families of tall sons and daughters who would have more sons. They had vitality, and from their kind came many of the best men the new land was to know.

With some awareness of what lay ahead, Matt Bardoul considered these things. He knew now that his days of hit-and-miss rambling were over. The west had been a gigantic field for exploration. He wanted to know, to see, to understand. Now, when he remembered the red gold hair and blue eyes of Jacquine Coyle, he knew the time had come to stop, to build, to make a life he could share.

So one by one he began to assay the metal of the men who were to travel with him. Of Brooks and Stark he had no doubt. These were good men, sincere men, strong men. Coyle himself was a man of civilization, yet he seemed to have the quality the frontier demanded.

There were others who would bare study. The lean, slab-sided Iry Jackson, burly Lute Harless with his foghorn voice and bulging eyes. Larson, the big, slow moving Swede, and the Jew, Rabun Kline. These men promised well, and no doubt there were others.

Of Pearson he already knew too much, yet he hesitated to form too decided an opinion, for experience might have wrought some change. Nothing Matt Bardoul had seen on the frontier impressed him with military men or their ability, even in their own field. Steeped in tradition, they were bound in a lockstep of ritual and a chain of command that throttled initiative. They were a mill that ground slowly and exceedingly fine, and more often than not by the time the grinding had ceased the need for flour was gone.

The Fetterman Massacre had only served to convince him of his judgment. He had seen Major Powell, an experienced Indian fighter, outranked for command of a rescue party by Fetterman. Then Fetterman, disdainful of the Indians' fighting ability, had gone out and pursued a few scattered Indians over a ridge. It was a trap in which his entire command was wiped out.

The only two men in the lot who fought with any skill or ability were two civilian guides who had been found, ringed with pools of blood where their enemies had fallen.

The case was not isolated. The mountain men fought the Indians when necessary, lived with them, hunted with them, and kept peace with them for the most part, but when they did fight, they usually won.

Pearson was a spit and polish soldier, narrow and self-centered, far from the best of his lot, but better than the worst.

They found Hardy's German sitting in front of his tent, a squat, red-faced man with cropped blond hair and a blond walrus mustache. His wagons were good and his teams better. When the trading was over, Matt had bought two wagons, Hardy another, and Murphy, despite his objections to encumbering himself, a fourth.

Twice during the two days that followed Matt glimpsed Jacquine Coyle from a distance, and both times she was with Clive Massey.

Matt wasted no time in preparations. His decision had been made and he hurried to buy the supplies he wanted, and then the three of them drove out to the rendezvous followed by a man named Bill Shedd whom Bardoul hired.

On the second day after the meeting the man had approached him on Sherman Street. "Seen you at the meetin'," he said. "I had me a wagon but lost her in a poker game. Coyle said if I could latch onto a job as a driver I'd still be one of the train."

"All right." Matt liked the look of the man. He was big, awkward, but kindly looking, and seemingly as powerful as one of the oxen he wished to drive. "You've latched on. Have you got a rifle?"

"Uh huh, a rifle an' a short gun, an' a fair to middlin' cowpony."

"What kind of rifle?"

"Winchester .44."

"Good! Mine's the same, so we won't be worried about having ammunition for you." Matt reached in his pocket and dropped a couple of gold coins in the man's hand. "That'll keep you until we leave, but be ready to go on time. Understand?"

By the next morning there were forty wagons at the rendezvous and most of them had come in during the night. Some of the wagons were carrying passengers with their weapons and tools. They were a rough, hard bitten lot, but good fighting men. Matt strolled aimlessly about, keeping his eyes open. Around the wagons of Deane, Bat Hammer, and a few of their like there seemed to be a preponderance of armed men. In each of those wagons rode two extra men, and a rough, surly lot they were.

"Murphy," he said thoughtfully, "we've got four wagons among the three of us, four men to four wagons, counting Shedd. I was just over near Deane's wagon. He's got two hard cases riding with him, and the wagon is loaded light for three men. Hammer has two riding with him, and so has Hatcher. Strikes me they are long on tough men, an' short on supplies an' equipment."

Murphy nodded, lifting one booted foot to a wagon tongue. He said nothing, but his eyes squinted toward Deane's wagon, and his expression was thoughtful.

The IXL Dining Room was crowded when Matt arrived in town Monday afternoon, but he pushed his way inside, looking for a table. His eye caught the eye of Brian Coyle who was seated at a table with Clive Massey and Jacquine. There was an empty chair, and when Coyle recognized him he stood up and waved for him to join them.

"Sit down, boy! Sit down! If we're all going on this trip together we might as well get acquainted!"

He gestured. "My daughter, Jacquine and Mr. Massey you've met. Jacquine, this is Matt Bardoul."

Matt bowed gravely, his eyes on Jacquine's, then he seated himself and slid his black hat under the chair. Jacquine lifted her cup and glanced at him over the rim, her eyes amused and faintly curious.

There was quality in this girl, something slim and handsome and finely tempered as a Kentucky thoroughbred. The red gold of her hair against the smooth beauty of her cheek stirred him, and he had trouble keeping his eyes from one flaming tendril of hair that brushed like living fire against the soft whiteness of her neck.

"You've been to the Big Horns?" Coyle asked, looking him over with interest.

"Yes, I was there a few years ago during the Indian trouble."

"You know the Sioux?"

He shrugged. "Some, I expect. Jim Bridger was probably the only white man who knew them well, but Phillips and Buffalo Murphy both know them."

"Will they make trouble for us?"

"Certainly." Matt buttered a piece of bread. "They won't attack a party of our size, although they might even try that, but they are more likely to try to pick off any stragglers or run off our stock. Most of the big chiefs of the Sioux and Cheyenne are on reservations now or in flight, and their statesmen, the ones like Red Cloud, Spotted Tail or John Grass have become men of peace."

"Statesmen?" Massey smiled, his dark eyes amused "That's scarcely the term for a savage, is it?"

"It's the right term for some of them, and especially for the ones I mentioned. A much better term than savage. There is always a question as to who is the savage and who is not. The Indian was a nomadic people who kept this country in a condition suited to his needs. He felt no necessity for complexity, he was content with the land, the buffalo, the beaver, and the wild game of other kinds. The land remained unchanged, and there was no necessity for change.

"The white man came and the beaver are gone, the buffalo are going. The white man cuts the timber along the streams so the rain rushes unchecked into the streams and causes floods that formerly the roots and brush held back. Already, in some places, he is putting too much stock on the grass, overgrazing the country.

"Time alone will tell what this will mean to the country, but for one, I don't like the look of it.

"As to being statesmen, what is a statesman? I think he's a leader who serves best the interests of his people, and the Indians I mentioned have done that, to the best of their ability against what some might consider a superior barbarism.

"If one is to consider oratory as part of a statesman as some people seem to believe, I believe the

Indian surpasses any people in history, not excepting the Greeks and the Romans. Had the Indians possessed a Plutarch, you might agree with me."

"You wouldn't compare Red Cloud to Cato?" Brian Coyle asked, interested but incredulous.

Matt took a swallow of coffee. Jacquine was looking at him, surprise in her eyes, and he was pleasantly conscious that her interest was intrigued. The subject interested him, and he nodded a response to Coyle's question.

"Yes, I would. For apt or picturesque expression I doubt if anyone could surpass the orators of the Sioux or Cheyenne, but their greatest asset is the greatest asset of any speaker . . . they have simplicity of statement, a gift for direct phrasing.

"In all recorded history there is no more tragic epitaph to a beaten, dying people who have been robbed of their birthright than that uttered by Spotted Tail when he said, 'The land is full of white men; our game is all gone, and we have come upon great trouble.' "

"You speak well yourself, Bardoul," Coyle said with interest. "Where did you attend school?"

"I didn't. And it seems to me the advantage of academic education is somewhat overrated. Excellent, perhaps, if one takes full advantage of it, but how many do? Benjamin Franklin and Abraham Lincoln were self-educated. As for myself, I've done a lot of reading."

Clive Massey studied Matt thoughtfully, aware of a growing uneasiness. He could sense Jacquine's interest and the growing friendship of Coyle himself, and it was no part of his plan to allow that. "From what I hear," he said casually, "you learned other things on the frontier besides sympathy for the Indians. I've heard you were quite good with a gun, good enough to have killed fourteen men."

Steel glinted in Matt's eyes, but he smiled. "We live as best we can in the west, and it isn't a tame country. Sometimes," his eyes were bland and innocent, "it is necessary to protect the innocent against the plans of the criminal."

It was a chance remark, but Matt saw Massey's face darken and knew he'd landed a good one. Massey started to speak, but Matt avoided the issue by turning to Jacquine. "You like the west?" he asked.

"What I've seen of it is wonderful!" she exclaimed. "However I don't believe all this killing I hear about is necessary . . . nor do I like killers!"

Her eyes flashed, and when he smiled, he saw resentment flare up.

"Now, Jackie," her father interposed, "that's not a good way to speak."

Matt pushed back his chair and got to his feet. "On the contrary," he said, "I like it. I'm a direct person myself, and I always believe in saying what I think and in expressing my intentions." He turned his head sharply toward Massey. "Don't you?" he demanded.

Clive Massey jerked. Then anger flooded him. The question had caught him off balance and that filled him with irritation. He looked up at Bardoul. *I'll kill you someday!* he thought, but even as he thought it, he smiled. "Yes, I do. Of course!"

Matt picked up his hat and turned away through the crowd, but as he went he saw a man standing against the wall waiting for a table. The fellow's eyes met his, and he looked away, blushing oddly. Matt glanced at him again. He was a slender fellow with brown hair and dark brown eyes, curiously soft. Oddly disturbed, he walked on outside.

Behind him, Jacquine watched him go. She turned toward Massey. "Who is he? I mean, what do you know about him?"

Massey shrugged. "A drifter and a gunman. He was a trail driver, and they are all a pretty rough crowd. He always has money and never seems to work, but just what he is or does I don't pretend to know."

"I think you do him an injustice," Coyle objected. "He strikes me as a strong, capable young man."

Clive Massey excused himself and wandered out to the bar. He was irritated and disturbed. That remark of Bardoul's about protecting the innocent against criminals hit too close to the truth to make him happy.

Could something of their plan have leaked out? He dismissed the thought. That wasn't possible.

He could surmise, but he could not actually know. He was irritated that his plan rested on such a shaky foundation, for he had hoped to eliminate all such men as Bardoul and Murphy, for they knew the Big Horns too well.

Something would have to be done about Matt Bardoul.

He thought of Logan Deane. It was too soon to use him, for Deane must remain a sheathed sword to be used only in dire necessity. A killing now might frighten off many of their best men if it was done by Deane, who was going along. Hammer was of no use for he had already backed down from Bardoul. If Bardoul were dry gulched now the finger of suspicion would point directly at Hammer, and Massey was under no misapprehension about his tool. Under pressure Bat Hammer might talk.

Then he thought of Spinner Johns.

That would serve a double purpose for then he would be rid of Johns as well. If there was a killing Johns could be persuaded into flight, and above all, Massey did not want him along. He was too volatile a substance, dangerous as a cobra, and uncertain as Texas weather.

Johns sat at a table occupied by Tate Lyon and Batsell Hammer. Massey avoided them as much as possible, both because he disliked the men personally and because it would do him no good to be seen frequenting the company of such characters. This was a necessity, and no time for hesitation.

Tate Lyon was a man of slightly less than medium height, always unshaven, always untidy. His buckskins were odorous and shabby, and between his lips he carried the stub of an old pipe. His lips were thick and loose, and he continually kept them working around the stem of the pipe, shifting it from place to place in his lips.

He glanced up at Massey, and put down the greasy deck of cards he had been riffling. "Look," he said,

"ain't there some way we can get rid of that Bardoul?
He knows that Shell Creek country, an' knows it a
durned sight better than I do. I'm afraid when he finds
out where we're headed he'll smell a rat."

"What difference would it make?" Hammer demanded. "They couldn't prove nothin', an' we could
always say they was tryin' to talk folks out of it so they
could get it all for themselves."

Massey drew a long black cheroot from his pocket
and lighted it. Tate Lyon had expressed his own fears,
and from the conversation at dinner he was aware that
if anything was to be done there was no time for delay.

Their plan was well conceived and with any sort
of luck could be carried through without a hitch. Once
the wagon train was well on the trail to the Big Horns
he would know how to handle the situation. Bardoul
and Murphy were the two most likely to dissent from
the carefully prepared plans laid down by himself, and
while he believed Coyle would listen to him, the men
had a good deal too much sense not to pay attention to anything Matt Bardoul would say.

There were going to be times when the movements of this wagon train would seem very erratic to a
man who knew the country.

"Gettin' rid of him ain't goin' to be so easy,"
Hammer said, "that Coyle has taken a fancy to him,
an' you all heard Phillips speak up for him. They all
know that, so we've got to be careful."

Spinner Johns' nose was like a parrot's beak and
his face was cold. He had been long in the west and
yet no sun seemed ever to tan his face. It was white
and still, almost without whiskers and without lines.
"Why not kill him?" he said. "Why fool around?"

Hammer glanced at him. "He ain't easy killed.
I've seen him throw a gun an' I don't want any part of
him."

"*You* don't," Spinner sneered. He lighted a cigar
and looked at Massey through the flame of the match.
"That doesn't speak for me. I'll cut him down, all neat
an' pretty . . . for a price."

Massey looked around the room uneasily. There

was no evading the issue now. He would have preferred to get Johns off to one side and make the issue plain without putting it into bald words.

He wanted Matt Bardoul out of the picture but he had no idea of eliminating himself. Under most circumstances he would have welcomed a fight with Bardoul, but at the moment it would have been the worst possible thing for him to attempt. Looking at the matter cold-bloodedly, he was quite sure he could kill him, but the reaction would be most unfavourable to his plans.

Spinner Johns would not hesitate to take the job, he knew that. The gunman from the Rio Grande was one of the most poisonous of the breed, a sure thing killer but one who was lightning fast. Left alone he was sullen and morose, contemptuous and irritable. When he killed he exploded into a blind, murderous rage that would not leave him until his guns were empty. He would kill a man without a gun as quickly as one who was armed. He would abide by no rules, and eaten by envy and hatred, he was like a rattlesnake during the blind, and would strike out viciously at anything that moved near him.

Clive Massey knew something of the man's reputation, and in a country where there were many bad men, Spinner Johns ranked with the worst. Born in Missouri he had migrated with his family to the Texas border country, and when sixteen he killed a man near Uvalde. The man was unarmed at the time, and Johns left the country with speed. Joining a trail herd from the Brazos, he rode north up the Chisholm Trail earning a reputation for being surly and dangerous, quick to flare into temper, yet when he cared to work, a top hand. He rarely cared to work.

In Hays City he downed two men in a gunfight, neither of whom died, but the fight served to class him, in the minds of many with that fast shooting Texas crowd made up of such names as Clay Allison, Manning Clements and Wes Hardin.

Idling about Abilene he was suspected of two cold blooded murders for robbery, but there was no proof. He left town and rode north with a trail herd for the Gallatin Valley in Montana, but his stay with the herd was short lived. In a minor argument at breakfast he drew and killed one of the hands riding the trail with him, and left the outfit hotly pursued by a dozen of the dead man's friends. He escaped, then rode back after dark and emptied his rifle into the men gathered around the fire, killing one and injuring two.

He killed his fourth man in Spearfish and then came on over to Deadwood.

Massey understood the nature of the man well enough. He had seen that killing in Spearfish and knew that Johns had lightning speed with a gun. If he killed Bardoul, and he was sure to, no one would blame anyone but Johns. If both men were killed, that would be best of all, and if the Spinner outlived the fight, then was dry gulched, there would be no more than a hearty sigh of relief around Deadwood.

First things came first, and Massey drew some money from his pocket and casually counted out two hundred dollars, then he looked up at Spinner.

With a sweeping gesture, Johns raked in the money with his left hand. "If anybody hears of this," the gunman's eyes pinned Hammer and Lyon to their seats as a collector pins an insect, "I'll kill more than one man!"

Hammer touched his tongue to his lips and swallowed. Lyon shifted in his seat and stole a look at Clive Massey. Tate Lyon was learning things himself, he was learning that he had failed to estimate Massey properly, and the knowledge frightened him. Massey was not just a money hungry and crooked tenderfoot as he had believed, but fully as cold blooded and a lot smarter than Spinner Johns.

For an instant, Johns let the cards run through his fingers to the table top, looking from one to the other of the three men. Then, he walked through the crowd, which parted before him, and stepped out on the boardwalk in front of the IXL. He had no idea where Matt Bardoul would be, but that he would be somewhere along this street was probable.

He stepped down into the dust and mingled with

the moving crowd, his guns loose in their holsters, his yellow eyes roving from side to side like those of a caged beast. Even those who did not know him avoided his path after one glance at the guns and the restless irritation so visible in the man.

The Spinner's eyes shifted, already ugly at not seeing Bardoul. He was going to earn this money quickly. It wasn't much but all he needed was a glimpse of Matt Bardoul, then he would kill him.

CHAPTER III

Jacquine arose from the table to see her brother push his way into the room. He waved at her over the heads of the crowd, then shouldered his way to her side.

His eyes were bright with excitement. The rough, masculine good nature, the shouts and yells, the cracking bull whips and jingling spurs seemed to have done something to him. Nineteen now, Barney Coyle had moved suddenly from a settled society and a regulated existence to frontier life, and for the first time he realized he was at home. This was his life, this was for him.

"Let's go see the town, Sis! There's no use you being cooped up in that crummy hotel room all day! The chances are you'll never see Deadwood again, so you might as well make the most of it."

"I'm not sure," her father's voice was dubious. This daughter of his worried him. Barney was falling into frontier life as though born to it, and Brian Coyle was enormously proud of his son, but Jacquine defeated him. He knew the frontier was no place for a girl, especially one as delicately nurtured as Jacquine had been. Yet there was a sparkle in her eyes and a lift to her chin that made him uneasy. What he had failed to understand was that she possessed just as much of the frontier spirit and his own blood as did Barney. "I'm not sure whether it would be a good idea," he continued, "this is a rough town, and some of these men would do anything!"

"I'll take care of her!" Barney loved his sister and was immensely proud of her. "Anyway," he grinned at her, "if anybody got hold of her they'd wish they hadn't. Believe me, Dad, this daughter of yours is bred back to a wildcat!"

"Barney!" she exclaimed reprovingly, but secretly the remark pleased her. She disliked the timid females who were all ruffles and flutters. She liked to be considered and treated as if she were self sufficient, and she knew that compared to most women, she was surprisingly so.

It had been one of the things she liked about Matt Bardoul. He looked at her as if she were a woman, and not as if the thought of sex would shock her to the roots of her being. He looked at her and treated her as an equal, without the usual soft talk or flattery men were always directing her way. She had grown to dislike the immediate change that came into their voices when they started talking to her.

She was beautiful and perfectly aware of the fact. Her common sense told her that few girls ever seemed as attractive to men as she, yet the thought did not impress her. While aware of her beauty, it had become for her one of the accepted facts of the life she lived, like the sun coming up and the stars appearing. The compliments it drew she received politely, but a little impatiently, for she was much more eager to be accepted and liked as a person.

It pleased her that Barney wanted her along, that he thought of her now, for she could see how the place had excited him, and how quickly he was fitting into the life around him.

The street was crowded with men. A huge, bearded man, even larger than Buffalo Murphy, turned to stare at her, his bold eyes sweeping her up and down in mingled admiration and astonishment. Half nettled and half amused, she stopped abruptly, put her hands on her hips and demanded, "What's the matter? Haven't you ever seen a lady before?"

The big man blushed magnificently, but through his embarrassment crowded some of his almost forgotten gallantry. He swept his hat from his head and bowed low. "Ma'am," he said sincerely, "now that I've seen you I doubt that I ever did see one before! And none half so beautiful!"

Jacquine blushed then, but her eyes laughed with him. "Thank you, sir!" she said, then turned and took Barney's arm.

He grinned at her. "Sis, if you start that out here you'll have the whole town fighting over you in no time!"

The street was scarcely more than a narrow alleyway of dust between the two rows of frame or log buildings, some of them false fronted, a few possessing boardwalks and awnings, but most fronting right on the dust, or occasionally hard packed earth of the roadway. Farther up the street near the tailor shop, a placer mine still occupied the center of the street, and traffic curved around it.

A six mule team was plodding down the street, the canvas cover removed from the high wheeled, heavily constructed wagon. Two men with broad hats and sleeves rolled up sat atop the load of logs. A bright new axe was struck into the log near one of them.

The signs were all of a pattern, long rectangles in shape each one extending out over the walks to catch the eye of all who glanced down the street. Deadwood Gulch was wide open, to the world and all its races and peoples, Indians, Chinese and Negroes mingled on an equal footing, ate together, drank together, and worked together. Already Deadwood was in a fair way to acquire the largest Chinatown ever acquired by any town of its size this side of China.

Suddenly a knot of men exploded out of a doorway and two of them hit the street in a lump. The first one up rushed at the other and aimed a kick at his head, but the fellow rolled out of the way and charged from a crouching position, his head butting the first man in the stomach and knocking him into the dust.

The fellow came up and as the redhead closed in, he swung a ponderous fist that missed, and then the two stood there, slugging furiously with no advantage either way. Suddenly the redhead stepped back and drew the back of his hand over his bleeding lips. "Oh, the hell with it!" he said. "Let's have a drink!"

The crowd roared approval, and mopping sweat and blood from his face with a torn sleeve, his opponent threw an arm over his shoulders and the whole crowd trooped back inside.

On the butt end of a log near the placer claim a drunk sat with his forearms resting on his knees, staring down the street through a haze of alcoholic wonderment and doubt. Someone at the other end of town fired a pistol into the air.

"Like it?" Barney squeezed her arm.

"Like it?" she looked about her with bright, excited eyes. "Oh, Barney, I *love* it! It's dirty, dusty, bloody and sort of awful, but it's wonderful!"

He nodded. "That's just the way I feel, Sis! Gosh, I'm sure glad Dad decided to come west! This is so much better than sitting around getting stiff and old in that town of ours! It was pretty, but this is a man's world!"

A man shoved by them, then turned and grabbed Barney's arm. "You're young Coyle, aren't you?" He glanced left and right. "Have you seen Bardoul? You know, that big fellow who runs with Buffalo Murphy?"

"Don't think I know him," Barney said, hesitantly.

"I do!" Jacquine said quickly. "What's the matter?"

"Somebody started the story around that Spinner Johns is gunning for him. For God's sake, if you see him before I do, warn him in time! Johns is a killer!"

Barney scowled, torn between excitement and duty. "Sis," he said doubtfully, "maybe I'd better take you back to the hotel. If there's going to be a gun fight I don't want you to get hurt!"

She caught his sleeve. "Barney, who is Spinner Johns?"

Barney looked at her, worried. "Sis, I don't know much about him, just sort of talk around town. He's a gunman. The kind we've heard Uncle Jack tell about, like those fellows down in Texas or Kansas. He killed a man just a few nights ago over in Spearfish."

He scowled. "Did you say you knew Matt Bardoul?"

"He was at our table last night for awhile and he's one of the men who are going on the trip with us. He rode up from Cheyenne alongside the stage I came up on, too. He seems nice."

As she spoke, she seemed to see him again as she had seen him last, rising from the table in the IXL Dining Room. How tall he was! And how easily and gracefully he moved!

She remembered the day she had seen him at Pole Creek Ranch, and how strangely the expression in his green eyes changed, eyes that could look so humorous and amused as if he always found something that brought a smile almost to his lips, yet they were eyes that could be filled with such fire that it startled and excited her. Yet she recalled the look she had seen him throw at Clive and there had been no softness or fire in his eyes then, only a cold green light, flat and deadly.

"He's a gunman, too, I think," she said, her eyes scanning the street for a glimpse of him, "but we should warn him, Barney. He's one of us, in a way."

"Come on, then! Let's find him!"

Barney took her arm once more and they started through the crowd, and as they moved she glanced up at this new brother of hers, amazed at the change in him. He seemed altogether different from the goodlooking boy who had courted the girls in Virginia with such casual grace and ease after they had come down from Washington.

There was new strength in him, new snap in his step, and a new confidence in his voice.

"Look!" Barney stopped, awe in his voice. "There's Spinner Johns now!"

She thought then that he need not have told her, for she would have known.

He was walking slowly down the very center of the street, a man just a little taller than she herself with a long, lantern jaw and flat, deadly looking eyes. He wore two guns tied down on his thighs and in his step there was a certain arrogance that seemed to command and empty the street before him.

Her uncle, Black Jack Coyle who had been in the west since before the War Between the States, had spun many yarns of gunmen, and their names were legend to her. Most of them were men alive now, men who had become legends in their lifetimes, men who had blasted fame out of a hard world with six-guns.

Wild Bill Hickok, Clay Allison, Wyatt Earp, Wes Hardin, Manning Clements, Ben Thompson, Luke Short, Billy the Kid . . . all were names she had heard, even as she had heard the stories of Bill Longley before them. Spinner Johns was a name new to her, but seeing him now, there was something about him that frightened her.

He wore a gray hat, and a gray shirt under a dark and rather dirty vest. A white handkerchief, an incongruous touch, fluttered from his left breast pocket. There was something slow and purposeful in his walk, and in his eyes as they swung side to side of the street, probing, judging, warning.

"I wonder where Matt is?" she whispered.

"I don't know, but I hope he gets away."

"Gets away?" she was astonished. "He won't try to get away, Barney!"

"He's a fool if he doesn't!" Barney spoke sharply. "Johns is poison mean." He frowned, and a puzzled tone came into his voice. "I wonder why he's after Bardoul?"

Her eyes, straying down the street, saw something visible to her that the gunman in the street center could not yet see. It was Buffalo Murphy!

She remembered seeing him in company with Matt in the store, and once later she had glimpsed them together on the street, walking with another man, a younger man.

Murphy had come out and was leaning now against the wall of the store, his rifle carelessly in the hollow of his arm. Then she saw the door push open, and the young man she had seen with them, Ban Hardy, came out and strolled casually across the street where he sat down on a box near the hitching rail. He lightd a cigarette.

"Barney!" she tightened her grip on his arm. "Something's going to happen! Stay here!"

They had walked on a few steps, going in the same direction as Spinner Johns now. At her tightened grip, Barney stopped, and just in time. Matt Bardoul stepped from a space between the buildings near them.

Johns was a good thirty yards away, and his eyes swung left, right. Then they swung back right and he stopped dead still in the center of the street.

He had seen Matt Bardoul.

The Spinner's feet were spread a little, and he stood there, poised and ready, on the balls of his feet, every nerve and sense keyed for what was to come.

Matt Bardoul said nothing, nor did he stop. He knew that to stop would be a signal and Johns would go for his gun, but Matt knew that standing only a few feet behind him, and right in the line of fire, was Jacquine Coyle!

He strolled across the boardwalk, his boots sounding clearly in the now silent street, his hands swinging easily at his sides. He stepped down into the thick dust.

Barney pushed his body in front of his sister's, his heart pounding with excitement.

Matt took another step before he spoke. "Hear you are lookin' for me, Spinner." His voice rang like a bell in the narrow, false fronted street. All along that street life seemed to have been suspended, caught suddenly by some strange wave and stricken into stark immobility. Standing in front of the IXL, a man heard his boot leather creak, and he could feel his heart pounding like a drum. "I heard you were huntin' me an' reckoned we'd ought to get together."

He continued to walk toward Johns with the same easy, careless stride. "Don't calculate to keep a man waitin', Johns, leastwise a man who wants to see me so bad he'll come a huntin' me."

Johns said nothing, only he seemed to crouch a little lower. Every nerve tingling, her eyes wide with fright, Jacquine watched Bardoul walk.

Was he never going to stop? Was he going to walk right up to the muzzle of that awful man's guns?

Scarcely a breath was drawn on the silent street. Awed, men watched as step by step the tall man in the buckskin shirt and black hat drew nearer to Spinner Johns.

"They tell me you're a bad man, Spinner. They tell me you've killed some men. Old men, no doubt. They tell me you're quite a bad man, Spinner, but I'm wondering what you do, when you face a man who isn't afraid? Is that the same thing, Spinner?

"I'm wondering who sent you after me, too. There had to be somebody. We've never had any words, Spinner. In fact, I never saw you until you were pointed out to me a few minutes ago."

Step . . . step . . . and still a further step.

Spinner's hands were like claws now, spread and eager. His eyes were blazing with a queer, leaping light and his teeth bared a little. His hands began to tremble now, with a strain. He was waiting, listening to the slow, even sound of that voice, and waiting for the one move . . . the move to kill!

Staring, her heart going faint from the strain, Jacquine suddenly glimpsed something in Matt's fingers. He had brought one hand forward very slowly, so slowly that no mistake could be made, and now he held that bright, highly polished brass shell in his fingers, belt high. A brass cartridge shell, and he was toying with it casually, carelessly. The brass flashed in the bright sun, then flashed again.

He continued to walk, and she was trembling, fearful of the sudden crash of guns she just knew would come, but then she saw something else.

Spinner Johns was uneasy. He was trembling, he . . . "What's Matt *doing?*" Barney whispered hoarsely. "What's got into him?"

No more than fifteen feet divided them now and Bardoul continued to walk, still playing with his bright brass shell. Thirteen . . . eleven . . . nine. . . .

"God!" Barney said. "Look at Johns! Look at him sweat!"

It was true. The killer's lips were twitching, his hands trembling. Poised to draw, the slightest sound or wrong move might set him off, but he was tense now, riveted to his place as though fascinated by this tall man who walked on and on, endlessly.

Nobody had ever walked up to him like this! They would always stop, there would be a breathless instant . . . then the round of guns. With a kind of sick horror he saw Bardoul coming, nearer, nearer.

Jacquine had a hand to her mouth now. How could anything human stand the suspense? The strain? They were so close now that neither man could miss, they were. . . .

The bright brass shell slipped from Matt's fingers and fell into the dust.

Half hypnotised, the Spinner's eyes followed it. Coolly then, Matt stooped as though to retrieve the shell, and then . . . incredibly fast, he scooped up a handful of loose sand and flipped it with a quick motion into the Spinner's eyes!

Caught by the sudden movement, Johns took the full handful of sand in the face. Blinded, he staggered, then clawed wildly for a gun, but it was knocked spinning into the street before he could bring it high enough to shoot. Screaming with excess of fury, almost babbling in his insane rage, he clawed at his eyes with one hand and grabbed for his other gun with his left.

The left hand was struck aside with a blow that almost paralysed his arm, then a blow struck him in the pit of the stomach that knocked his wind out. He doubled up gasping but a powerful hand caught his collar and jerked him to his tip toes, and then, standing there in the street, Matt Bardoul proceeded to slap Johns until his face streamed with blood.

The first slap was a backhand blow across the mouth that split his lips, the second a hardened palm that smacked him across the ear, stunning him. Then blow after blow that rocked his head on his shoulders until it bobbed as loosely as a cork on a string.

One gun was still in its holster but every time he tried to grab for it the hand was knocked aside.

Suddenly then, the six gun was jerked from its holster and tossed into the street. With a quick shift of hands. Matt caught the gunman by the shirt collar and belt, and swinging him off his feet, dropped him bodily into the waist deep water trough!

Johns went under the water, then came up, spitting and spluttering.

For a long moment, the street was breathless, and then somebody whooped, and suddenly the whole street was roaring with shouts and yells of laughter. Men slapped their legs and roared, then leaned weakly against each other, suddenly released from their tension, and roaring with appreciation. Matt Bardoul had walked up to one of the most feared gunmen in the west, slapped him silly and then dropped him into the water trough.

Had he killed him, the townspeople would have shrugged their shoulders and turned away, but this was something! This was a story to be told and retold! Spinner Johns slapped like a rag doll and then dropped into the trough!

Amid the laughter, Johns sprawled out of the trough into the dust, then he got heavily to his feet, and while the crowd behind him bellowed and cheered he turned and slunk down an alleyway between two buildings. Through his mind there beat the brutal realization that no one was afraid of him now, they would never be afraid of him again.

Clive Massey, standing in the door of the IXL, cursed under his breath, grinding his teeth in impotent fury. Portugee Phillips moved up beside him, grinning slyly. "Ever see the like of that, Massey? That took *nerve!* I'd ride through fifty blizzards afore I'd walk up to a gun fighter like that! Walked right up to him, took that crazy killer's gun away and slapped the livin' daylights out of him!"

Phillips looked up at Massey and his eyes were hard, knowing eyes. "If you're smart, Massey," he said softly, "you'll never tangle with Matt Bardoul. If you do, he'll kill you!"

"Shut up, damn you!" Massey wheeled, his eyes

ugly, then walked away, his feet slapping the board-walk in the violence of his temper.

Matt stepped up on the boardwalk and stopped in front of Jacquine. "Ma'am," he said, his voice sharp from nervous tension, "you'd do better to stay off the street when there's trouble! You might have been killed!'

Stung by the sharpness of his voice, she stiffened to her full height, angry and amazed. "Why . . . !" she gasped. "How dare you speak to me in that voice? If you think . . . !"

She might have forgiven him if he had not turned abruptly away leaving her with a furious temper and a mouthful of angry words for which she had no use. Angrily, she stamped her foot and stared after him. Then she flung herself around and started back to the IXL, her head high, her heart pounding. Barney heeled and started after her.

Murphy and Ban walked up to Matt. Murphy grinned at him. "You sure had me boogered," he said, "I figured sure as all get out he'd draw on you."

"What would you have done if he had?" Ban asked.

Matt Bardoul looked at him, surprised. "I'd have killed him," he said, "what did you think?"

They started up the street toward the Gem Theatre. "Jack Langrishe is putting on a show up to that theatre opposite Gold Street tonight," Ban suggested, "let's go have a look at it. I ain't seen a show since they took the first cows up from Texas!"

"Just so we get started for Split Rock in plenty of time," Matt said. "Bill Shedd's watchin' our wagons. He'll be on the job. He stopped by and told me this mornin' he was headed out there."

"That's good," Murphy struck a match on the seat of his jeans. "Stark's been keepin' an eye on 'em."

The three men stopped on a corner and watched the crowd passing. It was thinning out now, but the bars were filled. "Matt, what's wrong with this setup?" Hardy asked. "I don't like the look of things, an' never have. Logan Deane's hangin' out with Massey about half the time, an' Lute Harless tells me he seen Massey talkin' to Spinner Johns just an hour or so before he started huntin' you."

"That right?" It was possible, of course, Matt reflected, but somehow he had been divided between believing Johns was just out to get him because he had a sort of gunfighting reputation, or that Colonel Pearson had started the killer after him. That Clive Massey might have done it he doubted. It was possible, yet there would be no motive unless Massey had reason to fear him.

"Lute says there's sixty-two wagons out there now, all ready to roll. More than ninety men."

"That's a good lot."

"Enough to keep the Injuns off, all bein' armed like they are." Murphy shuffled his feet and shifted his pipe in his teeth. "Seen Abel Bain today."

Bardoul's head jerked around. "Did you say . . . *Abel Bain?*"

"Uh huh," Murphy looked at him shrewdly. "An' you know where? In Bat Hammer's wagon outfit!"

So? Matt rubbed his jaw thoughtfully. Now it was Abel Bain. The man was a renegade of the worst kind. A murderer, known to be a horsethief and a rustler. If Massey was taking on men like Bain there was nothing that could not happen.

The man had been run out of Virginia City, had narrowly escaped lynching once at Laramie. There had been no evidence to convict him of killing Ad Wilson at Tascosa, but the man was found dead in his bed one night with a knife wound, and he had been robbed. A horse was trailed to within a mile of Bain's ranch.

"He was keepin' out of sight," Buffalo went on, "an' they don't know I've seen him."

"I see." Matt kicked at a stone with the toe of his boot. "I think I'll advise Coyle to drop out of it."

"They won't listen."

"I know, but I'll advise them. It's the least I can do."

Hardy grinned. "Massey ain't goin' to like you!"

The crowd was already gathering for *The Banker's Daughter* when they went into the theatre and found seats. It was a noisy and profane crowd, but an interested one. Jack Langrishe always ran clean plays and he always entertained. He would do no less on this night. He had come from Dublin, and his theatres had been the bright spots in more than one western mining town.

Matt seated himself on a bench and stared around. The whole town had turned out and the place was jammed full of miners, stage drivers, bartenders, bull whackers and mule tenders. California Jack, faro dealer, Madame Canutson the lady bull-whacker whose profanity matched any man's, Scott Davis, shotgun messenger, Seth Bullock, Deadwood's sheriff, Cold Deck Johnny, Colorado Charlie, and many others. Names famous and infamous wherever miners, gamblers of the crowd that followed the boom towns gathered.

Suddenly, the door opened and a woman shoved her way inside, calling loudly over her shoulder. Whatever the remark was, everybody laughed. She wore a man's narrow brimmed black hat set at a careless angle atop her hair, and her rather long face, the skin olive, clear and smooth broke into a smile that suddenly made all who saw her forget that she was actually a plain woman.

"Ban," Matt said, "better take a look. There's a woman who'll be remembered after they've buried an' forgotten the rest of us. That's Calamity Jane!"

Hardy leaned forward, craning his neck for a better view. She wore a fringed buckskin coat that fitted loosely and was gathered by a broad leather belt. Her trousers were also fringed buckskin, and even now she was carrying a rifle. Under the buckskin coat she wore a man's plaid shirt.

"Heard a lot about her," Hardy said.

"She came into the Black Hills with Crook. Smuggled herself into the outfit when it left Laramie. She was one of the first to come in. Dead shot with that rifle, too. She's a hard case, but a good hearted one, give you anything you want, and funny thing, she being so much like a man in other ways, but she loves to handle sick people. Good at it, too."

Matt glanced at the late comers again, searching the crowd for the face he was eager to see. Then he saw her come through the door, laughing over her shoulder as Calamity Jane had done, but how different!

She was wearing a green gown that made a low murmur run over the crowd, and every head in the place turned toward her. She walked down the aisle, preceded by her brother and followed by Clive Massey. Matt felt the smile leave his face. He shifted his feet and turned his eyes elsewhere. He was aware that Buffalo was glancing at him out of the corners of his eyes, but he ignored it.

Nevertheless, he felt sick in the stomach and unhappy. He kept his eyes on the stage and the constant flurry of activity behind the curtain. Yet she sat in a position his eyes overlooked, and suddenly he realized she was looking for him. He saw her head turn slightly, glancing at the crowd, then after a moment, it turned toward him. Their eyes met, briefly. He nodded his head, and she replied with a cool nod, and then looked away.

The curtain started to go up. Quietly, he turned and left his seat. Murphy started to speak, but he shoved his way through the crowd to the outside. "The hell with it!" he told himself roughly. "The hell with it, I say!"

Shoving his hands deep in his pockets he stepped off the boardwalk and turned up the stairway that climbed the hill, walking out on the old, burned-over slope. When he had walked fairly well up on the hillside, he turned and looked back.

The town lay there in Deadwood Gulch, a scattered, loosely knit series of communities, some of them hidden away in small hollows or scattered in other ravines connecting with this. White Rocks loomed above him.

No woman was worth it. Telling himself that, he realized how much she had been in his mind lately, and they had exchanged only a few words, yet her face stayed in his thoughts with the memory of her voice. No woman had ever touched him like this before, and he was irritated by it, fighting the feeling as a broncho fights a bit. It wouldn't do. Clive Massey had the inside track, anyway.

Or there might be somebody back east who would come out soon to claim her. What did he know about it? She had frightened him today when he stepped out on the boardwalk to shoot it out with Spinner Johns, for she was right in the line of fire. It was because of her, and her alone, that Johns was alive. He had been forced to bluff him out because of the girl.

Ban Hardy was afraid Spinner Johns would come back, but Matt Bardoul was not. Johns would be heading for the brush now, heading for the brush with his horns sawed off. He would want to find a new country where nothing of his disgrace was known. Guessing something of what sort of man Johns was, Matt doubted whether he would ever be the same again. He had been called, been backed down, forced to take water. It did something ruinous to a man's morale, and never again would he face a man with the same fearlessness.

Matt walked back down the hill and headed for the stable to saddle his horse. He had thrown the hull on him and was adjusting the cinch when a voice spoke out of the darkness of a stall. Bardoul held perfectly still, not turning his head.

"Matt," he could not place the voice, "don't go on no wagon train. You staked me once when I was broke. I tell you that because I know you staked so many you won't remember. I'd git killed for this, if anybody knowed, but *don't go along with that wagon train!*"

"Why? What's going to happen?"

He waited for what seemed a full minute before there was a reply. "Dunno. But somethin' . . . ain't none of 'em supposed to come back alive."

"Who's the boss?" he demanded.

There was no reply. He waited a moment, then asked the question again, but there was no answer. His unknown informant was gone.

He bridled his horse, then led him down to the

IXL and tied him to the hitching rail. He stepped inside and made his way to the bar, his eyes studying the crowd, hoping to recognize a familiar face who might be the man he had staked. There were none.

Then the door opened and Logan Deane came in.

When his eyes found Bardoul, he smiled, walking up to the bar. "Nice job today," Deane said in his soft, pleasant voice. "A very nice job. I've heard of Wyatt Earp doin' somethin' like that with Ben Thompson, but nothin' like you did today."

"Spinner Johns wasn't Ben Thompson," Bardoul said truthfully.

"He was worse," Deane replied, "much worse! Thompson had brains, an' as much nerve as any man. He backed down for Earp simply because he knew if he won, he lost. He might kill Earp but he knew Earp would get him. There's no percentage in that sort of a deal.

"Johns was crazy. There was no tellin' what he might do."

Matt nodded. Then lifting his glass, he glanced over it at Deane. "How long have you known Clive Massey?" he asked.

The half friendly light vanished from Logan Deane's eyes and they turned flat gray. "I don't just remember," he said coolly, "I really don't remember!"

"Well," Matt said, "I know nothing about him, but I've got a feeling, Deane. It's a feeling that he should be lined up with us!"

Logan Deane's eyes studied him warily, but there was speculation in them now. "You mean, you think he's a gun slinger?"

"Yes, I do. Only Clive Massey would throw a gun only for what he could get out of it. Remember that, Deane!"

Logan Deane studied him. "Why tell me?" he said. "Why warn me?"

"Because someday you and I may shoot it out, Logan," Matt said. "I hope not, because I'm not a man who likes to kill, but if the time comes when we face each other, it will be fair and above board an' the best man will win. If either of us ever faces Clive Massey, it will not be until all the breaks áre on his side!"

Deane did not comment. He turned his glass on the bar, studying the wet rings left by the bottom of it.

"We'd have heard his name."

"Maybe we have," Matt suggested, "maybe we have . . . an' it might be a different one than the handle he uses now."

"Who?"

"You're as good at guessing as I am." Matt shrugged. "But a man could figure it out, maybe. Clay Allison has a club foot, an' Wyatt Earp has a different color of hair an' eyes. Also, he's an honest man. He's too big for Billy, an' I know Dave Rudabaugh, but he's one of them. I know he is!"

Matt was waiting on the street by the hitching rail when Murphy came up with Ban. Both men had stopped by after the show to get their horses, and now they were saddled up and ready to go. It was a good long ride they had ahead of them.

Bardoul glanced up and saw Brian Coyle going into the IXL, and saw Massey leave them at the door. All would be moving out soon, so if he was to speak, it must be now. Clive Massey was heading down the street, so without a word, Matt stepped up on the boardwalk and followed the Coyles into the hotel. Barney had joined them and the three were going upstairs.

They opened the door of Brian Coyle's room, and he lighted a light. When he lifted it, he saw Matt Bardoul standing in the door. They all three looked at him, waiting, trying to find some reason for his being there.

"I'd like to speak to you, sir," he said carefully.

"Very well." Brian was puzzled. "Come in and close the door."

"Sir," he said, "tonight when I was saddling my horse a man spoke out of a dark stall . . . I didn't get a glimpse of him . . . and warned me not to go on this trip. He warned me that nobody was to come back alive."

"Nonsense, my boy! Utter nonsense! Why, the

Sioux wouldn't think of attacking a train as large as ours!"

"He wasn't thinking of the Sioux. I believe he was thinking of the same thing I was, that there are too many outlaws on this wagon train."

Brian Coyle's face had hardened. "Just what is your motive for this advice, Bardoul? I'll admit I was aware there was some bad blood between you and Massey, but I ascribed that to nothing more than Clive's short temper and your own abruptness."

"Are you aware of the character of the men around him? Of Bat Hammer, or Abel Bain?"

"Bain? I don't believe I know him."

"You wouldn't. He's hiding in Hammer's wagon. He's known in all the camps as a thief and a murderer."

Coyle's face was stiff now, and his manner had grown chill. "Really, Bardoul, I think you've gone far enough. If you had such suspicions you should have voiced them at the meeting and not come to me here alone and by night. I'm afraid, sir, you're guilty of some very ungentlemanly conduct!"

Matt's face paled a little. His eyes shifted to Jacquine's but she glanced away coldly. "I was thinking of your daughter, sir. If there is trouble it would not be a good place for her."

"We, my son and I, are quite capable of caring for Jacquine's interests. You forget, Young Man, that I am one of the leaders of this wagon train, that I helped organize it, that I might say, I *did* organize it!

"Every man on this train is known to me, personally. Each one has been vouched for by one of my trusted friends. If there is any such person as Abel Bain, I have seen nothing of him.

"As to your tale bearing, and I'm sorry Bardoul, but there is no other name for it, I can only say that I have known some things about you and your past conduct for some days. I do not refer to the fact that you are an acknowledged gunfighter and a killer. I refer to other stories, known to the military, and they do not reflect well upon you, sir.

"Until now I had not mentioned those stories, nor did my son or daughter know of them, but under the circumstances, you leave me no other alternative than to mention them.

"Now, sir, let me give you a warning: you are going with us. I, myself, spoke for you against the wishes of Colonel Pearson and Clive Massey. But I know from what the Colonel has told me that you are a rebel and a troublemaker. We will have no trouble caused by you on this trip! Understand that! If there is, no one man on the train will be called upon to face you! We have organized our own force to keep the peace on this wagon train, and in the town until it is settled and an election can be held. At the first sign of trouble from you, you will be summarily dealt with!"

"Thank you, sir." Matt Bardoul's face was deathly white.

He turned abruptly and started for the door, then with his hand on the knob, he turned his head. "I know nothing of the personnel of your police force, or who its leader may be, but I'll make a little bet that Clive Massey is the commander, and that he chose the men to enforce the law!"

That time the remark got over. He saw Coyle's eyes narrow slightly with realization, and Matt knew he had been correct. He turned and walked outside, pulling the door shut after him.

Buffalo asked him no questions, and they mounted up and started out of town, yet when he turned off the trail to Split Rock and went by a different route, they made no comment. Buffalo was riding with his rifle across his saddle bows.

When he rolled out of his blankets at daybreak, the camp was already stirring. Fires were glowing over the bottomland where the wagons had gathered, and as he pulled on his boots he saw that Bill Shedd had a fire going.

The big man grinned when he walked up. "Little coffee goes good on a chilly mornin'," he said. "But she'll be plenty hot after that sun gets up!"

Bardoul nodded. "That's right. Did you refill those water barrels?"

"Yep, sho' did. We got plenty of water. More'n enough, most ways, to last us three days."

"We're liable to need it."

Hardy and Buffalo came up and joined them, but there was little talk. He had said nothing about his warning to Coyle, but he knew they were quite aware of what he had done, and approved it. From his actions they probably deduced the result.

Last gear was loaded into the wagons, and Murphy had already mounted the seat when Matt looked around to see a tall young man, very slender, approaching him. The fellow had blond hair that needed cutting, and a shy face. "Mr. Bardoul?" he asked. "Could you use another driver? I know you have one, and you probably want to drive your other wagon yourself, but I thought, maybe you . . . besides," he added suddenly, "I'd drive it for nothing! I . . . just want to be along. I want to go with the train."

"Did you talk to Brian Coyle?"

"No, I didn't. I talked with the other man . . . the tall one. The Army man."

"What did he say?"

"He said I couldn't come unless I had a wagon."

That decided Matt. "Can you handle an ox team?"

The boy's eyes brightened. "Yes, sir. I certainly can! Oxen or mules, it doesn't make any difference! I can keep your wagon in good shape, too!"

"All right! Mount up!"

He walked back to his horse and climbed into the saddle. From far ahead came the long, familiar call, "Ro-l-l-l-l 'em over!"

Whips cracked, and his wagon started. From the back of the zebra dun, he watched the wagons roll out and form up in four parallel columns, each almost a half mile long.

Gray dawn was lifting behind them, and he watched the oxen move out, a step, and then another step, in a slow, swaying, rhythmical movement, the covered wagons rumbling behind. Long grass waved in the light breeze, and far ahead, skylined on a hill top, Colonel Orvis Pearson lifted his hand theatrically, and motioned them on.

For better or worse, they had started. Now it only remained to wait and see what was to happen.

CHAPTER IV

Westward, the land lay empty. Behind them the rising sun threw their long shadows before them across the wind rippled grass. They were shadows not soon to fade from these virgin lands, but they were to lie long upon the plain and the mountain, darkening the retreat of the Indian.

The buffalo, of course, were gone. Here and there a lonely old bull, or a cow with a calf, wandered dismally and alone where once they trailed with their millions. The buffalo had roamed the prairies for countless years, and then the white man had come, and the buffalo were gone like a sprinkling of powder in a strong wind.

The Indians were a shattered few, defiant but defeated. In their last gesture, the swan song of a warlike people, they had met and defeated Custer. They had wiped him out.

After Custer the combined armies of Terry, Crook, and Gibbon advanced relentlessly, and against the scattered forces of the Indian they had little trouble. The warfare of the white man was never understood by the Indian, and if he learned at last, he learned too late, for his power was already broken.

To an Indian, a battle was a war. He did not think in terms of campaigns, and the winning or losing of a battle decided everything, and when it was over he returned to his tepee and his squaw. He had not learned to cope with the superior barbarism of the white man's warfare. The white man did not stop. He kept coming.

Yet somehow, even in defeat the red man contrived to come off best. Wrapped in his blanket like a

Roman senator in his toga, he stalked from the scene. The future might rob him of his morale, it might break him down, but he walked from the field a victor. If he was conquered later, it was never in full battle array. He was conquered by the slaughter of the buffalo and the relentless march of the white settlers even more than by the Army. It is still true that in the last major battle between the armies of the white man and the warriors from the Sioux and Cheyenne villages, that the Indian won.

Matt Bardoul loved the country into which he was riding. The blind drive after wealth and power had never seemed to him to be either worthy or comfortable. His own driving energies and his desire to see what lay across the horizon had moved him west, and once he saw the long, waving sea of grass, the rolling aspen cloaked hills, and the mounting ranks of the lodgepole pine, his heart was forever lost to this lonely, beautiful land.

The Big Horns still lay across that horizon, a image in the mind rather than the sky. Riding his long legged zebra dun on the side hill away from the wagon train, Matt knew that whatever the result, whatever the cost, this trip was worth the effort. This was his land, these were his people.

Riding alone, away from the dust of the wagons, he let the dun pick his own way, while his mind began ferreting a way down the winding burrows of passion and feeling that disturbed the people of the train.

In the clear light of day he was compelled to admit that he had no reason for any suspicion beyond his knowledge of the men around Massey. There was every chance that everything was strictly honest and straight forward. Father De Smet had always claimed there was gold in the Big Horns, and Tate Lyon's story might be true. If it was not true, why had they gone to such pains? Such effort?

Was he not prejudiced by his innate dislike of Massey? Or by Jacquine's seeming preference for the man?

Pearson had proved, some six years before, that as

an Army officer he was an inexperienced nincompoop
and a coward, but that was six years ago, and time
may bring many changes to a man for the better as well
as for the worse. It was true that so far Colonel Orvis
Pearson's only gesture toward leadership had been just
that . . . a gesture.

Seated upon a splendid horse, very straight in the
saddle, he had removed his hat with a sweeping gesture
worthy of Custer himself, and waved the wagon train
on.

Logan Deane was a killer, but as he had admitted,
he had killed men himself. On Deane he could reserve
an opinion. For Batsell Hammer there was no need nor
room for reservation. He was a renegade who stopped
at nothing. He was a thief and a murderer, and known
by all the frontier as such.

Abel Bain was worse. The huge, surly Bain was
a wolf where Hammer was a coyote. He was violent,
treacherous, brutal. However, Massey was new to the
frontier, apparently, and he might not know about Bain.

That Spinner Johns had tried to kill him shortly
after a talk with Massey, might be a coincidence. Johns
was the sort who might try to kill anyone, and with
slight provocation. If that fight had been an effort of
Massey's, the dark, handsome Clive had been grievous-
ly disappointed.

He was, he decided, building fantastic suspicion
upon nothing at all. There was no way in which Massey
could hope to gain.

The warning in the stable might have come from
someone who had tried for a place in the train and been
refused.

At the next stop the situation might reveal itself
more clearly, for then the elections would be held to
determine the captains of the four companies.

In his own group, aside from his two wagons
driven by Shedd and Tolliver, there were the wagons
of Murphy and Ban Hardy, Aaron Stark with one wagon, Rabun Kline with one, and the three wagons of
Lute Harless. Each of the latter was driven by a son of
Aaron Stark.

Still another wagon had joined them when they moved out that morning. Curiously, he dropped back alongside to see who was the driver. A big, wide shouldered man hunched on the wagon seat, a man with a wide smile and a ready laugh. But as he looked at Matt his eyes were shrewd, intense.

He waved to Bardoul. "You in command?"

"Nobody is. The election is tonight."

Matt touched the dun with a spur and cantered ahead until he drew alongside Murphy's wagon. The big mountain man grinned at him. "Reckon this route will take us by the Stone Cup? Never forget the place. Holed up there three days once, standin' off some thievin' Crows."

"Be good to get back," Bardoul agreed, "I like the Big Horns."

"Wonder where at that gold is? I've been runnin' it over in my mind, an' I can't seem to figure it out. I never seen none, my own self."

"You weren't looking for gold, Buff. It could be there, all right. Personally, I don't care. I've an idea of finding myself a ranch over in the basin and runnin' a few cows."

"Who does know where we're goin', I wonder?"

"Coyle, probably. Certainly Pearson an' Massey. Then Lyon has been there, and Portugee Phillips will have been told. We'll get the lowdown tonight, but until then nobody is supposed to know. Frankly, I haven't even tried to guess."

Murphy glanced at him. "Seen that girl of Coyle's a few minutes ago. She was ridin' a mighty pretty spotted pony. Said Clive Massey gave it to her."

Matt offered no comment, and Murphy lighted his pipe and settled to driving. All morning Matt had avoided thinking of the girl, feeling that whatever consideration she might have given him had been erased by last night's discussion at the hotel. Clive Massey, much in her father's favour, would have all the advantage, nor was he a man likely to lose any time in making the most of the opportunity.

Studying his own position, Matt Bardoul could see

that it was scarcely enviable. Colonel Pearson had studiously avoided him, which was understandable, for Matt alone knew of the man's fearful incompetence. Brian Coyle, who had been Matt's one friend among the leaders could be considered a friend no longer. As for Massey, he knew the man would like nothing so well as to see Bardoul out of the wagon train.

When they pulled up for a brief lunch, Bardoul loped the dun down to the fire. It had been Stark's suggestion, eagerly accepted by the others, that his girls do the cooking for all, and that they have a community cooking, with each bringing a share.

Stark was sitting on a log near the fire when Matt swung down from the saddle and began loosening his cinch. "Howdy!" Stark called. "Who's the feller tied on behind?"

The man walked up just in time to hear the question. He looked around the group, smiling widely. "Name of Ernie Braden! Mornin' folks!" he boomed. "I reckon we're all friends here! So you just call me Ernie!"

Stark glanced at his empty hands, took his pipe from his mouth and spat, but said nothing.

Braden picked up a cup and held it out to Sary Stark. "How's about some coffee, Ma'am? From those purty hands of yours, it'll seem plumb sweet!"

Lute Harless walked up with the three Stark boys. Jeb sat down on the log beside his father. "Wished night would come. I'd sure enough like to know where we're headed!"

Braden looked around and winked. "I could give you a hint," he said knowingly, "You ever hear tell of Shell Creek? That's my bet!"

Buffalo Murphy stared at the fire, then he lifted his eyes, squinting at Braden. "You ever been to Shell Creek?"

"No," Braden admitted, "I ain't. Only," he winked, "I hear a few things."

"You tell 'em, too, I reckon," Jeb Stark said.

Braden seemed not to hear. He glanced around at

the group, slapping himself emphatically on the stomach. "Well, tonight's the big night! Election! Don't reckon there's any party lines here, but it's a mighty big thing, choosin' a leader. A captain, that is. We sure want to pick somebody who has the confidence of the leaders of this outfit. Then everything will go along much better."

"I wonder who that would be?" Hardy asked innocently.

"Well," Braden was thoughtful, "Stark here would be a good man, Harless another. Needs a man free of a wagon, of course, an' I reckon both Stark an' Harless are tied down."

"That lets you out too, doesn't it?" Hardy suggested.

"Matter of fact," Braden admitted, "it doesn't. I got me a good driver. He's helpin' with another wagon today, but actually he's with me. He'll be over before election time tonight. Name of Bunker."

"Looks like you might be the likely choice for captain, then," Hardy suggested gravely. "That is, if you have the confidence of the leaders. How do you stand with Colonel Pearson?"

Braden glanced around wisely, then held up two fingers. "Like that!" he stated emphatically. "We understand each other, the Colonel an' me!"

"Well," Hardy said, "that sure is a relief to get that problem settled. Sure takes a load off my mind. Wouldn't do to get the wrong man as captain." He glanced around at Murphy. "Say, that reminds me: what ever happened to that wagon boss we had out of Fort Phil Kearney that time? The one we didn't like?"

Murphy scowled thoughtfully. "That one? Why, sure! He was the one I shoved off the seat when we were swimmin' the river durin' flood. I sure hated to do it, but it saved shootin'."

"That ain't the one." Ban was insistent. "I mean that tall one, with the sandy beard."

"Oh, him?" Murphy slapped his leg. "Hell, how could you forget him? That was the one we tied on

the buffalo bull! Last we seen of him was that bull,
tearin' off with the herd, an' that wagon captain tied
stark naked atop him! I reckon he's goin' yet!"

Stark stirred the fire, and Braden stared at first
one and then the other. "You're funnin'?" he suggested.

"Funnin'?" Murphy looked up. "Of course we was
funnin'! Got to do something along the trail for laughs!
When you got a wagon boss you don't like, get shet of
him, quickest way you know how!"

Aaron Stark took the pipe from his mouth and
glanced over at the tall young driver sitting beside Bill
Shedd. "You're Tolliver, eh? Any kin to the Tollivers of
Sandy Run?"

Tolliver glanced up. "Yep, sure thing. We're full
cousins. You know 'em?"

"I should smile! My wife's sister married up with
Clyde."

"That would be Aunt Jane, then? That makes us
practic'ly kinfolks."

"I reckon."

"Well," Braden suggested, "when election comes
tonight we sure better pick the right man. Don't know,"
he said with a glance at Hardy, "if I'd care to be captain of this outfit, treatin' wagon bosses the way you
do, still, if I'm elected, I'll serve. I'll sure do the best I
know how to keep us at the head of the train all the
time, too!"

When they were mounting their wagons again,
Stark glanced at Bardoul. "Talkative sort of feller, ain't
he?"

Matt grinned. "Kind of. Reckon he'd sure like to
be boss of this company."

"Reckon he would," Stark agreed. "Reckon that's
what he was sent for."

"Ro-o-l-l-l out! Roll 'em o-o-over!"

The call swept down the line of wagons, picked
up by many voices, and once more the oxen leaned
against the harness and the wagons began to move.

In some respects the prospects for the wagon
train could not have been improved. The time of year
was good, although water would be scarce for the

spring rains were far behind and the fall rains had not yet begun, however, the prairies would be firm and the hauling not too heavy.

Trouble with the Indians was possible but improbable. Only a short time before Crazy Horse had surrendered, closely followed by the surrender of Two Moons and Lame Deer. Of the wild Indians, only Sitting Bull, the medicine man who aspired to be a war chief, remained free, and he had escaped to Canada. American Horse was dead, and Dull Knife of the Cheyennes was helpless to offer any opposition. Red Cloud, who had once compelled the Army to abandon the forts along the Bozeman Trail, had become a reservation Indian, occasionally going east on lecture tours.

A few young braves might kill a straggler if any was found, or drive off some stock, but the prospects of any organized band being large enough to attack the sixty-two wagons of the train seemed out of the question now.

Trouble, if there was to be any, must spring from within the wagon train itself.

Twice, Matt sighted Jacquine Coyle, and each time she was well ahead of the wagons, riding beside Clive Massey. He saw no evidence of Logan Deane.

Pearson, of course, was always in sight. Astride his magnificent bay he made a commanding figure of a man, fully conscious of the effect he created.

The sod was firm, and as the four columns of wagons kept well apart, the travelling was fairly good. This route had not been used before, so the grass was long and the sod over much of the way was solid enough so that dust was late in starting. Several times when Matt was near his own wagons he saw young Tolliver glancing back toward the rear of the train.

When he caught Matt watching him, he waved, but kept his eyes to the front as long as Matt was in sight. His actions puzzled Bardoul. Had Tolliver had trouble in Spearfish or Deadwood? Was he expecting to be pursued? Certainly, his actions gave every evidence of it.

Once, sighting an antelope, Matt rode away from

the column long enough to kill it. He brought the fresh meat back to the wagons and passed it to Sarah Stark. She smiled at him. "I guess we won't starve none!"

She was a pretty girl, and Matt had noticed the way Ban Hardy kept his eyes on her. He chuckled, and grinned at the girl. "Sary, you'd better keep your eyes open! There's a young cowhand on this wagon train who's lookin' you over!"

"Let him look!" she said, with spirit. Then, her curiosity aroused, she asked quickly: "Who do you mean?"

"Ban Hardy, that Texas trail driver. I hear those Texans are plumb romantic. Of course, he probably sees you're all taken up with that Braden fellow."

"Braden?" Sary was aghast. "Why, I'm no such thing! Wherever did you get that idea? Why, if he was the last man on earth . . . !" She snorted indelicately. "Him! Of all people!"

When they circled for camp that night they had made eighteen miles. It was a good day's travel, neither the best nor the worst a wagon train could expect.

Clive Massey rode up during supper. "All of you come over to the Coyle wagon when you've eaten." He glanced at Braden, a faintly questioning look, then rode away.

Ernie Braden was being very expansive. He offered his tobacco pouch around, and the men by the fire gravely helped themselves. When he held forth at some length on his past experiences with wagon trains they listened respectfully, and said little.

Finally, Murphy got up and rubbed his hands on his buckskins. "Might as well go over," he said, "this is where we get the lowdown."

Brian Coyle had taken his stand behind a barrel, as before. Behind him, Colonel Pearson waited, standing at ease. Clive Massey conversed in low tones with Jacquine. Some of the men sat around cross legged, and the others filled in behind them,

"You've all seen the gold we had," Coyle began abruptly. "beyond that you've made this trip on faith. Now to announce our destination, and I doubt if it will mean much to you. It certainly meant nothing to me. We are going to the forks of Shell Creek, the other side of the Big Horn Mountains. That's where the gold was found."

A low murmur went through the gathered men, but the talk died when Coyle began to speak again.

"In any such group as this there is certain to be some trouble, so as is the procedure in any well regulated community we have appointed a man whose duty it will be to maintain order. That appointment fell upon Clive Massey. I hope you will all give him your utmost cooperation."

There were a few scattered cheers, but most of the men held their silence. Brian Coyle glanced around, then continued, "He has named ten men who will assist him in maintaining order, with Logan Deane as his second in command."

Murphy glanced at Bardoul and spat. "Well, what else could you expect?" he said.

"Now," Coyle continued, "for the next order of business. Slips of paper are being distributed to be used in voting for your company commanders. The four companies will be designated as A, B, C, and D. Choose your captains carefully, for they must be men capable of leadership, and men who have the respect of all others in the group.

"Company A," Coyle indicated the column with which Massey and Deane travelled, "will vote first."

"That'll be Massey," Stark suggested, "you wait an' see!"

It was. And Brian Coyle was elected captain of B Company. Herman Reutz, the former storekeeper, was elected captain of Company C, and then D Company voted.

The votes were collected by Barney Coyle and delivered to his father. Matt glanced over at Braden who was talking to Clive Massey. As Coyle called for silence, Braden turned toward him confidently.

Brian Coyle lifted the first ballot, opened it, and read, "Ernie Braden!" Braden smiled.

He lifted the next ballot. "Matt Bardoul!" he called.

Coyle lifted the third ballot, hesitated a little, and called out, "Bardoul again!"

The smile on Braden's face grew forced. The next vote was for Braden, and then all the rest for Matt Bardoul.

Murphy nudged Matt as his election was announced. "Look at 'em! They don't like it, not even one little bit!"

Clive Massey's face was stiff, while Braden looked black and ugly. He had been so confident of victory, so sure he had won them over.

"Before we break up," Coyle said, "the captains will meet at my wagon for a conference."

Ban Hardy got him. His eyes crinkled with dry humour. "Luck," he said to Matt, "don't let 'em fast talk you."

Matt strolled over to the wagon and leaned against the wheel. He dug out his tobacco and rolled a cigarette. Jacquine was only a few feet from him, talking to her brother, but she avoided his glance, so he paid no further attention to her.

Pearson hesitated a moment to gain the attention of the group, ignoring Matt. "After talking with Lyon and Phillips," he suggested, "we have chosen a route that is indicated on this map I have drawn with the help of Miss Coyle. As there will be several river crossings it will be well to prepare your wagons for them."

Matt studied the map thoughtfully. It was going to miss the Stone Cup, the best waterhole between Deadwood and the Big Horns, and would take them through very dry country. Yet it had advantages even if there would be less water.

"You've been through this country, Bardoul," Reutz said suddenly, "what do you think of the route?"

Matt hesitated, noting the irritation in both Pearson and Massey. "It's a good one, but for the scarcity of water."

Pearson touched a point on the map. "There's fresh water right here, at a logical stopping point."

"That's right, Pearson," Matt replied, "but that's a slough. The water is stagnant, usually covered with green moss, and with a lot of cat tails growing in it. The water should only be used by humans in an emergency."

"We appreciate the information," Pearson said sarcastically. "Knowing you, I couldn't expect to find any plan that would please you!"

"Knowing you," Bardoul returned sharply, "I can't imagine you drawing a route that would be practical. That second waterhole," he added, "is almost pure alkali. I mean the one at Pumpkin Buttes."

"My information is different!" Pearson snapped.

Bardoul shrugged and lighted a cigarette, glancing at the others. Clive Massey was smiling a little, Brian Coyle looked irritated, and only Herman Reutz looked thoughtful.

"My point," Matt said evenly, "is simply this: We are all in this together, and any personal animosity should be dropped until the trip is over. Any information I have as to the route, is yours for the asking. I only volunteered what I knew because I felt it was well to know these things beforehand."

"That's fair enough," Reutz said. "Weren't you in the planning of this trail?"

Matt did not reply, and a dead silence fell over the group. Pearson shifted his feet uneasily, then cleared his throat. "Company A will lead off in the morning."

When a few other details had been settled, the meeting broke up. Matt walked back to his wagon in time to see young Tolliver mounted and riding away. Bardoul started to call after him to warn him of Indians, but there was something so surreptitious about the way he was leaving that it puzzled him. Yet Tolliver was already some distance off and going fast, riding as if toward a definite objective.

Matt shrugged, then walked back to his wagon and shook out his bed. It would be completely dark in a matter of minutes. Hearing a footstep he glanced up to see the German storekeeper walking toward him. Reutz sat down on the wagon tongue. "You know this country pretty well, don't you?" he asked.

Bardoul nodded. "I've been over this particular route twice before. It's a good route but for the lack of water."

"Pearson's pretty sharp. Has he got it in for you about something?"

"Yes, I guess so. It's an old story now, but I served with him as a civilian scout for awhile. We didn't get along."

"I figured something like that." He paused and lighted his pipe. "You don't like our trail?"

"It isn't bad. Not much brush, mostly open country, good grass, and only a few streams to cross. At this time of year they may be dry or almost dry. Those waterholes I spoke of are useless."

"Maybe they have changed?"

"I talked with a Crow at Spearfish. He says they are still bad."

"You've some good men in your outfit."

"Some of the best. I doubt if Braden and his driver will stay with us now."

"He told Massey he would be captain. I imagine he was quite sure of it." Reutz rubbed his chin thoughtfully with the stem of his pipe. "Bardoul," he said suddenly, "you've done some talking about Deane and Hammer. What do you know about them?"

"What everybody in the west knows. Logan Deane's a gun slinger and a killer. I haven't much room for talk, because I've thrown a gun a few times myself. I will say that I was pushed a good deal, or I wouldn't have. Probably that was the way with Deane, too. As for Hammer, the man is a thief and a murderer."

Reutz tossed a stick into the dying blaze. "There's something I don't quite understand," he said, "Massey and Deane have selected ten men to maintain order in this outfit. You'd think we were a lot of troublemakers."

"Ten? Why, that's more than they ever had in Dodge, I'd guess."

"Sure, and this Hammer is one of them. There's a man named Bain who is another."

"*Bain?*" Matt swore. "Why, he's the worst cutthroat in the western country! What's Coyle thinking of? This wagon train is being placed right in the hands of the outlaws!"

"That's what I was afraid of," Reutz said, "and I don't like it."

The following day they made fourteen miles. Matt glanced thoughtfully at Tolliver who was on the job bright and early. He looked tired, and must have been gone much of the night, but Matt had not heard him return.

Had the young mountaineer ridden back to Deadwood? It did not seem reasonable to suppose he had unless there was someone back there whom he intended to tell of the caravan's destination. Yet Bardoul was instinctively drawn to the young man, and could not bring himself to believe that Tolliver was betraying them in any sense. Matt made no comment, preferring to await results.

During the night he had got out two extra pistols he carried and loaded them carefully. Then he concealed them in a bale of goods where they would be out of sight yet easy to his hand. He did the same thing with a shot gun.

Why he did these things he could not have said. He had that streak of caution in him that so many adventurous men have. Having seen much, they come to a natural way of life that prepares and considers every eventuality.

He had no idea of what to expect, however, he could now allow himself some reason for doubt. When ten lawless men are put in charge of policing a caravan of some hundred odd people, and these men who were to maintain the law were of the stamp of Bain and Hammer, then trouble was truly impending.

As to Shell Creek, if there was gold in the Big Horns it could as easily be there as elsewhere. In fact, the towering knob of Bald Mountain not far from where the creek headed up could be gold country. Certainly, there was evidence of some mineral in the rocks around there.

At daylight on that second day the barrels they carried were filled to the brim once more. When the wagons pulled out and started west, he took his rifle and kept well off to one side of the line of march, saving his horse and keeping it free of the dust that would increase thirst. Ernie Braden and the surly Bunker, his driver, were still with his company.

Matt Bardoul turned at right angles to the line of march and put the dun down a ravine, crossed the branch at the bottom and mounted the opposite slope through the trees. A half hour of easy riding brought him no sight of game, so he turned and cut back toward the trail. It was then he sighted the wagon.

Matt reined in sharply and swung the dun back under the cover of the trees.

It was a light spring wagon, much lighter than any other in the train, and pulled by four mules. Two men sat on the front seat, and studying them as they drew up opposite him, he saw they both seemed very young, and from their resemblance, must have been brothers. They were travelling alone, and a good four miles behind the wagon train.

They kept the mules at a steady gate, and seemed to be talking in lively fashion. One of them was the young man he had seen leaning against the wall of the IXL Dining Room in Deadwood.

Tolliver had ridden back this way last night. Had he seen this wagon? Or had he known they were here and come back to visit them? If not, why had he not mentioned them when he returned? Circling back through the trees, Matt caught up with the wagon train, and just before he reached it he bagged three turkeys.

Two days dragged by slowly, and in those two days they covered thirty miles. It was on the evening of the fifth day out that trouble started.

Herman Reutz, who had been spending more and more time with Matt, was sitting with him on a pile of rocks near the wagons, talking over the events of the day. Buffalo Murphy and Aaron Stark had come up to join them, and then Barney Coyle.

Suddenly a scream rent the air, and leaping to their feet, the men stared down toward the shadowed ravine where a stream, shallow but clean and clear, flowed over the rocks into a pool among the trees. As one man they started to run.

Matt was the first one through the brush, and what he saw brought a rush of anger to his face.

Sary Stark, who had evidently been bathing in the pool, was struggling, only half clad, with the huge, bearded Abel Bain!

With a lunge, Matt grabbed the big renegade by the collar and kicking him behind the knee, jerked him free. Then he hurled him staggering back into the trees. Stark took one glimpse and his rifle started to lift, but Reutz knocked it up.

Bain was on his feet, glaring at Bardoul. "I ain't wearin' a gun," he said, "but if I was . . . !"

Matt shucked his guns and passed them to Reutz. Bain lunged at him, and there was a bright sliver of light in his hand! Bardoul ducked, blocking the knife with his left forearm. Then he slugged a wicked right into the big man's stomach. Bain gasped, and Matt chopped him on the arm, forcing him to drop the knife. Then he stepped back and jabbed swiftly, three fast, knife like punches to the bearded face. One ripped a gash over his eye, the other widened it, the third pulped his lips.

Bain was a big man and powerful, but he was no match for Bardoul. Fast, and smooth on his feet, Matt stayed in close, ripping the big man with short, chopping, brutal punches. In less than three minutes the big man was gasping for breath his face battered to a pulp of blood and beard. Then Bardoul swung a right, a low, lifting hook, half uppercut, to the body. It just cleared Bain's belt. The renegade gulped and staggered.

Men charged through the trees. "What goes on here?" Massey was in the lead, his face dark with passion. "Drop your hands, Bardoul, or I'll kill you!" he roared.

Four or five of Deane's men were with him. All carried guns. "Like hell you will!" Stark covered Massey with his rifle. "You raise a hand an' I'll kill you! Bain's gettin' what he deserves! Rightly, he ought to be hung!"

Matt walked into the battered, reeling man and setting himself, threw another of those wicked punches, then a third. Bain sank to the grass, groaning.

"Bardoul," Massey said, "you're under arrest!"

"Just a minute!" Reutz passed Matt back his guns. "Hadn't you better ask a few questions, Massey? This man Bain assaulted Sary Stark. Found her bathin' here alone. Bardoul stopped him. I'd say hangin' would be too good for Bain."

"He's had it comin' for a long time," Buffalo added grimly. "I'll furnish the rope."

"There'll be no hanging here. You men all get back to the camp. Bardoul, you stay here."

"What's the matter, Clive?" Barney Coyle said. "Why are you so set on jumping Matt Bardoul? I think it was time we held a trial for Bain."

Massey's face was ugly, but his lips tightened. "I'll say who's to be tried!" he flared.

"No, you won't." Aaron Stark spat. "I reckon you've got some mistaken ideas about just who you are, Massey. Your men are to enforce the law, regulate peace, not to say who is to be tried and who is not. I reckon you all had better start with your own passel of men. Bain's the guilty party here. Furthermore, I'm servin' notice that no man is molestin' my gals. You git rid of Bain, or I will!"

"I think," Bardoul said calmly, "that we should have the trial of Bain. I think also we should have a meeting of all the people on this train and decide just where your duties begin and end, Massey!"

For a moment, Clive stared at him, hatred in his face. Then he turned abruptly. "Bring Bain to camp!" he said, and walked rapidly away.

Slowly, the group trooped back toward the wagon train. Barney Coyle fell in beside Bardoul. "I saw that," he said. "I was right behind you, and saw that beast grabbing that girl, trying to tear her clothing! Why, Sis or nobody is safe with that kind of an animal around!"

"I'm glad you were there, Barney," Matt said sincerely, "it begins to look like there was trouble ahead, and a lot of it. I have a lot of respect for your father, and for you and your sister. My warning that night was sincere. I knew Bain. He has narrowly escaped hanging for molesting women on several occasions."

"You sure gave him a beating!" Barney said grimly. "I never realized a man could hit that hard with his fists! I couldn't have beaten a man that way with a club!"

Matt grinned. "I had a good teacher," he said, "an Englishman I met in New Orleans, name of Jem Mace. He used to be the heavyweight champion. I boxed some with John Morrissey, too."

Buffalo Murphy, Stark and Reutz were waiting near Matt's wagons. As Barney walked off, Murphy said abruptly. "I reckon this begins it! Ever' man better keep a gun handy from now on."

"You, Matt," Stark said, "had better watch your back. Bain'll kill you if he gets loose!"

"He ain't getting loose!" Reutz said grimly. "I'm having a talk with Pearson and Coyle right now!"

But he did. In the morning Abel Bain was no longer with the wagon train. He had "escaped" during the night.

CHAPTER V

Company D led off on the following morning. The trail was bad, much the worst it had been at any time since they left Spearfish. Matt knew the terrain, and twice circled large hills. He was beginning his third swing when he heard a sound of galloping horses, and turned in the saddle to see Colonel Pearson and Clive Massey riding toward him. With them was Barney Coyle.

"What's the idea?" Massey demanded irritably. "If we keep winding around all the time, we'll never get there! You've swung over three miles north of the route we're supposed to be taking!"

"I know," Matt agreed, "and I'm trying to miss some hills. There's a mighty rough spot ahead."

Tate Lyon had ridden up. Massey turned on him. "Tate, is there a place up ahead that we can't cross with our wagons?"

Lyon laughed, his eyes avoiding Bardoul's. "Hell, no! Just like this, an' a few low hills. Nothin' to bother."

"Then swing back on the route!" Massey ordered.

"No," Bardoul said, "I won't. If you or Pearson want to take the lead from here on, you can. I say you've got some nasty bad country ahead of you unless we go at least three miles further north of the route we are taking."

"I'll take the lead!" Pearson swung his bay. Bardoul shrugged and fell back alongside his lead wagon.

Tolliver glanced up at him. "Is it purty bad up there?"

"Rough country," Bardoul said, "we'll have to use ropes and chains to get the wagons down. Probably have to double up on the teams, too."

He rode his dun back along the line of the company wagons, telling them what lay ahead, and explaining the procedure to be adopted when they arrived. Then tying the dun behind his head wagon, he got in and dug out of the pile of stores the necessary chains and equipment.

When he remounted his horse, Barney Coyle was alongside. "It looks all right up ahead," he suggested, waving a hand at the waving grass lands.

Matt nodded. "Look, Barney," he said, "watch the oxen. They are moving slower, leaning into the harness more. Notice their tracks. The hooves are digging in at the toes more than they did. There is nothing here by which we can judge other than that, but we have been climbing steadily for the last two hours. It will be that way for at least two miles further, and then the prairie will break off sharply."

"You've been through here before?"

"Not exactly here, but I know there are miles of very rough country ahead of us, and we should have sighted it. We might be lucky and find an easy way down, but I doubt it."

The two rode on, side by side, then Barney suggested. "Why not ride ahead and have a look?"

"Good idea!"

Pearson stared at them as they cantered past, but said nothing. The grass was knee high to the horses here, and good feed. They were not far from the Belle Fourche River, but from where they rode, it could not be seen.

The break came suddenly, almost three miles from where they left the wagon train. The shelf of the prairie broke sharply off, and although they scouted the rim for a mile in either direction, they found no way down. Matt reined in on the edge and studied the steep hill carefully.

The rim was sheer for about six feet, and then

sloped steeply away toward the bottom. It would be impossible to use horses or oxen here. They would have to be led down.

Matt had picked up a shovel before he left the wagons, and now he dismounted and trailing the bridle reins, began to dig away the lip, pushing the dirt down hill. After a few minutes Barney relieved him. By the time the wagons were in sight they had cut a run way through that first sheer drop so that it slanted steeply down to the main slope below.

Bardoul mounted and rode back. He reined in alongside of Pearson. "Colonel, I'm having my company wagons fan out on the rim up here, or a few yards away from the rim. The wagons will have to be let down one by one. I'd suggest the other companies find likely spots further along the rim. If we use one place, it is going to take much longer."

"Is there really a rim up there?" Pearson demanded. He stared sharply at Matt, as if this were some plot of his.

"Yes, there is. It's no more than three hundred feet to the bottom," he added, "and the oxen could handle the wagons after the first half of that distance."

His orders had already been given, so he dropped back and told Reutz what lay ahead. The German listened. "I see," he said finally, "how do you propose to lower your wagons? By hand?"

"No, with a block. I have three in my wagons. I'll keep one team up here to hold the block. Reeve a line through it and we'll pay it off gradually, letting the wagons roll down on their own wheels, just using the line for a brake. I expect we could work at several spots, though, letting two or three wagons down at once, but I was afraid that would spread us out too far in case of Indians."

When he got back to the rim his own wagons were already arriving and Tolliver had unhooked his oxen after swinging the wagon's rear end toward the cut Barney and Matt had dug.

Shedd took his team down the cut to the bottom to pick up the first wagon that came down and start it moving. Then one by one the wagons were rolled back to the lip of the cut by all hands, and with the oxen doing the holding, the line was slowly paid out and the wagons rolled, one by one to the bottom.

It was gruelling work, despite the blocks they used. Yet the planning had prepared the way so there was little wasted time. Ahead of them the country looked rocky and rough with many shallow dips, a few dry stream beds, and some thick brush.

Glancing down the rim, Matt saw Coyle and Pearson standing with several of their men on the edge of the drop off, discussing ways and means. When the last of his wagons was on the bottom, only Herman Reutz had a wagon down. Bardoul's wagons hooked up and they moved off in the gathering dusk.

A mile further along they camped, and as they sat around the fire eating, they heard the cursing of men and the sound of rolling wagons. It would be hours before they all made it to the bottom. Matt ate a few bites, then arose abruptly and walked to his horse which he had kept saddled. Then he rode back toward the rim where the men still toiled. After much searching he found Coyle.

The man had his coat off, his face was dirty and he was sweating. He looked up at Matt, and his mouth seemed to tighten.

"Howdy," Matt said, "I've got some blocks. Want 'em?"

Coyle's irritation was close to the surface. He started to say no, then hesitated. "I could use 'em," he said lamely, "I guess this was one thing we didn't plan for."

Matt had brought two of the blocks along. He dropped them to the ground at Coyle's feet. "If she'd like," he said, avoiding Jacquine's eyes, "your daughter could ride over an' sit with the women from my company. They've got a fire an' some hot food. That coffee tastes mighty good."

He looked up, and his eyes met hers. For an instant, they held, then she nodded. "I think I will, Father," she said coolly, "if there's nothing I can do here."

"Ride along with her, will you, Bardoul?" Coyle asked. "Since this morning I'm not sure I like her riding around alone."

"You won't need me here?"

"Thanks. With these blocks we'll get along."

They turned their horses and rode along the rim toward the cut he had made earlier. When they reached it, Jacquine reined in and turned a little in her saddle. "Well," she said, "you were right about Bain."

"He's a frontier character," he said noncommittally. "A lot of men know about him."

"Clive didn't."

So it was Clive now? The thought angered him, but he said nothing. She waited for his reply, but when it did not come she said quickly, "You think he did know?"

"I don't know whether he did or not," Matt said quietly, "but Logan Deane knew. He is Massey's right hand man. I should think if he knew he would tell Massey."

"Just what are you hinting at?" Jacquine demanded, a thin edge of anger in her voice. "You advised us not to come. You said it might not be safe. Why?"

"I don't know," he admitted frankly. "I don't know at all. I only know that from the first there has seemed to be something wrong here. My feeling was increased when Massey picked the men he did as his law enforcement group. They are a lot of outlaws!"

"He says they are not!"

"Well, I offer Bain as an example."

"You can't judge them all by one."

"In this case you can. Some are better, and some worse than Bain. The fact remains that Massey claimed he did not know Bain was with the wagon train. Your father obviously did not know. Yet he was here, concealed until we left Deadwood. He showed his true colours at the first opportunity.

"Moreover, I see no reason why we should have ten men to enforce peace in a wagon train that is over half composed of men and their families. The only possible trouble-making elements are in that group themselves."

"You don't like Clive, do you?" Jacquine demanded.

"Frankly, no. However, that may be a matter of personalities. Some people simply can't get along. Yet I think there is more to it than that. He didn't want me on this trip. It was only Portugee and your father who made it possible for me to come. Why didn't he want me? Was it because I knew too much about the Big Horns?"

"Perhaps it was because of your experiences with Colonel Pearson!" she flared, nettled by him, yet disturbed.

"Possibly." He indicated the cut. "Shall we ride on?"

For an instant, she hesitated, then she started her horse down the cut ahead of him. At that instant he felt a sharp sting of pain along his shoulder, and the report of a rifle rang out!

He wheeled his horse and rode like a streak at the direction of the shot. There was another hurried shot, then a sound of falling gravel, Matt's six shooter came up and he fired quickly, once, twice, three times in the direction of the sound.

Men came running, rifles in hand, but Jacquine was beside him first. "What happened?" she demanded.

"Somebody tried to kill me," he replied shortly.

"Oh, you're just being dramatic!" she protested. "Probably a rifle went off by accident!"

He swung his horse broadside to hers and grabbed her wrist roughly. With a jerk that nearly lifted her from the saddle, he took her hand and pressed it against his shoulder.

"Oh!" she gasped. "You're bleeding!"

"It's all part of the drama!" he said roughly.

Massey, Coyle, Pearson and several other men had come up. "What's going on here?" Pearson demanded.

"Somebody took a shot at me," Matt replied. "In the morning I'm going on the trail."

"An Indian, probably," Coyle suggested, "maybe he figured it was a good chance to catch a straggler."

"It wasn't an Indian." Matt's voice was positive. In the darkness he could see Pearson's head come up. "I heard the sound of boots on gravel."

"Nonsense!" Pearson snapped. "Who would shoot at you?"

"At least a half dozen men, Colonel," Bardoul said coolly, "on this wagon train."

"You're referring to talk of trouble between you and Logan Deane?"

"No. When and if Deane ever shoots at me it will be an even break. Say what you want to about him, he's not yellow!"

"Thanks." Deane had ridden up in the darkness. "Thanks, Bardoul."

"I'll wait until daybreak," Matt said, "then I'll get on the trail."

"You'll do nothing of the kind?" Massey flared. "This wagon train sticks all together. We can't have each individual running off on errands of his own."

"You heard me say I was going," Bardoul felt anger mounting within him. He did not like Massey, and tried to fight against the feeling, knowing it interfered with the clarity of his judgment.

"I forbid it!" Massey snapped.

Matt shucked. "You forbid it? Then go climb a tree, friend Massey, because in the morning I'm going after that dry gulcher. If you want to stop me, come prepared for it!"

"Now, now!" Coyle interrupted nervously. "Let's not start fighting amongst ourselves. We have trouble enough ahead. If he wants to trail the man, Clive, let him go. After all, it is his own business and if he doesn't come back, the fault is his own, not ours."

"All right!" Massey turned his horse. "Do as you damn please!"

They had made six miles during the day.

Daylight found them ready to roll, but Matt saddled the dun, then turned to Buffalo. "Lead them today, will you?" he said. "We'll strike a big hill about noon. As we get to it, better bear off to one side. Have them double up the teams for that pull, it is going to be hard enough, and that will make it easier on the stock."

"I recall that place," Murphy bit off a chew. "You goin' huntin?"

"Uh huh. I don't like bein' shot at. I don't like it at all."

"Be a swell chance for them to get you, alone."

"They won't get me. But you might keep an eye open. If you or Ban see anybody startin' to leave the train, you might stop 'em."

"We'll do that!" Murphy said positively. "You got a theory?"

"Bain."

Matt Bardoul swung into the saddle and turned the dun back toward the rim. Clive Massey watched him go, and his face was bitter. "Bat!" he said.

Hammer came up. "Go after him, Bat. I don't want him to come back."

Hammer touched his lips with his tongue. "How about some help? He's a tough one, that Bardoul. Got eyes like a hawk an' ears like a lynx."

"Damn it," Massey said sullenly, "can't anybody do anything around here?" He wheeled, and his eyes fell on a loitering half-breed. Buckskin Johnson was part Crow and part white and all coyote. "Go with him!" he said.

Ban Hardy saw them go. He was glancing back from his wagon seat. Barney Coyle had just ridden up. "Take this wagon, Barney," Ban said, "I'd better go have a look."

Barney Coyle glanced around. "I'll go!" he said eagerly. He wheeled his horse and started for a low hill where he might cut them off. Hoof beats sounded and he glanced around to see Murphy riding toward him. "Come on," Buff said heartily. "Maybe this'll be fun!"

They put their horses to a fast run, shielded from Massey's view by the dust and wagons. Cutting down into a ravine they raced along its bottom, then around the edge of a wash and out on a hillside. Murphy reined in. "Now, just hold it," he said. "Keep your rifle ready."

It was only a minute until they heard horses, and then Bat Hammer and the breed rode into sight.

"Hold it, boys!" Murphy kneed his horse into the road, his rifle ready. Coyle was beside him, his heart pounding.

"You're strayin' a bit far from the wagons, better get back!"

"We're huntin' some fresh meat," Hammer protested. His eyes shifted from Murphy to Coyle. He did not understand Coyle's being there, and did not like it.

"Maybe," Murphy agreed pleasantly, "but you'll find the huntin' better up ahead of us, or off toward the Belle Fourche. Suppose you start that way? An' fast?"

Hammer hesitated, his face darkening, then with a curse he swung his horse and followed by the Indian, rode away.

Matt Bardoul took his time, he was quite sure Bain was his man, and there was every chance that he might circle around and rejoin the wagon train. If that happened it was sure to precipitate trouble. The trail began on the steep slope down which they had lowered the wagons.

Matt found the place where the man had been lying when he fired his shot. The shell was still there, and it was from a Winchester .44. He looked over the bank, and saw a place showing muddbaj boot tracks. Scrambling over the edge, he found the place where the man had landed after his leap, a little further on he found a spot of blood. "Winged him," Bardoul said thoughtfully. "Well, that makes it more simple!"

Returning to the zebra dun, he led the horse down the cut in the rim, and then back to where he had found the tracks and the blood. For the next three hundred yards the trail was not difficult. The wounded man was getting out of there, but fast. It had been dark, and he was not concerned about his trail.

At the bottom of the slope down which he had come on an angle, the trail led up a winding wash. Mounting his horse, Matt followed at a walk.

The sun was up now, and already hot. In the bottom of the wash it was like an oven. Once Matt found a place where the wounded man stopped to bandage his wound. There was more blood here, and a piece of faded blue cloth had fallen to the ground, evidently a piece torn but unused. After that there was no more blood, yet the trail remained fairly easy to follow.

Yet after a mile, the man circled back toward the original place until they reached a small copse where there were a few willows and some cottonwood. Matt lost time here, approaching cautiously, and searching inch by inch through the bottom. Finally he found where a horse had been tied, and he studied the tracks of the animal.

The mounted man now rode rapidly, heading due north from the route of the wagon train. Matt settled down to following, keeping a wary eye on the terrain around him. He knew very well the manner of man he was following. Abel Bain was a fighter. The man had cause to hate him, and would never rest until he had killed Bardoul or was killed himself.

As yet Bain did not know he was trailed. That was obvious from the route he chose and the way he travelled. It had still been dark when the wounded man had covered this country. He had moved fast once he got aboard the horse, and he was making no effort to swing around in a circle to rejoin the wagon train.

It was mid morning before Bardoul found any change in the trail. Then he reined in suddenly. Here the wounded man had stopped, dismounted, and walked up to the crest of a hill among some rocks. He had stopped to have a look at something.

Matt's eyes narrowed. It was still too new a trail to have been made in daylight, so that meant that Bain could not have been looking back over his own trail. He would know he could not be followed until daylight made his tracks visible. What then had he been looking at?

It had to be a fire. Nothing else would have been visible at that distance at night. Yet what distance? Where had the fire been?

Suddenly, Matt recalled the light wagon and the two men who had been following the train, the two men he suspected Tolliver of knowing. Were they instead, friends of Bain?

Bain had remained here for some time, watching that fire. Three cigarette stubs lay on the ground among the rocks. Bain had been in Texas and like most of the men who had picked up cigarette smoking from across the border, he had. Anyway, the butts were fresh and had obviously lain there but a short time.

From the position of the stubs, Matt deduced the approximate location of the fire Abel Bain must have watched. Mounting once more, he started out over the prairie, riding back and forth to find that fire.

He found it a half mile from the rocks. A few charred bits of wood and some still smouldering buffalo chips. Nearby were the narrow wheel tracks of the light wagon, and the tracks of the mules. There were the tracks of three persons, but those of the last man, and Bardoul recognized them as the tracks he had followed from the rim, were those of Abel Bain.

Had Bain come to the fire during the night? Or the following morning?

The wagon had moved out, probably at daybreak. Scouting the area carefully, Bardoul could find no way of determining whether Abel Bain had stayed with the wagon or gone on, for here a number of tracks merged, part of them being the trail left by one column of wagons on the previous day.

Disgusted, he rode his horse under cover of some trees and rested, after loosening the cinch and removing the bit from the dun's mouth. After an hour, he mounted and started on the trail of the wagons, moving very cautiously now.

If Bain was with that wagon, he would most certainly be keeping a sharp lookout, and if he was not, he might be trailing it at a safe distance.

Here was a confusing situation. Who were the two men in the light wagon? Were they friends of Tolliver? If so, what was Bain's connection with them? And if Tolliver's friends, why had not the young mountaineer approached him on the subject of their joining his company?

The trail now was following the Belle Fourche, and within a short time, Matt came within sight of the wagon train. The long hill ahead was a hard pull, but apparently the system adopted by Murphy at his suggestion was being followed by both Coyle and Reutz, for he could see most of them were doubling their teams for the long haul. Yet the absence of the light wagon worried him. Somehow he had missed it, and the wagon must have been concealed in the brakes near the river.

For a time he debated returning to search the wagon out, then decided to wait, riding back to his own company.

They had surmounted the hill. Barney Coyle was there, sitting his horse near Murphy, and his face broke into a grin as he saw Matt. "Find him?"

Bardoul shook his head. He took out a handkerchief and mopped the sweat from his face. "No." He offered no explanation except to add that he was quite sure where he was.

Later, beside Tolliver's wagon, he said casually, "You ever know Bain before?"

Tolliver glanced up, surprised. "Me? No, I never knowed him. I ain't been in this country no great time."

Bardoul looked at him searchingly. If ever a man seemed without guile it was Tolliver. Yet he was connected in some way, Matt was sure, with the wagon trailing them.

When the column was lined out again . . . they followed a route a little to the right of the company ahead . . . he rode up alongside Murphy.

"We'll make a long dry trip of it tomorrow unless he swings closer to the river," Murphy suggested.

"I think he'll change course a little. It looks to me like he was going to go north again, but that will leave the river to cross, maybe several times if we hold the route I think he's figuring on."

Colonel Pearson and Massey both avoided him,

remaining away from the train. Once, he saw Jacquine. The girl was riding with Barney, and when they drew near him she rode closer.

"How is your shoulder?" she asked. It was impossible to tell whether she was really concerned or merely being polite.

"All right," he said, "it wasn't much. Just cut the skin."

"Do you think it was somebody shooting at you?"

"Sure, and he made a good shot of it, too. I turned in my saddle just then or he would have had me. I must have been outlined against the sky, and he could hear my voice from where I sat."

"Do you think it was Bain?" Barney wanted to know.

"I'm sure of it. I trailed him a good distance. I think I know where he is."

"In the train?" Jacquine asked quickly. Matt thought he detected a little worry in her voice.

"Not exactly." He avoided the subject, not wanting to go on with it.

"Has your father said anything more about the route?" he asked Barney.

The younger Coyle shrugged. "No, he hasn't said much. I believe the general trend is northwest, however. Around the northern end of the mountains and then south to this Shell Creek."

They forded the Belle Fourche three times during the day, and then turned into an abandoned Indian trail which led to a vacant Indian camp, only recently abandoned. Despite the long hill the wagons had done well, and they made eighteen miles more.

Matt saw supper started, and then he swung into the saddle and headed off along the wagon trail. Just before he dropped over the crest toward the river bottom he saw a horseman cut out from the wagon train and start after him. His jaw hardened and his eyes narrowed with thought. It looked like Tolliver's horse.

He smelled the smoke of a fire before he came up with the wagon. Instantly, he swung down, and loosening his guns in his holsters, he started moving carefully through the brush, leaving his horse standing. When he drew nearer, he heard voices. For an instant, he froze in place, sure that one of them was a woman. Then when they spoke again, he was sure he was mistaken.

The wagon had been drawn up in the trees near the stream, and one of the two men was bending over a fire. The other was gathering sticks. Seated on the ground, his back against a wheel, was Abel Bain.

Huge, hairy, and dirty, he lounged there with a rifle across his lap. His shirt was bloodstained, but from all appearances Matt's shot had done no more damage, except in loss of blood, than Bain's own bullet. His face bore the marks of the beating Bardoul had given him. There was a deep cut over one eye, and a blue swelling, two fingers wide, under the other. His lips were puffed and swollen, but there was a deep cut visible on one of them.

"Hey! You by the fire! Come over here!" Bain called abruptly.

Bardoul noticed the man picking up wood had straightened and turned toward Bain. Matt noticed that he wore no gun. From the look of things, Abel Bain was an uninvited guest.

The boy by the fire had not moved.

"Come here, I said!" Bain roared. Matt eased closer under cover of Bain's diverted attention. He glanced quickly at the other fellow, and could see his face was white and tense.

The boy started a few steps toward Bain, then stopped. Bain got to his feet and put the rifle down. He stared hard at the boy. "Hell!" he exploded suddenly. "You don't look like no boy! I think you're a girl! Come here!"

"Don't go!"

The man nearer Matt spoke sharply. "Don't go any nearer!"

Bain turned and glared at him. "Keepin' her all for yourself, huh?" he said. "Purty smart, dressin' her like a man! Well, by . . . !"

The remark lost itself for Abel Bain was face to face with death. He had shifted his eyes to see Matt

Bardoul standing just on the edge of the brush, feet apart, facing him.

Bain's face lost the sudden look of triumph. He looked now like a trapped wolf, but one still full of viciousness and fight. He crouched a little. "So you trailed me, huh? I was a watchin' for you!"

"And you tried to kill me, Bain. I don't like people who sneak shots at me."

"Well, you found me!" Bain snarled. "I hate your guts, anyway, Bardoul! I always did!"

Matt saw the sudden widening of Bain's eyes as he went for a gun, and Matt palmed his own. He never knew when he drew, only his gun was out, and he drove two hammering shots through Bain's left shirt pocket.

The big renegade's eyes glazed and the gun slipped from his fingers. His knees sagged, and then he stumbled one step and fell.

Matt fed shells into the gun and holstered it. Then he looked up sharply. "What happened here?" he demanded.

"My name's Joe Rucker. This here's my brother. This feller come sneakin' up on us about daybreak. He got the drop on me an' took our guns. Said as how he was figurin' to ride with us for a ways. He had the drop, an' there was nothin' we could do about it."

"All right. The sign read that way, so I'm takin' your word for it."

A horse crashed through the brush, and Matt wheeled, gun in hand. It was young Tolliver, and his eyes went from Matt to the body of Bain. His face was pale.

"These people friends of yours, Tolliver?" Matt asked kindly.

The young driver nodded, embarrassed. "Sort of," he agreed. "I met up with them in Deadwood."

"Why don't you join my company, Joe?" Bardoul asked. "Be glad to have you."

Joe's eyes shifted to his brother. "Reckon I'd better not," he said. "Reckon we better foller along to ourselves."

"This is Indian country."

"I know. We'll stick it."

"All right." He glanced at Bain's body. "Have you got a shovel? If you have, I'll bury him."

"You go ahead," Tolliver suggested, "I'll bury this hombre."

Together they dug a grave on the bank of the Belle Fourche, and then Tolliver burned words on a board with a hot iron, and they put it up as a marker.

ABEL BAIN . . . OUTLAW

HE DRAWED TOO SLOW

Killed 1877

Matt Bardoul swung into the saddle and loped back toward the wagon train. He was circling toward his own wagons when he saw a group of men standing to one side. They all looked up as he drew near.

Colonel Orvis Pearson, Brian Coyle, Herman Reutz, Buffalo Murphy, Barney Coyle and several others, including Clive Massey and Logan Deane.

Matt pulled up, glancing over the group. Then his eyes shifted to Massey. "You might like to know," he said grimly, "I just buried Abel Bain!"

Clive Massey's face darkened, and Matt saw Logan Deane lift a tobacco sack from his shirt pocket and start to build a smoke.

"You *what?*" Massey demanded.

"I trailed Abel Bain, the man who shot at me. I found him. He tried to draw. He's dead."

Massey's face was a study of doubt and anger, then suddenly, his eyes changed, and he turned toward the group with a shrug. "See? This is what I meant! If such men are allowed to keep their guns there will be continual shootings, such as this!"

Reutz glanced up at Bardoul. "Pearson suggests we collect all the guns and keep them in a couple of wagons, under guard. To prevent shootings."

"He's got a lot of nerve," Bardoul said flatly. "I

wouldn't give up my gun for any man! And what would happen if we run into hostile Indians?"

"We could deal them out, then collect them again," Massey smiled. "I didn't expect you to agree, Bardoul, but these others are peace loving men."

"And what do we do for protection if some more of your law enforcing outfit start tryin' what Bain did?" Matt demanded.

"Bain was rough, I'll admit. You seem to have taken care of that, and it is scarcely liable to happen again. I think the guns should be collected and kept in a safe place."

Matt stared thoughtfully at his horse's head. There was more to this than appeared on the surface. Here, he felt sure, was a clue toward Massey's ultimate plan. Yet what could he gain by disarming the entire wagon train? Except, of course, to put them completely in his hands, for his group of nine men would still keep their weapons.

"For myself, I say no. I think I can speak for those in my company."

"That's right!" Murphy agreed. "They are against it!"

"We can always take them!" Massey flared.

Matt chuckled. "Now wouldn't that be sensible? Startin' a war out here on the plains? No, if it comes to a strong division of opinion, we could split the train. I'd take my group an' go my own way."

"If you do," Herman Reutz said, "count me in. I'll go with you."

Surprisingly, Massey smiled. "Well, maybe I was rather drastic. Perhaps it is expecting too much to ask you to give up your guns even if they could be distributed fast enough in case of trouble. It was just a suggestion, anyway. Something calculated to keep some men who have a natural bent toward killing from going too far."

"If you mean that for me," Bardoul said calmly, "forget it. I never shot at any man except in self-defense. I trailed Bain because he tried to kill me an' because he was a mad dog. He drew. It was his tough luck, however, if you take a poll of the women in this train, I think you'll find they all will rest easier when they know he's dead."

"Then that question is settled," Coyle said, obviously relieved. "What about the route?"

"We follow the one we chose," Pearson said. "It has been very good so far."

"What about that route, Bardoul?" Reutz asked.

"It is a good route so far. Tomorrow it will be rough, but still good, and the next day. After that, I'd say we'd better change. That waterhole is not good and we will make it only after a dry camp."

"Nonsense!" Pearson said. "Our information is of the best. Lyon says that waterhole is good. Phillips says he thinks it is."

"We'll continue on the way we're going," Coyle said. "How about it, Massey?"

"I'll take Tate Lyon's word. After all, he's the guide on this trip."

"That's good enough for me," Coyle added.

"Well," Reutz shrugged, "might's well give it a try."

Massey turned on Bardoul, and there was a cool, measured triumph in his eyes. Jacquine Coyle had just ridden up. "By the way, Bardoul. What about that wagon of yours that is trailing behind us?"

They all turned, eyes on him. Suspicion mounted into the eyes of the German. "What wagon?" Reutz asked.

"Why, the light wagon that's been trailin' us. Two men in it."

"What about it, Bardoul?" Coyle wanted to know.

"I know no more about them, than you. My driver, Tolliver, seems to know them. Bain had climbed in their wagon and was holding them under his gun. The oldest one's name is Joe Rucker, but both are mere youngsters, and perfectly harmless!"

He turned his horse and started back toward his wagons, Murphy falling in alongside of him. How much they believed, he neither knew nor cared. Yet he was conscious that Jacquine's eyes followed him, curious, questioning.

CHAPTER VI

The air lay dead and still upon the long, dry grass lands, no breath of wind stirring the pale green and brown of the prairie. A haze covered the sky, a high haze that seemed to gather and intensify the heat while increasing the humidity and making every breath an effort.

The oxen were irritable and erratic, no longer content to bow their necks and pull, but wanting to wander from the trail, to spread out, to escape the eternally rising and enveloping dust.

Stones mixed themselves with the grass, and although the heavy wagons tacked and yawed, they could not escape them all. The going was heavier now, and occasionally the sheer weight of the pull dragged the teams to a stop, and then under the cracking of the bull whips they lunged into the harness once more, straining inch by inch through the grass.

Pausing to give the oxen a chance to breathe Murphy glanced up at Matt, who had stopped beside him, "Sultry as hell! We may get a storm!"

"Uh huh. A little rain would help."

"If we get it now, it won't be a little rain."

Twice more they crossed the river, but the water was running very low. Once, far away to the south, they sighted a few antelope, and although Bardoul tried, there was no getting close to them. They were restless and wary, seeming to feel the same tension that disturbed the oxen.

Glancing back he noticed that Joe's wagon was following them closer now, staying within sight of the wagon train.

This was Indian country, and several times he had seen Indian sign around. Murphy noticed it, too.

During the late afternoon, Matt relieved Tolliver, and walked beside the oxen while the young mountaineer rode back to talk to Joe and Joe's brother. Matt told him to warn them about keeping a sharp lookout for Indians.

Company C, led by Herman Reutz, was next to him on the south. The storekeeper had seven wagons, all heavily loaded. Two of his company had four wagons each. Aside from Brian Coyle's, no wagons were loaded so richly as these, although Matt knew his own load was valuable enough.

If the Sioux should wipe them out they would certainly make a rich haul. Probably no wagon train had ever moved toward the west as richly laden as this one. Each man was chosen and each had been advised as to his cargo, and the loads they carried were at least eighty percent pay loads.

At prevailing prices, Matt figured, his wagons were worth easily . . . it hit him like a bucket of ice water.

He stopped dead still for an instant as the idea hit his mind, and then he began to walk on, but he was scowling. Why, in freight and animals alone, not counting weapons or money carried on their persons, this wagon train must be worth more than three hundred thousand dollars!

Work cattle brought thirty to forty dollars a head in St. Joseph or Council Bluffs, although often the price varied from month to month. They were selling for still higher prices in Deadwood, but in Oregon they would command at least twice that amount. There were a number of milk cows being driven along, and nearly every wagon had at least one saddle horse trailing behind. Some of Coyle's company were driving a few sheep.

Each wagon carried from two thousand to twenty-five hundred pounds of freight, most of it in clothing, ammunition, tea, flour, coffee, sugar, beans, bacon and dried fruit. As the wagon train was supposed to supply the basic needs of a town that was expected to grow, there were also tools, bales of clothing and other dry goods as well as extra weapons.

It would be a rich haul, a very rich haul for the Sioux . . . or anyone else.

Supposing the personnel of the wagon train were unarmed? How very simple to slaughter them and take over!

That, he knew, was the only way it could be done. The west was already too crowded for a wagon train to be looted boldly without making every man of the attacking party an outlaw. The only way it could be done would be mass murder.

Nor would it be the first time it had happened. White men were known to have run with Indians, and to have guided them to selected wagon trains. Jules Reni, for whom Julesburg was named, had long been suspected of doing just that. The richest wagon trains had invariably been looted after leaving his post, and escaped prisoners told of seeing white renegades coming and going among the Indians.

Abel Bain had been known to be one of these, and Bat Hammer was suspected of being another. Bardoul had once accompanied a relief party that started out to drive off the Indians attacking a wagon train, and while trailing the Indians, had personally seen a man riding a steeldust horse, such as Hammer rode at the time, among the pursued. Although there had been no evidence, feeling was so high around Julesburg that Hammer had left the country.

Certainly, if that were the plan, to lead this wagon train into the remote Big Horn basin and loot it, the planning had been shrewd. Precautions had been taken to select only men who would bring good stock and a rich cargo, and to keep anyone from knowing their destination.

Where, in all this, did Colonel Pearson stand? Despite his dislike for the man Matt could not bring himself to believe that Pearson was a criminal. He might be a coward, and was without doubt a fool, but he was at least a reasonably honest fool.

Yet Brian Coyle was one of the planners. The

project had been conceived by Pearson, Coyle and Massey, and Tate Lyon had offered the gold that was their talking point. That Lyon was a part of the scheme, Bardoul could easily believe, for the man was of a type with Bain and Hammer.

Was Coyle an unwitting dupe of Massey? Or was he involved himself? If he was involved, would he bring his daughter? That was the best argument in Coyle's favour, and yet Coyle had done most of the planning and organization. Many a man had been drawn into crooked dealings when he believed it could be done without being exposed, and to them this should seem a foolproof plan.

Whether or not he had guessed correctly, it would be wise to plan with this answer in mind. If it were not the right one they would at least be ready for whatever came. It would be well, too, to have a talk with some of the more trustworthy men of his own company as well as those of Coyle and Reutz. They must not be trapped.

There was another point to be considered. Where would the attack be likely to occur? Would it be soon? In the Big Horn basin? Or would they wait until they reached the bank of the Shell?

It was logical to assume that they would wait. The further the place of attack from Deadwood, the easier it would be to destroy any possibility of information ever getting out as to the fate of the wagon train. Also, the wagons would be closer to the market probably selected for the goods which would certainly be further west. When he thought of the market problem, he at once recalled the mining towns northwest of them where everything was priced out of reason.

When Tolliver returned, Matt mounted his horse, and mopping perspiration from his face, turned the horse toward the open country to escape the dust.

He was no more than a quarter of a mile away from the train when he saw Jacquine Coyle loping her pony toward him. "Oh? It's you?" She looked at him curiously. "Somehow I didn't recognize you."

"Disappointed? Or is my horse so dusty he looks black?" Clive Massey often rode a black horse.

"No, it was neither. Only, I thought . . . well, I'm glad to see you, anyway. I've been wanting to tell you how sorry I was for being sarcastic the other evening when you were shot. It's just that I was never near anyone who had been shot before, and it seemed so fantastic. I thought something would happen, a big noise, or a scream or something. It was scarcely even exciting."

He chuckled. "Next time I'll grab my chest with both hands, scream and fall off my horse."

"Oh, didn't mean that! But. . . ."

"I know. It surprised me at first, too. So many things that are so dramatic or exciting when you read about them actually happen so simply and quietly. We humans like to consider ourselves important to creation and to the world, and we expect that whenever death comes it should be with a crash of thunder and wild shouts or something, or with soft music around and people looking grave and serious. We always have it that way in the theatre because it makes us believe in our importance. Most of our life is a matter of dressing ourselves up to believe in just that, dressing ourselves in attractive clothes, in titles, in reputations. Actually, at base we all realize that we're just a frightened bunch of animals, still afraid of the unknown, still afraid of thousands of things that can separate us from life, and trying to shield ourselves from our own smallness."

Jacquine stared at him curiously. "You're a strange man. You talk like a philosopher. Does your wound bother you now?"

"Itches a little in this heat. It wasn't much."

She turned a little in her saddle. "How does a man become what you are?" she asked. "I mean . . . well, Barney heard some stories about you. About your fight with Lefty King at Julesburg, and how you were at the Wagon Box fight, and Ban Hardy told us how you stood off sixty Kiowas all alone once, down in Texas."

"Ban talks too much. Anyway, I was in a buffalo wallow, and they couldn't get to me."

"Then on the stage coming up from Cheyenne I heard Elam Brooks talking to a man when we stopped at Pole Creek Ranch and he said you were one man Logan Deane would want to stay clear of. Are you such a dangerous person then?"

"Me? Lord, no! Only I've had gun trouble a few times."

"What do you think about Logan Deane?"

"I think he's a brave man, as much as any of us are."

"Barney heard that he was suspected of holding up the stage out of Cheyenne, once."

"I wouldn't know. He doesn't talk much. He has a reputation as being one of the fastest men alive with a gun."

"Do you think you'll have trouble with him?"

Matt glanced at her curiously. Was this simple curiosity? Or was she actually seeking information? And if it was information she wanted, was it for herself? Her father? Or for Clive Massey? If he said he expected trouble, and within himself he was sure it would eventually come, it could be twisted to mean that he was hunting trouble. Massey would stop at nothing to put him in a bad light, to get rid of him.

"I doubt it. He has a reputation as a gun hand. So have I. Often two such men hunt each other up just to see which is best, and the men of this wagon train know that. They like to talk about such things over a camp-fire, and men always have. I expect that in the days of the knights in armour the various fighters would go miles to find each other, and before them cavemen with stone clubs.

"The trouble is that such talk will often lead to a fight, for gun fighters are often jealous of their reputations, and they hear a lot of talk about who is the fastest, until finally they begin to wonder themselves. From there it is just a step to an actual fight."

"Like you and Spinner Johns?"

"That was different."

"You mean," she asked carefully, "that you believe he was sent to kill you?"

"Where did you get that idea?"

"Barney heard it. He likes you, and he hears a lot of gossip among the men. Some of them believe he was sent to kill you."

"I don't know why he came. I had never seen him before."

"You've heard that silly talk about Clive sending him?" She looked at him searchingly.

"Yes. Did Barney tell you that, too?"

"No, I heard that from two other men. Mr. Reutz and Elam Brooks thought it curious."

He changed the subject deliberately. "That brother of yours is quite a fellow. He's considerable of a man, if you ask me. This country is made to order for him."

"If he doesn't become a gunman, he has been practicing."

"He should. It might come in handy, sometime. After all," he looked at her quickly, anxious that she understand this point, "this country is still wild. There are Indians here, and white renegades that are worse. These men are savage, they understand only the law of force, and if one is to live in such a country one must be prepared to protect those one loves and the things one lives by.

"But you need not worry about Barney. He isn't the stuff of which gunmen are made."

She looked around at him suddenly. "Who's your girl? Is it that pretty Stark girl? Sarah?"

He blushed suddenly. "Gosh, no! I don't have a girl."

"Or is it that girl in the light wagon back there?" There was genuine questioning in her eyes now and he realized she had been leading up to this.

He hesitated only an instant. "What girl? You mean Joe's brother?"

"I heard Joe's brother was a girl."

He was not sure of that, but he believed Abel Bain's guess could be right. There was certainly something mysterious about that light wagon.

"Whoever gave you that idea?"

"Clive. He says you're keeping a girl back there, dressed as a man."

"He's mistaken. If there is a girl back there, it is none of my business, and I don't know that there is."

"Are you still suspicious about this wagon train? I remember how you tried to warn us in the hotel."

He avoided the issue by seeming to misunderstand the question. "You mean, do I doubt there is gold along the Shell? No, I can't say that I do. There is very likely to be gold there, and certainly, whether there is or not it is one of the most beautiful regions in the west. For myself, I don't care whether there is or not. I have other plans."

"What sort of plans?"

"A ranch in the Big Horn basin. A ranch where I can see the mist rising over the valley in the morning and where I can see my cattle grazing on the long grass. A place of my own, just a long, low rambling place with lots of comfort and security, with good, cold water, a lot of beauty around me, and a chance to do something that will add to the country instead of just looting it."

"A wife? Or have you a wife somewhere?"

"No, to the last question. I have no wife, and haven't had. As to whether I want one: of course. Schopenhauer said that happiness was born a twin. I believe that. Nothing is quite so beautiful as when you share it with someone else. There is no purpose in working unless one work for someone, for something."

"A gunfighter who quotes Schopenhauer! What next?"

"You'd be surprised at some of the men you see in the west. Don't get an idea because they wear guns and use them that all these men are ignorant and un-educated. Some of the most brilliant men in the world have come west as pioneers, men of intelligence and ability in every line. Around these campfires I've heard men discuss questions of philosophy in a manner that would do justice to Berkeley or Hume."

"Then it isn't gold you're looking for?"

"Of course not. Gold can mean power, luxury, women, liquor, and whatever a man wants in that line, but gold always means struggle, war. I don't want that. I'm a man who knows what he wants, a home, a ranch, time to work without strain, and time to live. Why fight my life away to have as much as or more than someone else? Soon the years are gone and all there is to remember is a lot of empty struggle, and one is too old to enjoy what was gained."

"What was the trouble between you and Colonel Pearson?"

He looked around at her quickly. "What is this? An inquisition?" He shrugged, smiling. "It was quite important at the time. We had a difference of opinion about a little matter of tactics in an Indian fight down south of here, a long way south."

"Was he in command?"

"Yes. I was a civilian scout."

He studied the horizon, his eyes narrowing. "We're going to have a storm, and a bad one. We'd better start back."

Without actually being aware of it, they had ridden on ahead of the wagon train. They were far out of sight of it now, and Matt could see the thickening along the horizon. He knew how quickly storms could strike in this region, and how fierce they could be.

Even as he spoke a wind had begun to stir the tall grass. It was gratefully cooling, but he could feel the rain in it. They swung their horses and started back for the wagon train. The horses were eager to run, so they let them go, and behind them the wind suddenly swept down, bringing with it a spatter of rain. A moment later the plain went gray before them with a steel streaked curtain of pounding rain.

The rain stirred the dust bringing a queer smell from the hot dust lying in the grass, and from the grass itself. Jacquine glanced over at him, her eyes bright with laughter. He grinned in response, the rain soaking his shirt and running down his body under his clothes. The dun had turned black now with rain, but the horses seem to welcome the coolness after the long heat of the day.

They rode down on the wagon train, riding neck and neck at a dead run, soaked to the skin and laughing. As they reached the train, she swung off toward her own wagons, lifting a hand to wave at him, and he swung along side of Tolliver and ducked his head into the back of the wagon for his slicker.

It was only then he recalled his earlier thoughts, his decision about what must be done. He must see Lute Harless right away. Lute, Stark, and the others.

A half hour later it had become too dark and too muddy to travel. They swung the wagon train in a circle within a circle, and gathered the stock inside it. Tonight it would be dangerous to let them graze outside, for they would drift for miles before the driving rain and wind. Usually, the oxen could be safely turned loose, for they rarely travelled far. It was one of the many advantages they had for use on the plains.

Matt found shelter for the zebra dun, and rubbed it down. He thought over what he would tell the others while doing it. Supper was a hurried meal, a matter of getting a plateful of food and rushing to a wagon to eat. Otherwise the pounding rain wrecked and chilled the food.

When he had finished eating, Matt got up. He glanced around at big Bill Shedd. "Stick close by, Bill. Keep an eye on both wagons. I'll be gone for awhile."

Shedd glanced at him thoughtfully, lighting his pipe. "All right." He inhaled deeply. "Them wagons in A Company," he said suddenly, "loaded mighty light, ain't they?"

Bardoul nodded.

"Seems funny. Goin' west to organize a town, an' one of the main stems ain't carryin' much."

Matt pulled on his slicker again, looking past the lantern at Shedd. The big man puzzled him. He was huge, fat around the belt, and usually untidy, but sometimes there was an expression in his eyes that made Matt wonder if he was the big, simple sort of man he seemed. "You think about that, Bill," he said, "but don't talk about it."

He buttoned his slicker, then ran his hand inside the pocket to make sure he could lay a hand on the butt of his gun. "Bill, just why did you want to come on this wagon trip? You don't strike me as a gold hunting man."

"I ain't. Rightly I'm a bullwhacker an' a farmer. Maybe I'll find me a farm farther west. First I got me a job to do."

"A job?"

Shedd puffed for a moment on his pipe. "Yeah. A job. I ain't no gold huntin' man. Right now I'm a man huntin' man."

So that was it. Matt looked at Shedd thoughtfully and with new eyes. It was strange how often you accepted someone at face value or what seemed face value and without thinking much about them. Bill Shedd suddenly took on new significance. Bardoul was aware of a new impression, a startling, deep impression. If he were the man Bill Shedd was hunting he would be worried, very worried. There was something sure, inexorable about the big, ponderous fellow that gave him a sudden feeling of doom.

"What man, Shedd?"

"You got things on your mind, you don't talk about 'em. Neither do I." He glanced up at Bardoul through the thin smoke of his pipe. "Meanin' no offense." He paused. "Funny thing is, I am not sure."

"We'll have to talk about that, Bill. I'll be back."

He slid out of the covered wagon and dropped to the ground. The first heavy rush of rain had let up now and it was a steady if not a crashing downpour. The going would be very bad tomorrow. Bowing his head to the rain, he walked back toward Murphy's wagon, and thrust his head inside. Ban Hardy was sitting there with him. So was Jeb Stark. "Stick around, all of you. I'll be back."

Pulling his head back, a cold drop of water went down the back of his neck. It never failed, he thought. Cover yourself as you would, be as careful as you will, one drop will always fall down the back of your neck.

Lightning streaked the night, and he could see the picketed animals in the center of the huge circle, their backs wet and glistening. Around them, like the coils of a huge snake, were the gathered wagons, each only a few feet from the next, the wet canvas glistening in the reflected light. He splashed through a pool and stopped by Stark's wagon.

He scratched on the canvas. "Come in!" Stark yelled.

Matt pushed his head in. "My feet are wet, an' I'm dripping. Stark, come over to Murphy's wagon, will you? Little medicine talk."

He withdrew his neck and went on to Lute Harless' wagon. He hesitated, after speaking to Harless. Beyond was Rabun Kline's wagon, and next to that, Ernie Braden's. He hesitated over the idea of Kline. He had never talked much to the little Jew. Nor did he have any idea how the man stood except that he kept his team and wagon well, and had seemed a stable, reliable man.

That he was a friend of Herman Reutz, he knew. But was he too close to Pearson and Coyle? Would he talk?

Bardoul shrugged, then turned and moved toward Kline's wagon. He scratched on the canvas, and at a word, thrust his head inside. Rabun Kline was lying on one elbow, reading a book. He wore square steel rimmed glasses, which he took off as he saw Bardoul. "Oh?" he was surprised. "Come in, will you?"

"Some other time. Now, we've got a talk coming up. Medicine talk."

"Where?"

"Murphy's wagon." Matt took off his hat and wiped his wet face. "Kline, we've never talked much, but I take it you're an honest man."

"Thank you, sir. I hope that I am."

"Up there at Murphy's wagon there's a talk for honest men, but one that may mean a mess of trouble. Maybe gun trouble."

Kline folded his glasses carefully. "Shall I bring my gun now, sir?"

Bardoul grinned. Suddenly, he liked this square built man with the placid face. In the west you knew men quickly, and he knew this one now. "Not necessarily," he said, "if it comes to that, it will be later."

Within ten minutes they were all there, gathered in a tight little group in the crowded confines of the wagon. Murphy, fortunately, was carrying less than most of them, and had space.

Matt glanced around at their wet, serious faces. "Men," he said softly, "I had a brainstorm today. I want you to hear me out, answer my questions, and then decide if I am crazy or not."

He turned to Lute. "Harless, you have three wagons. What would you say your wagons, teams, and cargo are worth at prevailing prices?"

Lute's brow furrowed, and he rubbed his chin with the stem of his pipe. "Reckon I could figure it. My wagons are carryin' upwards of two thousand pound each. All told I've got about two thousand pound of flour in all three wagons, scattered amongst 'em. Flour is sellin' pretty general at ten dollars a hundred, some places more. You can figure that flour at two thousand dollars, all right."

He studied the problem for a few minutes while the rain pounded steadily on the canvas over their heads, and dripped from the sides of the wagon bed to the sod below. "Countin' sugar, tea, tools, an' ammunition, I'd say I have about ten thousand dollars tied up in my outfit. Ever' cent I brought west, an' what I took out of my claim in Deadwood."

"Reutz and Coyle would have more, wouldn't they?" Matt asked.

"Sure. A good bit more."

"Then," Matt suggested slowly, "at a rough guess this wagon train would have a total value of nearly or maybe more than, three hundred thousand dollars?"

"I'd say a little more than that," Rabun Kline said. "Perhaps half again as much. Coyle and Reutz have richer loads than we."

Matt nodded. His voice was low, reaching only the crowded circle of intent faces. "What a nice, rich, juicy plum to knock off the bough . . . if someone had the idea!"

Aaron Stark's chewing stopped with his mouth open. Murphy took the pipe from his mouth and stared at Matt, then slowly he put it back in his teeth. "Well, I'll be damned!" he muttered.

"Think it over: we were all carefully selected as men who had money enough to put a good, substantial outfit on wheels. We all were led to indicate our cash position by buying shares in the venture, the money being held by Clive Massey. We were advised as to what stock to buy, all valuable merchandise. Every effort has been made to see that this is the richest wagon train on wheels!"

"So!" Harless stared at him.

"Understand, I am accusing nobody. Understand also that I know nothing the rest of you do not know. I told you of my warning in the livery stable, and some of you are aware of my doubts of Massey, my questioning of Hammer's presence, and that of Bain.

"Buffalo can tell you that Abel Bain was a notorious renegade who raided many wagon trains out of Julesburg, and was almost lynched for it. Portugee Phillips knows the same thing."

"I've heard that," Harless said.

"Hammer has been suspected of the same operations. So was Buckskin Johnson. Their wagons carry more men than goods, heavily armed men, all with tough reputations. A little while ago Massey tried to get us to give up our weapons, too."

"You figure," Stark asked, "that they plan to murder us all an' lay it to the Injuns?"

"Something like that. Understand, I know no more than the rest of you. I may be doing honest men a grave injustice, but I've called you here to tell you and let you make up your own minds. If it is in the wind, we can set our canvas for it and be ready. If it is not, what can we lose?"

Hardy straightened a leg, then drew it back. He was getting stiff from the cramped position. "I'd say we'd better figure it that way. Massey lays out the guard plan. Any night he wants he could have only his own men awake. We'd be caught asleep, and wouldn't have a chance!"

"Or he could have some of us killed on guard," Murphy offered. "It's been done."

Harless shook his head. "It doesn't seem possible they would do a thing like that," he protested. "After all, they are white men!"

Stark snorted. "I'd sooner trust an Injun!"

"Mr. Coyle's a fine man," Kline added, "you don't think he would be a party to such a thing?"

"I doubt it, but I don't know. The only thing we can do," Matt continued, "is to carry weapons and ammunition at all times and keep our ears and eyes open. Who is, or who is not in it, I wouldn't know."

"Somebody let that Bain get loose," Stark added. "He wouldn't have got loose had it been me. Sary still wakes up nights shiverin' an' scared."

"What would you advise, sir?" Kline asked, looking up at Bardoul.

"Only what I've said. To go armed and watch. It would pay to remember the suggestions of Murphy and Ban, and keep an eye on that guard list, too. And any time any of us are on guard, it would pay to keep an eye on the camp as well as outside the camp."

"We could bust up an' go on by ourselves," Harless commented, "but that might lead to trouble right now."

"Uh huh." Matt thought of Jacquine. "Personally, I'm stayin' with this outfit. I think that's best. But I'll have a talk with Reutz about this. The rest of you keep mum."

They sat in silence for a few minutes while the rain fell steadily. All of them were thinking ahead, realizing what this might mean. To a man, those in the group had invested every dime in this venture. To lose it would mean all they possessed was gone, more, it would mean life itself, for not one of them could imagine the deal being attempted other than by a massacre.

Bardoul knew they were thinking, and even with his suspicion rising so strong within him, he could see how little he had to go on. Nothing but the merest suspicion. There could be plausible reasons for the presence of Bain and Hammer. Yet he could not convince himself that he was mistaken.

He knew the country that lay ahead, and knowing it, he was doubtful of any early attempt being made. Every effort should be taken now to prevent any surprise, but if the attack came, he was doubtful if it would come before they reached the Big Horn basin. In the meantime, much might happen.

"What about the division of friends and enemies?" Kline asked. "Wouldn't it be well to consider that a little? To try to draw some line of demarcation? What do you think, Mr. Bardoul?"

Matt studied the matter. "We can't be sure. I would say all in my own company are honest men with the exception of Ernie Braden and his driver. I believe they are doubtful."

"I agree," Stark said grimly, "that Braden's a liar an' a four flusher."

"Most of the men in Reutz' outfit are good men. Elam Brooks, certainly is. There are others."

"The total number of people now with the company," Kline said, "is one hundred and forty-four. There are sixty-two wagons. Fourteen of those wagons are in Company A, where Mr. Bardoul seems to feel the greatest danger lies. They are lightly loaded wagons, but some of them carry goods belonging to Brian Coyle, and to Weber, who is in Coyle's company.

"Fifty-three women and children, which leaves ninety-one men. The question is, how many of the ninety-one can we depend on?"

"We'll have to study that," Stark said, "I reckon there's nigh thirty men in that Company A, an' we can figure them as again us right to start. I reckon until we do some figurin' we better count on nobody but ourselves. Matt here smelled this out, an' he ain't drivin' much of the time. Let him study out which ones we can figure to stand by us, an' which won't."

"I agree, sir," Rabun Kline said, "and until then we do no talking?"

"Right!"

Matt Bardoul drew his hands along his trouser leg. He was remembering the cold face and the flat deadly eyes of Logan Deane. Sooner or later that would have to be settled, too. Strangely enough, at that moment he began to wonder about Deane. Somehow, killer though the man was, he did not seem to have a place in such a scheme as this.

Thinking of him, Matt recalled their conversation at the bar after his fight with Johns when he had suggested that Clive Massey was himself a gunman.

Who?

One by one he began to chalk off the names of those he could not be. Clay Allison and Wyatt Earp and Billy the Kid could be eliminated. Not Masterson, Luke Short, or Billy Brooks. Not Ben Thompson or Wes Hardin. Try as he would, he could not think of who Massey might be, but instinct told him the man was a gun artist.

There were many such, however, who had never become known and Massey might be one of these. In the Clements' clan in Texas there were dozens of gunmen. Manny himself, Jim Miller, and many others, but the shadow of Manny Clements and his cousin, Wes Hardin, had obscured the names of the clan members.

Further west in the mining camps of California, Nevada, and Utah there were other gunmen, such as the Plummer gang of Montana, Pearson of Pioche, and many others who never acquired the fame given to the gunmen of Texas or the cattle trail towns. It might be that Massey came from such a group.

Every sense in his body sounded a warning when near Massey. The man was a killer, and unless Matt was mistaken, a cold blooded killer with deadly speed. There was something in the way he looked at a man, something in his movements that was a challenge.

"Well," he said looking up, "I guess there's nothing more. If any of you learn anything, by all means come to me with it."

"What about Phillips?" Harless asked.

"I don't know," he replied honestly, "I really don't

know. He was one of the first to hint that something might be wrong with this whole trip, but we hadn't better count on him until we know."

Suddenly, he noticed a slight bulge in the canvas that had not been there earlier. He lifted his finger for silence, then stepped over the knees of the men between him and the door. There must have been some subtle movement of the wagon, for he heard a slight splash outside and hurled himself at the opening, gun in hand.

He caught one fleeting glimpse of a dark shadow vanishing in the direction of the other wagons, and he dared not shoot, for the wagons, some of them containing women, were directly in line with the running man.

The others piled out beside him. "Who was it?" someone demanded.

"I didn't get a look at him." Matt went around beside the wagon, and crouched there in the rain, striking a match that he cupped in his hands.

There were tracks there, partly in the mud, partly in water. The man had shifted his feet several times, so he might have been there for some time. There was no identifying mark.

He got to his feet and looked around at the circle of intent faces. "Well, maybe he was friendly, and probably not. From now on, every waking and sleeping moment, we've got to be ready!"

As the men scattered toward their wagons, Matt Bardoul turned his head and stared off through the dwindling rain at the large, white topped wagon where Jacquine Coyle lay sleeping.

This night might have changed everything. Walking back to his own wagon, he crawled inside. When he was ready for bed, he drew his guns, and one by one, with loving care, he cleaned and reloaded them. Now, he was ready. They could start any time.

CHAPTER VII

Back in the wagon after her exciting ride through the lashing rain, Jacquine changed into dry clothing, but while she changed her mind was not at rest, nor had it been at rest for some days.

She understood herself quite well, and she was perfectly aware that something had happened that day when she got down from the stagecoach and looked up to see Matt Bardoul leaning against the awning post in front of the IXL.

Just what had happened or how much she did not know. There had been little further contact to allow them to know each other, and on the other hand, there had been the obvious dislike on the part of Colonel Pearson as well as Clive's subtle but biting comments. The stories she heard of Bardoul in Deadwood were not favourable, nor were those after she left Deadwood until Barney became interested.

Barney was very little older than she, but Jacquine, although she never said as much, had come to entertain a high respect for his judgment. She saw, too, that what Matt had said was true, that Barney was growing, that he was becoming a man in balance and judgment. Had he remained in the relatively safe and even tempered eastern atmosphere, he might have been eight or ten years acquiring the manhood he had acquired in eight or ten months.

At first she had dismissed Matt's warning as sheer nonsense. She shared her father's anger and irritation that he should go so far as to make such veiled accusations of men they knew and liked. Also, she felt it

110

was a reflection on her father's judgment if not his honesty. Yet the thought was planted, and her eyes opened. She began to look for evidence to refute his warning, to prove him wrong, and scarcely had she begun this observation than she became aware of a vague but increasing doubt within her.

The incident of Abel Bain's attempted assault on Sary Stark she could dismiss. In the rough, new western world all kinds and types of men came together, and such things might happen. The fact that Matt Bardoul had warned of his presence in the wagon train and that Clive had dismissed his charge as unfounded, stayed in her mind.

Yet this was but one thing. Riding about as she was, she soon became aware of the subtle differences between the three companies of men commanded by Reutz, Bardoul and her father as compared with that commanded by Massey. The men of the latter group were an untidy, sullen, hard drinking crowd, and no women among them. It was from this group that Clive had chosen his law enforcement group.

She heard of all the disputes in the wagon train, for her father often discussed or complained about them. Barney brought her the rest of the news, and she was usually present when any discussion came up. She knew that Matt had warned them about the trail, and that this warning had proved correct. She noticed also that his wagons reached the bottom fastest and with less trouble than the others. She knew his loan of the block and tackle had helped her father and Herman Reutz.

Clive rarely talked about the gold fields any more. They had occupied a great part of his conversation while in Deadwood. Now she noticed that he was quieter, more watchful, but when he did talk to her there was a boldness and assurance in his manner that was new and different, nor did she like the change.

The following day, riding ahead of the train, she galloped up to join Colonel Orvis Pearson.

He was a fine figure of a man, tall and commanding. He rode as if perpetually on parade, and there was something dashing and theatrical in his manner. More and more she was becoming aware that he was merely a facade, a figurehead. It was her father and Clive Massey who directed the affairs of the train. And more and more she was aware of growing strain, and of the tendency for many of the men to draw closer to Matt Bardoul. Herman Reutz, for instance, had definitely aligned himself with Bardoul.

"Good Morning, Colonel! The air is nice after the rain, isn't it?"

"Beautiful! As you are beautiful, Miss Coyle! We should make a good many miles to-day, if this holds."

Most of the rain had already sunk into the parched, thirsty soil, and before the day was over the sun would erase what little impression it had made. Several times as she rode beside him, Jacquine started to speak, to ask the question she was dying to ask.

"Colonel," she said suddenly, "weren't you and Matt Bardoul in the Army together?"

His face stiffened, and when he spoke, his voice was sharp and cold. "He was never in the Service! Bardoul is a disobedient, recalcitrant ruffian!"

He turned his head abruptly. "Has he been talking to you about me?" There was something in his manner that savoured almost of fear. "Has he?"

"Oh, no! Someone, I've forgotten who, just said you two had been in the Apache country together."

"He was a civilian scout. I was in command. He should have been court martialed and shot!" Abruptly, he changed the subject. "Life in a frontier town will be difficult for you, won't it? You know there are few of . . . ."

The conversation drifted on, but her interest was gone. When she could conveniently escape, she dropped back. Matt was far away on the flank, riding his zebra dun. Her curiosity was thoroughly aroused and she intended to get to the bottom of the story, once and for all. Her father had hinted that it was disgraceful, that Bardoul had been discharged in dishonour.

Clive had hinted that in a panic of fear, Matt had fled from a battlefield.

Murphy was his friend, and would be prejudiced. Suddenly, she thought of Portugee Phillips.

She had never talked to him. Bits of information about him had drifted to her from time to time, but he held himself aloof, rarely talking with any of them. She knew him by sight, his black pointed beard, and his narrow, cynical eyes with a hint of ugliness in them. He seemed a surly, taciturn man. Yet she knew the story of his ride from Fort Kearny to Laramie, two hundred and thirty-six miles through a driving blizzard, hordes of Indians, and thirty degrees below zero weather.

He had staggered, half frozen, into the glare and gaiety of a dance at Laramie, told his story and fainted. That story started a relief expedition to Fort Kearny and prevented the Sioux from wiping out the small garrison. Phillips had nearly died, but his name had become a byword in the west.

She knew well enough what that ride must have been. Probably at no time could he have seen more than a few feet before him, yet unerring as a compass course, he had ridden through that blizzard, without wandering or circling. He had killed Carrington's splendid Kentucky thoroughbred on that ride, and nearly killed himself, but the horse lasted until he reached Laramie and died at the steps of the officers' club where they were holding a Christmas Eve dance.

Portugee Phillips was not a nice man. He had been reported by Malcolm Campbell to be dangerous and hard to get along with, but courage has never had anything to do with virtue. On that fatal night after the Fetterman Massacre when the dark fury of the blizzard swept down over Fort Phil Kearny, Carrington called for a volunteer to ride to Laramie for help. Phillips was the only one who would attempt it. And he did it. The run from Marathon was a child's play by comparison. As a feat, it stood by itself.

Jacquine rode her spotted pony out to where Phillips lounged in his saddle, a half mile from the wagon train. He looked at her as she rode up, his eyes amused and somewhat cruel. Although now there was curiosity in them, too.

"You've been in the west a long time, haven't you?" she asked.

He nodded. "I reckon."

"Do you know the country west of here?"

"Some, no mor'n Murphy or Matt Bardoul."

She looked at him quickly. "Do they know more about it than Tate Lyon?"

His yellowish eyes shifted to her, amused, calculating, ironic. "Yes," he said, "they do. Lyon says he knows the route to Shell Creek or the Rottengrass. Maybe he does. He don't know much else."

"Do you know anything about the trouble between Bardoul and Colonel Pearson?"

He was frankly studying her now, and he grinned suddenly. "I take it your interest is personal," he said.

For a minute or two they rode in silence, then he nodded. "I heard about it before I knowed either of 'em. Couple of soldiers told me. They was there."

He spat. "That Pearson! He's no leader! Massey's doing what he damn' well pleases with this whole outfit! Pearson's just along for the ride!"

Phillips bit off another chew of tobacco. "It was down Mexico way, 'most to the line, right in the heart of the Apache country. Pearson was in command of eighty men, followin' the 'Paches to punish them for raidin' some wagon trains an' ranches. Matt Bardoul was a good bit younger then, but he knowed Indians, an' he knowed the west.

"They come up with the Indians about sunup in the morning. Up to then they hadn't seen hide nor hair of an Indian, only the trail. These Indians fired an' then disappeared into a valley. Matt went up ahead, an' he saw maybe fifty 'Paches campin' in the bottom alongside of a stream. He rode back and told Pearson, then warned him it was a trap.

"Pearson laughed at him. Said let them try! He'd show 'em! Bardoul warned him again. Said it wasn't Indian nature to camp so open like. It wasn't Indian nature to be in camp that late in the morning when there were soldiers close by. Pearson told him flatly that he was either a coward, a traitor, or a fool, and he led his eighty men down into that canyon.

"Ma'am, you never fit Indians. They are uncommon shrewd folks. When the soldiers rode down into that canyon, those Indians vanished into the rocks, and then suddenly other 'Paches, layin' in ambush, opened up on the soldiers.

"Indians mostly was bad shots. But the first volley four of the soldiers went down. Matt, he yelled at Pearson to come on, wantin' to make a run for it out of that trap, Pearson ordered his men to dismount and deploy. They did, and then they looked for a target, an' no Indians in sight: Then the 'Paches stampeded their horses, an' they were trapped for fair. It was a good half mile of travel out of that canyon, an' on foot they would have been slaughtered to the last man.

"Pearson, he was still all confidence. He'd show those Indians. Wait until they attacked!

"Only they didn't attack. They had no intention of attackin'. The soldiers were there, they had no horses, very little food, and almost no water. Down in front of them, maybe a hundred yards from where they lay, was the stream. They could hear it runnin' over the rocks. Right back of it were a lot of 'Paches. Actually, there was more'n two hundred Indians there.

"Two more soldiers were killed, one wounded. They lay there, waitin' for an attack. Matt, he warned Pearson they had better try findin' a way up the cliffs. He volunteered, an' Pearson ordered him to stay where he was. Pearson was still thinkin' they would attack. Hell, Ma'am, them 'Paches are fighters! They knew they could wait.

"That night three soldiers were knifed by 'Paches that snaked up on 'em through the rocks. The soldiers were scattered out wherever they could get cover.

"The second day passed, too. Water ran short, then gave out. It was all mighty hot. One soldier tried to get down to the stream for water, an' the Indians shot him in the legs. A man started after him, and they shot him. Then they laid there, an' ever now and again they would fire into that wounded man's legs, tryin' to get the soldiers to come after him.

"Pearson decided to try to charge 'em. Bardoul told him not to, an' they nigh come to blows. They tried the charge, an' lost eight men. On the third day, Pearson couldn't take it. He broke up.

"Matt, without waitin', had been crawlin' around back in the rocks, and he done found a way out. It was only a crevice, but it was a chance. So he went to Pearson with it, an' Pearson was in no shape to give any orders. His second in command was dead, an' there was only some noncoms left. Pearson ordered Matt back to his 'post' an' said they'd stay right there. Actually, they all said he was half out of his head, he was so scared.

"Pearson's like a lot of men. As long as things go well, he's tough an' tight on discipline, but when he gets into a situation that's different, he doesn't know what to do. What little sense he had left told him no soldier ran from an Indian. Only thing was, he never had much good sense at any time. He was a garrison soldier, not a fightin' man, an' there is a sight of difference.

"Matt Bardoul didn't hesitate. He got four or five of the sergeants and corporals together. He told them flat what a spot they were in. That the Indians would pick them off one by one or let them die of thirst. It was move or else. He said he could take them out. They hesitated some, because it meant goin' agin orders, but they followed Bardoul. When he told Pearson, the colonel frothed at the mouth he was so mad. Then started to shout, an' Matt knocked him out with a six shooter, tied his hands an' gagged him. Then he led them up through that crack in the rocks an' out of the country.

"That is, out of that valley. They circled around and got at the stream up water of the Indians. They got a drink, an' they filled their canteens. When they took stock, they found that of the eighty-two men who had ridden into that canyon, fifty-three had come out, almost half of them with some kind of a wound.

"The 'Paches was mad. They trailed 'em down, an' Bardoul had got the soldiers back to a place where the stream banks were high, an' they caught the 'Paches followin' their tracks. Bardoul had out figured them Indians. After they got some water an' moved on, he had the soldiers stagger around on purpose. When they stopped he had them dip bandages in water, then rinse them over rocks to make it look like there was more wounds and more weakness than there was."

Jacquine was watching her horse's head, her mind far away, seeing them as they must have been, that beaten, bloody, bedraggled bunch of men in dusty, blood-stained uniforms, their leader still tied and gagged luring the 'Paches into a trap.

"Well, Ma'am, she worked. Them 'Paches, they weren't used to soldiers actin' like that. They figured sure enough the soldiers were all in, an' they come after 'em. Them soldiers was sore! Plenty sore! They opened up when those 'Paches wasn't no more than twenty feet away, an' they mowed 'em down.

"It was quite a battle, but before the last scattered 'Paches got out of that creek bed, there was sixty of them dead. Bardoul took ten men an' followed 'em a little way, an' they killed eight or ten more."

"But what happened when they got back to the Fort?"

Phillips shrugged. "Pearson, he filed charges against Bardoul an' several of the noncoms, but nothin' ever came of it. After awhile Pearson was transferred east. They smeared the whole thing with white wash to cover up for Pearson. That's the Army way. Sooner cover up a mistake than admit he was wrong."

They had left the river now, and were moving out over the plains, travelling west by north. Jacquine rode alone or with Barney most of the day. Matt was keeping to himself, far out on the flank opposite his own wagons.

It was late afternoon before Clive came up to her

on his fine black horse. "Looks like we'll make twenty miles today!" He was beaming, and evidently very pleased. "We're striking across toward the Powder now, and we should reach it somewhere near Fort Reno."

"Are there soldiers there now?"

"I think so, but not very many. The Sioux haven't been making much trouble since the Custer battle."

"Clive, I've been thinking. You've never told me what you intend to do when we get to the Shell."

"Do?" He looked at her as if he had no idea what she was talking about. "How? What do you mean?"

"Well, Father is opening a bank, and he intends to buy the gold the men get from the creeks. Mr. Reutz is opening a general store, and I heard Lute Harless was planning to start a freight line, and everybody I've talked to has something in mind, so I was wondering what you planned to do."

"Oh, I'll try working a claim for awhile, and keep my eyes open for something better."

She accepted his answer without comment but was far from satisfied. Somehow she believed the question had never occurred to him, and for all Clive Massey's temper and temperament, she knew he was ambitious, and it was unlike him to go into any enterprise such as this without some definite plan.

Of course, some of the business was to be co-operative. He might manage some of that. Yet she could find no solution to the problem that seemed to fit Clive Massey.

Riding along beside him, she began mentally comparing the two men. Matt Bardoul, tall, lean and quiet, his eyes faintly amused, his manner always thoughtful. She remembered the respect and trust that men like Ban Hardy and Murphy had for him, and she knew from her talks with the Stark girls that Aaron Stark swore by him. Clive was even bigger, a powerful man, handsome, always perfectly dressed. He laughed a lot, and had beautiful teeth, but his eyes were level and hard.

"Where were you born, Clive?" she asked suddenly.

He laughed. "You're full of questions today! Why, I was born in New Orleans."

"In New Orleans? Oh, you should meet that big man who drives for Bardoul. He's from New Orleans, too!"

Any enthusiasm in Massey's voice was restrained. He glanced at her, and shrugged. "A lot of people live in New Orleans. It's scarcely possible that I've ever met him. What's his name?"

"Bill something or other. I don't know."

They made a dry camp at noon that day, the first after leaving the river. Matt found a pool that was partly filled with water from the rain, and led his teams to it. Stark and Harless watered their teams before the pool went dry. By a little scouting, they found two more shallow pools and watered the rest of the stock in the company.

In the afternoon the going was harder. The grass was high, and the ground smooth for the most part, but slightly up hill. Then after about an hour the grass thinned out and the land became more rocky. When they made camp that night it was near a slough, but the water was thick with green moss and unfit to drink.

Morning found them starting on. The going was very bad, and they were forced to make several detours and the day ended with just fourteen miles behind them, and they made a dry camp. Matt used their water sparingly, and strolling around the other companies, found they were in worse shape than his own.

The horses and oxen were very restless, their longing for water after the hard, hot day being reason enough. The moon was bright, so after a brief meeting of the captains it was decided to move out at one o'clock in the morning. It was a slow start, and a hard pull.

The only thought now was water. Matt used the last of what he carried in the barrels, and stared thoughtfully into the night. It was a clear, beautiful night, however, and after the first two hours they made better time. At about four o'clock they came up to the huge circular mass of Pumpkin Buttes. A rider from the Coyle company had found water but it was bitter as gall and white as milk. After a dry breakfast, they moved on.

At their noon halt they made dry camp once more and Herman Reutz walked over from his company. He nodded to Stark, then sat down beside Bardoul. "How much further to water?"

Matt shrugged. "I don't know of any closer than Fort Reno, now. It's on the river. Or near by. It's another good day, and maybe a shade more. Will your stock make it?"

Reutz shrugged an expressive shoulder. "Maybe. I think so. But what comes after that? I'm beginning not to like this set up."

"Neither do I like it," Stark said. He forked up a slice of venison and loaded his plate with beans. "I don't like anything about it. I'm for cuttin' off to ourselves. I'm for a showdown."

Harless shook his head. "Not yet. There's no use us bringin' something to a head too soon. Let's see what happens. We won't be took by surprise now that we're warned."

"If I could only place the man!" Bardoul said aloud. "I'd swear he's a gunfighter and killer."

Bill Shedd shifted his seat on the wagon tongue. "The Texas trails didn't breed all the gunmen. You thought about the river boats?"

Bardoul swung around, giving Shedd all his attention. "You mean the riverboat gamblers?"

"Yeah. Some of them are mighty slick. Several of them most p'tic'lar slick. Dick Ryder, for instance, or Sim Boyne."

Stark looked up. "I heard of him. The Natchez killer. From the Natchez Trace. Used to say he rode with Murrell, but he ain't hardly old enough. He's a mean one, though."

Stark looked thoughtfully at Shedd. "You from that country?"

"Sort of. Lived along the Trace when I was a boy. I was raised up on stories of Murrell, Hare an' two

Harpes. First job I ever had was at Natchez under the Hill. Leastwise, the first job off the farm."

"What about Ryder and Boyne?" Matt asked.

Shedd finished chewing a mouthful of beans and reached for his coffee cup. "Killers, the both of 'em. No kin. Which was the worst, nobody could say. As late as the beginning of the War Between the States there was still a sight of money goin' over the Trace, but Sim Boyne started there as a boy. Must have been about sixteen when he began killin' travellers an' robbin' 'em.

"Showed up in New Orleans, finally. Got him a job down there in a gamblin' joint as a gunman, from that he went to gamblin' on his own. Durin' the war he took out and went to South America." Bill took a gulp of coffee, then put down his cup. "He come back, though, an' took up with Dick Ryder and some guerillas. Done a lot of robbin' and killin' before the war was over. Ain't been seen since."

By the middle of the afternoon they began to see mountains. Matt Bardoul was riding off on the flank as usual and keeping a sharp eye out. Twice during the day he had seen fresh tracks, obviously made by Indian ponies. One of the groups must have been forty or more braves, and the other slightly smaller. Such a group might not attack the train, but they would try to run off stock or attack stragglers.

The peaks of the Big Horns were snow capped and they caught the brilliant sunlight, flashing it back into his eyes.

The grass was sparse now, and very parched. Dust arose in clouds. The air was hot and heavy and the oxen were making heavy going of it.

Brian Coyle rode over toward him. The big man's face was dust covered and he looked tired. He shook his head at Matt. "Reckon we should have listened to you, Bardoul. How far off is that Stone Cup Spring?"

"Too far now," Matt said with genuine regret. "It is over forty miles to the north of us. It is better now to keep right on to the river. We'll hit it somewhere near Fort Reno."

Coyle mopped his brow. "Those mountains look good. Are there trees?"

"You bet! Some of the finest stands of lodgepole pine you'll ever see in this world! Lots of grass, too, and plenty of water. That's a good country."

"Jackie tells me you plan to start a ranch over there."

"That's right, back over in the Basin. Some fine grass land in there, and I know some of the Indians. I won't have any trouble."

"How about a market?"

"I won't worry much about that for a couple of years. I want to stock my range well, first. After that I can always sell some beef to the mines in western Montana. Or drive to the railroad in southern Wyoming. A market won't be any problem.

"Once I get my buildings set up, I'm going down to Cheyenne and contact some of the Texas cattlemen and get some cattle driven in here for me."

"Sounds like a good investment."

"In good times there's none better. They increase very rapidly. The cattle business, unless you lose a lot by drought or bad cold spells, is a good business. I've had some experience with cattle. So has young Hardy."

Elam Brooks galloped his horse over to them. The moment Matt saw his face he knew something was wrong.

The former stage driver reined in front of Brian Coyle. "Coyle, what's going on in this wagon train, anyway? There's hell to pay back there!"

"What do you mean?" Coyle demanded. "What's the trouble?" He turned in his saddle to find his company was stopped and there was a dark bunching of wagon horses and men.

"Logan Deane an' Bat Hammer took Ben Sperry's guns off him!" Brooks declared. "Sperry had a fight with Hammer this mornin' after he found Hammer goin' through his wagon. Ben knocked Hammer down, an' they fit for three, four minutes. Ben, he's a strappin' big bull whacker an' Hammer had no business fightin' him. He whupped Bat fair an' square. Then a few minutes ago Hammer came up with Deane, threw a gun on Sperry an' started takin' his guns."

They were riding swiftly toward the Coyle wagons. Worried, Matt noted that the other companies were moving on, although Massey's men were lagging a little. Neither Reutz nor any of his own men appeared to have noticed the trouble.

Sperry was on the ground when they rode up. Blood was streaming from a cut in his head, and his wife was crying. One of Massey's men was holding her back, and Bat Hammer stood over Sperry gun in hand. His face was livid with fury.

"What's going on here?" Coyle demanded.

Deane swung around, his eyes shifting from Coyle to Brooks and Bardoul. They darkened a little and his lips thinned when he saw Matt.

"Just enforcin' a little law," Deane said bluntly. "Hammer was investigating Sperry's wagon on my orders. Sperry found him at it, and beat him up."

"On your orders?" Coyle's voice was suddenly even, and Matt looked up at him. He was surprised, suddenly. All the good fellowship and easy congenial manner was gone. Brian Coyle was crisp and hard. "Just what reason had you to give any such orders, Deane? I'm in command of this company, duly elected by the personnel. If you had any complaint you could bring it to me."

Bardoul's eyes shifted suddenly to Deane, and he saw the gunman was disturbed. Coyle, he realized, had fooled him as well as Bardoul. Only a glance was needed to tell not only that Coyle was angry, but that he was not a man to be trifled with. Under pressure, Coyle had it.

"He's been accused of stealin'," Deane said. "Hammer was searchin' for stolen goods."

"Ben Sperry? Of *stealing?*" Coyle stared in blank and angry astonishment. "Logan Deane, I don't know what your game is, but you'd better know this: I've known Ben Sperry for twenty years and a more honest man never lived. Hammer," Coyle's head jerked around, "you put that gun up and get out of here!"

"Just a minute!" Deane snapped. "I'm in command of the law enforcement on this wagon train! Hammer's under my orders!"

"All right, then! You order him out of here!" Brian Coyle's eyes were blazing. If he thought about Deane's gunfighting there was no sign of it in his manner. Coyle, Bardoul realized, with a queer, leaping satisfaction, was the sort of man who would beard the devil in hell and feed him hot coals.

Deane hesitated only an instant, his eyes bleak. At least twenty of his men were behind him. Brian Coyle was sided by only two, Elam Brooks, the hard bitten former stage driver, an Indian fighter and mountain man, and Matt Bardoul.

Yet Logan Deane was no fool. No doubt there entered his mind the thought that by tomorrow they would be coming up to Fort Reno and its soldiers.

"All right, Bat. Go back to your wagon!" Deane said.

Hammer glared at him for an instant as if he did not believe his ears. Then with an oath he stepped back and holstered his gun. Ben Sperry got slowly to his feet. "Not much man in you, is there? Pistol whup a man after he whupped you man to man! Hit him while that damn' gunfighter holds a gun on him!"

"That will be enough of that, Ben!" Coyle said. He swung to Logan Deane. "Deane, when you have any complaints about the personnel of my wagon company, you come to me. If any wagons are to be searched, I want to be there to search them with you! I want the complaint to have a public hearing."

"I reckon," Matt said quietly, "that goes for my company too!"

Deane's eyes shifted and his glance lay upon Bardoul like a rapier touch. For an instant their glances crossed, Deane cold and ready, Matt completely relaxed and smiling half amused. Yet his eyes were alert.

"Maybe," Logan Deane said, "we'll have something to settle one of these days!"

Bardoul smiled. "Maybe we will, Logan," he said quietly, "maybe we will. An' maybe again you'll realize what a stinkin' mess you're walkin' into of your own accord." He reined his horse around. Then turned in his saddle, his right hand on the cantle, he said, "I have an idea, Deane, there's a lot more honest man in you than most folks think!" Brian Coyle's eyes shifted from one to the other, puzzled. Then as Bardoul started to move off, he moved up beside him. "What did that mean, Bardoul?"

"Nothin', maybe." He glanced over at the father of Jacquine. "I don't want to ask for trouble, Coyle, but why don't you put this alongside of that Bain affair and what I warned you about back in Deadwood? It might make some sort of sense."

As he rode back to his own company he was scowling. He knew why Logan Deane had backed down. The answer, of course, was Fort Reno. On the other hand, what had Bat Hammer been doing in Ben Sperry's wagon? It was unlikely that he would be doing any petty thieving at this stage of the game. If not that, then what could he be looking for?

Clive Massey had been up ahead with Barney Coyle. Had Massey been back there, what then would have happened?

One reason for the ending of the affair, and perhaps the only reason, had undoubtedly been Brian Coyle's reaction. It was totally unexpected, and Matt Bardoul grinned at the startled look in Deane's eyes, and the shocked expression of Bat Hammer when Brian Coyle interfered. They had all taken the man too lightly. This might be a new sort of life for him, but he might have a lot behind him. After all, he must have been through the war. When faced with a situation Coyle had reared right up on his hind legs and told them off. No wonder Barney and Jacquine had fire!

Somehow Matt realized, they were going to have to draw Coyle into their councils and acquaint him with their suspicions, for there was every chance he would put all this down to just a minor squabble and not to a symptom of something more serious.

Yet the lines were drawing sharper and cleaner

now. The pattern had not yet displayed itself, but the cleavage had appeared, and the sudden strength of Coyle might cause them to rearrange their plans. However, there was small chance that anything would happen between this time and their leaving of Fort Reno. After that, it would be every man for himself unless he was greatly mistaken.

Dust arose in a cloud over the wagon train. The oxen moved with slow, ponderous steps, barely crawling over the Prairie that was almost a desert. In the distance the snowcapped peaks beckoned them with uplifted fingers. Dust caked the faces and lay in a mantle over the clothing of everyone in the train. Once, late in the afternoon, riding far off on the flank, Matt found a pool among some rocks. He filled his canteen, and a spare he was carrying just for that purpose. Then by the time the dun had drunk, the pool was only gray mud, slightly damp.

He rode back to the train and stopped it. Then carefully, they walked along, sponging out the mouths and nostrils of the oxen. With care, they succeeded in giving a little attention to all the oxen in the company. Then they moved on, crawling slowly along the flank of the main body.

It was almost dark when Matt Bardoul dropped back toward the light wagon that still lagged behind them. Joe and Joe's brother sat side by side on the wagon seat as he came alongside.

"We're pulling up to Fort Reno," he said, "and we should make it shortly after midnight. Why don't you join my company from there on in? We'd be glad to have you."

Joe shook his head. Bardoul doubted if he were more than twenty, and his brother, if brother it was, looked even younger. "Thanks, we better stay to ourselves."

"Then keep an eye open for Indians. This is the old Bozeman Trail country, and the Sioux never did like the white men coming in here. Now, they have resigned themselves to it on the surface, but whenever they get a chance, they attack and kill stragglers."

"Thanks again, we will."

He rode back toward his own wagons. There was something here that puzzled him, something he did not understand. Certainly, Joe's brother might be a girl, but if so, why wouldn't she welcome travelling closer to the other women of the train? Especially, after the fright she must have received from Abel Bain.

It was long after midnight before Matt, riding far ahead, sighted the first lights of Fort Reno. He turned then and rode back along the line of the wagons. The movement was painfully slow, and the drivers sat heavily on their seats or walked beside the teams, sodden with weariness. The big wagons seemed scarcely to inch along, each turn of the wheel a special effort, each step a dogged battle with deep lying dust and the cumbersome weight of the wagons.

Even Jacquine was in the saddle. She showed up beside him suddenly as he remounted after putting his shoulder to the wheel to get the wagon over a rock.

"Are we almost there?"

He nodded. "Right over that rise. Thank God, the last little way is down hill. If it wasn't, I doubt if we could make it."

"Two of Dad's teams have stopped. The last three or four miles a lot of them have been dropping out."

He glanced ahead. They were the first houses they had seen in days. They had come fifty-five miles without water.

Several uniformed horsemen were riding toward them. The officer in command reined in. "Are you in command here?" he demanded of Bardoul.

"Only of the company. Colonel Orvis Pearson is in command of the entire train."

"*Colonel Orvis Pearson?* Well, I'll be damned!" He noticed Jacquine. "Oh? I beg your pardon!" He looked back at Bardoul. "We've orders to search this train," he said, "we're looking for a woman, Rosanna Cole. She's wanted for murder!"

CHAPTER VIII

"Rosanna Cole?" Bardoul shrugged. "Never heard of her. I'm quite sure that Colonel Pearson will lend you every possible aid, however." Matt hesitated. "For murder, you say? Where did all this happen?"

"In St. Louis. She has been traced as far as Deadwood, but they lost track of her there."

"Since when did the Army start doing police business?" Matt grinned at the young officer.

"The Army does everything out here!" He looked from Matt to Jacquine. "My name is Lieutenant Powell."

Bardoul's eyes crinkled at the corners. "My name is Bardoul, and may I present Miss Jacquine Coyle?"

"Miss?" Powell's eyes brightened. "Say, that's jolly! I was sure you two were married when you rode up! Something about the way you look."

Matt grinned. "Sorry, I got that cut over my eye in a fist fight."

The burly sergeant sitting behind the lieutenant spoke suddenly. "Sir?"

Powell turned. "What is it, Sergeant?"

"This man is Matt Bardoul, sir."

Matt glanced quickly at the sergeant. He had never seen him before. The name evidently meant something to the lieutenant for he turned quickly and looked at Matt again. "Sorry," Powell said, "I didn't connect the name. We've heard a lot about you, sir. You'll find friends at Fort Reno, a number of them."

Powell smiled at Jacquine. "I hope you can stay a few days, Miss Coyle. We see all too few women at Reno."

The sky was already turning gray and the long shadows were drawing back reluctantly toward the snowcapped mountains in the west. The air was very fresh and cool, and without talking, Matt rode on ahead, Jacquine keeping pace with him. When they reached the stream they stopped and their horses waded gratefully into the water, drinking and blowing.

It was very still. A bird called in the aspens down stream, and the darkness that lay on the water lifted. There was a damp freshness in the air, and the smell of trees and some faint, barely discernible perfume from some blossoming vine hanging in the trees.

"You know," Matt said suddenly, "sometimes I wish we could have met under other circumstances."

Jacquine looked up quickly, then away. "What circumstances?"

"Oh, in the town you came from. In your home, at a dance, at another home. This way, well, there's almost everything against us at the beginning. The things you heard about me, the dislike your father has for me . . . all of those things."

"Maybe they aren't important."

"Perhaps not, but again they might be much more important than either of us realize. Now, in a few days, we will be nearing the end of our trip. We go north now, and then around the Big Horns into the Basin, and we will come to the Shell. Then or sooner, a lot may happen."

"You think there will be trouble?"

"A lot of trouble. I think we may have things happening from the day we leave Fort Reno."

"You know that I think you're mistaken?"

"Yes, of course. I think I know how you feel. Frankly, while I warned your father about bringing you along, I'm glad you came. In fact, that's why I came."

He shifted in his saddle, pushing his hat back on his head. In the growing light she could see him clearly, and see the grave seriousness of his eyes, yet there seemed to be some hint of dancing deviltry in them, too. That same look that had excited her in front of the

IXL, and later when he arose to leave the table in the dining room.

"You mean you came because of me?"

"Sure," he took out the makings and began to build a cigarette, "I'll admit I might have come anyway, but as it happens, I made a decision back there at Pole Creek."

"At Pole Creek? The stage station?"

"Uh huh. I decided then and there . . ." he touched his tongue to the cigarette, then put it between his lips, "that you were for me. I made up my mind that come hell or high water, you were going to belong to me."

She looked up. "Is this a statement of intentions or a proposal, or just what?"

"It's not a proposal. I don't believe in them very much. It's much safer to tell a girl than to ask her. Saves a lot of wear and tear on their minds. Women are such contrary creatures, they have to stall or say no. So the thing to do is to tell them, and let that settle it."

"And they have nothing to say about it?"

"Of course not!" he grinned. "Although they would probably say plenty!"

"Where did you learn all of this about women?" Jacquine asked, a streak of perversity made her add: "From Rosanna Cole?"

His head jerked around. "From who?"

"Rosanna Cole . . . the girl in the wagon that has been following us."

"You know as much about her as I do," he said. The thought had taken hold of his mind. Why hadn't he considered it before? When Powell first mentioned the wanted woman? "If her name is Rosanna Cole this is the first I knew of it."

"You expect me to believe that?"

"That," he said gently, "is your problem. I've told you the truth."

"It seems very strange that the story would be all over the wagon train if there was nothing to it. I've heard several people mention it as unquestioned truth."

Irritation mounted in him, but he fought it down.

"It isn't strange to me when Clive Massey is so anxious to discredit me."

"You do him an injustice, Matt Bardoul! Clive has never said anything against you! Nor has he given me, or my father, any reason to believe all your vile suspicions about him. I don't know exactly what you have in mind, but I can tell you that you're wrong! Dead wrong! Clive Massey is a gentleman, in every sense of the word! I've been associated with him a great deal more than you have, and I think I should know."

"You may be right," he agreed quietly, "if you are, all my instinct and judgment of men is at fault."

"It's simply because you two are at cross purposes, and have been from the beginning! There's nothing wrong with Clive, and I think he has done a good job with this wagon train. Father admires him very much."

It was light now, and behind them they could hear the first of the wagons. Upstream some of the horsemen were already watering their stock, and beyond them, on the parade ground of the fort, the troops would be lined up for reveille.

Somewhere downstream a loon called, and a dove mourned in the deep brush. The zebra dun lifted his head, ears pricked, all attention. Jacquine said nothing, and Matt fumbled in his pocket for his tobacco. In his impatience he had thrown down his cigarette half smoked.

"If that is Rosanna Cole," he said thoughtfully, "Tolliver knows something about her. I wonder how much? And where are they?"

"You are going to warn them?"

He shrugged. "The Lieutenant may have found them by now, or no one may guess who they are. Somehow, well . . . they seemed such nice people. Kids, both of them. As far as that goes, I've nothing on which to base a conclusion that one of them is a girl. Abel Bain believed it . . . but I don't know."

Jacquine listened without comment. She did not know whether to accept this as truth or to believe it was said to convince her she was wrong. She had never really believed the story, but it had been going the rounds in the wagon train, and a number of the women had repeated it.

Something else came to her mind suddenly. "Matt, did you ever hear of anyone named Sim Boyne?"

His head jerked around so quick that he spilled the tobacco from the cigarette paper. *"Sim Boyne?* Where did you hear that name?"

"Who is he? What is he?"

He studied her, his eyes narrow. "What have you been doing? Listening to someone talk around the camp fires? Sim Boyne is a killer and a murderer. He's one of the last of those renegades that made the Natchez Trace a synonym for blood and death. They were worse than any Indians. Bill Shedd told me a lot about them, but everyone who has been to Natchez or New Orleans knows a lot about them."

Jacquine frowned, then started her horse. As they rode up the opposite bank, he reached out and caught her bridle. "Where did you hear that name? It's important that I know!"

Their eyes met and held. "Matt," she said, "I heard that Sim Boyne was on this wagon train, and another man named Dick Ryder . . . *and that both of them were in your company!"*

"Now, listen . . . !" He was apalled. In his company? But who could . . . he stared at her. "Jacquine, tell me where you heard this and how. Who in the world could have such an idea, and who did they think these men were?"

Jacquine's eyes were level. "Matt," she said quietly, "I just overheard some talk in a wagon I was passing one night. I heard one man say that he knew Dick Ryder, that he had seen him, that he was now in your company. He also said that where Ryder was, Sim Boyne was not far away. Then he described Sim Boyne."

"Described him? What was the description? Do you remember?"

"Yes. I remember very well, although at the

**Enjoy the Best
of the World's Bestselling
Frontier Storyteller in...**

THE
LOUIS L'AMOUR
COLLECTION

**Savor <u>Silver Canyon</u> in this new hardcover
collector's edition free for 10 days.**

At last, a top-quality, hardcover edition of the
best frontier fiction of Louis L'Amour. Beautifully
produced books with hand-tooled covers, gold-
leaf stamping, and double-sewn bindings.

Reading and rereading these books will give
you hours of satisfaction. These are works of
lasting pleasure. Books you'll be proud to pass
on to your children.

MEMO FROM LOUIS L'AMOUR

Dear Reader:

Over the years, many people have asked me when a first-rate hardcover collection of my books would become available. Now the people at Bantam Books have made that hope a reality. They've put together a collection of which I am very proud. Fine bindings, handsome design, and a price which I'm pleased to say makes these books an affordable addition to almost everyone's permanent library.

Bantam Books has so much faith in this series that they're making what seems to me is an extraordinary offer. They'll send you <u>Silver Canyon</u>, on a 10-day, free examination basis. Plus they'll send you a free copy of my new Calendar.

Even if you decide for any reason whatever to return <u>Silver Canyon</u>, you may keep the Calendar free of charge and without obligation. Personally, I think you'll be delighted with <u>Silver Canyon</u> and the other volumes in this series.

Sincerely,

Louis L'Amour

Louis L'Amour

P.S. They tell me supplies of the Calendar are limited, so you should order now.

time I did not know who Sim Boyne was, and since I have mentioned this to no one. The description . . . but why tell you, Matt? You know, *because you're Sim Boyne!"*

She touched spurs to her pony and was gone in a pound of hooves. Blankly, Matt stared at the trees. "Well, I'll be damned! I'll be forever damned!"

He sat by while the wagons crossed the stream and moved up to the camping ground and drew in a tight circle of their own. Reutz was also pulling in, and his wagons joined Bardoul's. The storekeeper shook his head. "Man, if we'd had three miles further to go none of my wagons would have made it. As it is, three of them have fallen out and after we water the stock we'll have to go back an' pick them up."

"We'll be following the river from now on. For several days, anyway. You hear about the trouble Ben Sperry had?"

Reutz nodded. He stoked his pipe. "Matt, my crowd are about ready to break off from the rest of them. Some of them are getting scared. There's a lot of bad talk going around, and from all I hear, Sperry's wagon isn't the only one that's been searched."

"Anything missing?"

"Nothing anybody noticed. But that doesn't make the women folks any happier, knowing there are men like that Hammer prowling about the wagons. Nothing much has been said in meeting, but my boys are getting about ready for a break. If we make it, will you lead us?"

Matt stripped the saddle from the dun. "Damn it, Reutz, I'd like to, but right now I'm not anxious to break away from the train. If my boys want to break, however, I'll stay with them. I know Aaron wants to. He's said so in so many words. Lute ain't so sure."

"Could you take us to the Shell?"

"Surest thing you know. Get you there faster than Lyon will take this bunch."

"What about Phillips? Where does he stand?"

"Portugee might go with us, but he's an uncertain quantity right now. I figure the man has some idea of his own cooking around in that head of his. What it could be, I don't know."

He thought of telling Herman Reutz about Jacquine's comments on Ryder and Boyne, then decided against it. No use giving such a story more importance than it had. Yet it was a story sure to be repeated. Odd, how such a preposterous story could get started, but when it came to that was the story so preposterous? How much did he know about the men in his own wagon train? Of them all, the only ones he had known before, were Ban Hardy and Buffalo Murphy. Stark, a hard bitten man, came from the country of the Natchez Trace, or not far from it. Lute Harless . . . well, under that bluff, amiable exterior he might be a lot of things. And he knew nothing of young Tolliver or of Bill Shedd. Nor, and here he might be striking the right note, of Ernie Braden or Bunker.

Space was cleared for dancing that night, and many of the men from the three companies stationed at the Fort came over for the festivities. Buffalo Murphy and Ban Hardy routed out their best and so did the others. Brian Coyle, accompanied by Jacquine and Barney, came over, followed in a few minutes by Clive Massey, handsome and distinguished in a black broadcloth suit and a white ruffled shirt. His black hat pulled low upon his brow, he looked everything the southern gentleman should be.

Bat Hammer was there, loitering with Buckskin Johnson and several more of the toughs from the Massey wagons. Logan Deane, silent and alone, leaned on a wagon wheel off by himself in the half darkness. There was plenty of food, and from somewhere came a barrel of liquor, and in a matter of a few minutes the camp was roaring with laughter. Murphy, in fine fettle, started a song and everyone joined in.

Thoughtful and watchful, Matt loitered on the edge of things. When the dancing started, he saw Jacquine move out into the circle with Clive Massey. They made a handsome couple and he felt a pang of actual physical pain as they moved together.

He smoked thoughtfully, staring across the firelight at the moving figures. A dozen couples were dancing now, and he noticed Lieutenant Powell move in and claim Jacquine for a dance.

Jacquine puzzled him, and he puzzled himself. Usually, he talked easily and fluently when with women, but when with Jacquine he always seemed to be saying things he had not wanted nor planned to say. They had talked little enough, but what he had said on those occasions was never what he wanted to say or should have said. He felt drawn to her as to no other woman he had ever met, but it irritated and angered him that she could like Clive Massey so much. At the same time, he could see that the man was attractive, yet she seemed unable to sense what he felt about Massey, that the man was evil, dangerous and definitely cruel.

He turned impatiently away from the fire and strode off into the darkness, swearing to himself. He wanted to ask her to dance but how would she receive him? If she refused, and well she might, he knew it would hurt like the very devil. Besides, he had no wish to be laughed at by the ruffians that hung around with Hammer.

Thinking of that, something occurred to himself suddenly that he had not considered before. What had been in the mind of that sergeant today when he suddenly told Lieutenant Powell who he was? Were they looking for him, too? Was something wrong? The sergeant was a stranger, and so was Powell. The Lieutenant had said he would find friends here . . . who?

He paced back and forth, smoking and thinking, trying to find his way into the mind of Massey that he might ferret out the plans for the wagon train. This would be their last contact with civilization. Going should be good for awhile, and in a couple of days forty or fifty miles would separate them from Fort Reno, and each day would move them further and further away.

Yet he held to his original view. If there was to be an attack, it would come when they were in the Basin, or at the north end of the Big Horns. That would be the logical place. Fort C. F. Smith would not be too far away, yet probably no one on the wagon train knew its exact location. And it would be too far away to do any good. It was, he believed, abandoned and in ruins, anyway.

He turned and walked back to the fire. Jacquine was standing across it, in conversation with Clive Massey. He had his hat off, and his patrician features looked clean and hard in the firelight. He was staring at Jacquine, and saying something. Then she laughed, and he caught her arm and laughed too. Fury bubbled up in Matt's brain and he hurled his cigarette down.

He knew he was being a fool, but . . . he turned abruptly and walked around the fire. The fiddles were tuning for another dance. Matt started for Jacquine, walking swiftly. Suddenly a hand caught his arm. "Sir? The Captain would like to speak to you."

He looked impatiently at the tall redheaded soldier. "Damn it, Man! There's a dance on!"

"Sorry, sir!" The soldier grinned. "I know what you mean, but it's urgent, sir."

"All right!" He turned abruptly and walked away after the soldier. He did not see Jacquine's eyes following him.

Captain Gordon Sharp stood behind a small fire at one side of the camp. There were no other soldiers around. The orderly led Bardoul to him, then saluted. "Mr. Bardoul, sir!"

"All right, thanks, Graves. You may go."

Sharp was a short, compact man who carried himself erect, and had a square good-looking face. He might have been forty, but was probably a year or two younger. He thrust out a hand. "Bardoul? Sit down, will you? I've been wanting to have a talk with you."

"With me, sir?"

"Yes. As you may know, we have the job on our hands of keeping some kind of order in a side section of territory. It is a pretty thankless job, as you can imagine. My men are nearly all recruits, just out from the east, and few of them have any idea of working with Indians. Also, we suffer from a division of sentiment.

Certain interests want the Indians driven still further west, others consider them noble redmen who can do no wrong and are badly abused. We naturally try to strike a middle course that we imagine is somewhere near the right one.

"We've an added problem now. Partly due to some vigilante efforts in the mining camps to the north and west, we are getting an influx of bad men. White men who are out for their own ends. They have been causing us just as much trouble as the Indians. Knowing the Sioux, you understand our problem. They strike here, then there, and we can never seem to catch up with them or pin down any certain bunch as the offenders. The result is that my men are riding themselves and their horses ragged, and not doing much good."

Matt nodded. "I know how you feel. Unless you know the country, you wouldn't have a chance."

"There's something else, too." Captain Sharp picked a blazing twig from the fire and lit his pipe. "Ever hear of Sim Boyne?"

Bardoul chuckled. "Never knew much about him, but the last few days I've been hearing a lot!"

Sharp looked at him with quick, hard eyes. "You mean, you've run into him? Or met someone who has?"

"No, not that. Just talk. We've got a man along who came from Natchez and another from up at the north end of the Trace. They were both telling stories about him."

"I see." Sharp smoked thoughtfully. "Bardoul, we've got some pretty good authority that says both Ryder and Boyne are headed out this way or already here. According to the story, they have an idea of organizing some sort of an independent power out here in the west. It sounds fantastic, I agree, yet it could create a lot of trouble. Murrell had the idea, you know, and before him, Aaron Burr had it. You'll still find a lot of people who swore by Murrell's fantastic secret organisation. However, whether that's the idea or not, Boyne and Ryder are both dangerous men, and they are believed to have come west.

"We've word from several places that a lot of bad men are headed this way, and it looks like something big may be afoot. We've heard that they intend to ride in and take over Bannock and some of the mining towns, completely clean up and then leave. We've heard all sorts of fantastic stories. This is 1877, and you'd think people would stop dreaming, but apparently some of the best of them do."

"You mean, you have orders to look into such things? That it is considered so serious the Army is putting troops to work on it?"

Sharp laughed. "You make it sound fairly silly. No, as a matter of fact, it is just talk. And I have no orders along that line at all, just some talk with higher ranking officers. Of course, you know what the Army is, always seeing wars around every mountain and behind every treaty. Maybe it isn't a bad thing: somebody should be on the alert.

"No, as a matter of fact, this isn't my job. It's yours."

"Mine?"

"That's right," Captain Sharp reached into his dispatch case. "I have a commission for you as Deputy United States Marshal for the area; it's a special appointment. They made an attempt to catch you in Cheyenne, but you had already gone on to Deadwood Gulch. And they failed to get you there, so this was sent to me to deliver to you when you passed here."

Matt Bardoul stared at the document. He remembered vaguely some talk in Cheyenne about this, but he had supposed it to be only talk. He had been footloose and fancy free, and when asked if he would accept such an appointment he had said that he would, but at the time he had not dreamed O'Connor was serious.

"Just what," he asked, "does this mean? What am I supposed to do?"

"Your orders are there, folded in with your commission. I think, however, you are simply to enforce law in Wyoming, and particularly that area in the Big Horn range country. What they really want is the scalps of

Sim Boyne, Dick Ryder, and a few scattered members of the Plummer gang. There have also been some renegades around. I know there are warrants out for Abel Bain."

Matt looked up. "Bain is dead." Briefly, he explained. Then he said, "What about this Rosanna Cole affair? Lieutenant Powell was looking for her this morning."

"Yes, we have been asked to keep our eyes open. She was a youngster, scarcely more than a girl, married to a very wealthy man in St. Louis. Well, she shot him and killed him, and not much that anybody knows about it except that he was found dead with a bullet through his body, and she was gone.

"Some say her lover did it, others maintain she didn't have any lover. Our only job is to ship her back to St. Louis if we find her. Frankly, I don't like the job, and am not much interested. It isn't the Army's business and but for some political bigwig, it wouldn't be of interest to us. To you, however, as deputy marshal, it would be."

"Do you have a description of her?"

Sharp smiled. "Only a very poor one, brown hair and blue eyes, five feet three inches, weight about one hundred and ten. That is all we have, and that could fit a lot of women."

Matt slapped the paper thoughtfully into his palm. This could be both good and bad. He looked up at Captain Sharp. "I'll take this, but I don't want it. I never really expected it would come through. For your information, I am not looking for Rosanna Cole . . . as for Boyne and Ryder, I'll bring them in if I can find them.

"In the meanwhile, how many know about this appointment?"

"We two only. It was the business of nobody else."

"Good!" Matt smiled. "Then mention it to no one. I'll put this is my pocket and go on with that wagon train. I've an idea that's just where a Deputy United States Marshal will be needed."

He turned away, but Captain Sharp's voice stopped him. "By the way . . . you have, Lieutenant Powell said, a Colonel Orvis Pearson in command of your wagon train?"

"Yes, we have. An Army officer."

Sharp glanced up. "A *former* Army officer. You might tell him, just this and no more, that Arch Schandler is dead."

"That Arch Schandler is dead?"

"Yes, that's enough. He will understand thoroughly." Sharp grinned suddenly. "Say, Powell tells me you've got an uncommonly pretty girl along. Could I meet her?"

"Huh!" Matt smiled wryly. "You and the whole United States Army!"

Jacquine was standing by the fire again, talking to Sarah Stark. She looked up as he approached, then glanced from Captain Sharp to Matt.

Matt bowed very formally. "Miss Coyle, the Captain is very eager to meet you and I thought it best he have his chance." He put his hand on Sharp's arm. "Captain Gordon Sharp . . . Miss Coyle." Matt stepped back and started to move away.

"Well!" Jacquine said. "Are you going to leave just like that? Have you forgotten our dance? I was waiting for you!"

Humour glinted in his eyes. "Forgotten?" he said gallantly. "How could I possibly forget? But with Captain Sharp and Lieutenant Powell, I didn't think you would remember."

They moved out over the grass, dancing. She looked up at him. "I don't believe you were even going to ask me!"

He smiled. "I wasn't. It seemed the situation was well taken care of, and far be it from me to step on Clive Massey's toes!"

"You're not stepping on his toes!" Jacquine's eyes flashed at him. "Just because I've talked to him a few times . . . ." Her voice trailed away and she felt her pulse quicken as his arm went around her waist. She looked up at him, half frightened by the expression in his eyes. It was an expression that was half tenderness and half . . . well, something no nice girl should even think about. But it was something that made her feet falter suddenly . . . and she wondered afterwards why they should falter right there, at the darkest side of the circle.

Almost before she realized what had happened, he swung her swiftly into the darkness behind one of the wagons, and almost before she stopped moving he bent his head and their lips met. There seemed to be a roaring in her ears and her muscles seemed to melt and her body folded against his, caught in the onsweeping tide of passion. He held her close and their lips clung together and she felt her breast heaving against his chest and her head was back and his lips were on her neck, her ears . . . she tore herself free and stood there, staring wildly at him.

"Jacquine!" he said. He started toward her.

"No, please!" She tried to hold herself straighter, and his hand caught her elbow.

Holding herself tightly, her breath coming in gasps, she tried to straighten her hat and her bonnet. She looked up at him swiftly. "We'd better get back," she said, "they are still dancing!"

All the next day the stock rested. Bardoul lay on his blanket under the aspens and chewed on a leaf of grass, trying to think his way out of the situation. He had no idea what Jacquine felt about him. That there was a strong physical attraction, he knew, but he was also aware that it wasn't enough, and that it could exist without anything else.

Yet he knew he was in love. There was no doubting that. He sat up abruptly. It was not a new thing, for actually he had known it all along. He had known it since that day at Pole Creek Station, and all he had seen and felt or learned since had merely confirmed him in his belief.

How did she feel toward Clive Massey? And how was she going to feel when matters finally came to a head? Was Brian Coyle in the clear, or was he a party to Massey's schemes? One thing was sure, his actions now would have official sanction. Now it would not be merely a matter of self defense, for the law lay in his hands.

The law was something he understood and respected. It was a trust, a sacred trust. He knew that not many frontier marshals considered it so, but it was his belief, and had always been. In what was to come he must act without malice and only upon evidence, yet he knew well enough that in this case there would be no need for evidence to present before a court, In this situation he would have to be judge and jury, and perhaps executioner.

Coyle's reaction in the case of Hammer and Sperry might have been the legitimate action of a just and angry man. It might also have been the anger of a man who saw a well planned scheme endangered by a clumsy action.

When they moved out tomorrow, events would move more swiftly. Knowing that, he got up quickly. He must see Jacquine. He must see her and settle this thing that was between them. Then he stopped. For the time at least, he had better wait. For if he spoke his mind, and by some chance she loved him, it would be that much harder when he was faced with his duty and shouldered with the protection of these people of the wagon train.

Swearing softly, he started toward the encampment.

Several soldiers were loafing about, and he saw Herman Reutz talking with Lute Harless. He started toward him, but when they looked up and saw him both men turned swiftly away and walked in the other direction.

Matt stopped so suddenly he almost fell. There could be no mistaking their action. These two . . . two of his best friends on the wagon train . . . had deliberately turned and walked away from him!

Puzzled, he turned and walked on in the direction of the fort. Then he shrugged. Probably they had been discussing some business deal, some little plan of their own that was confidential. There was a wagon drawn up near the crude palade and several soldiers gathered around. Bat Hammer was there, and Logan Deane. So were Johnson, Sperry, two of the Stark boys and Bill Shedd. As he walked up Clive Massey came through the gate beside the wagon and their eyes met.

He was shocked at the sudden blaze of passion in Massey's eyes, but the man avoided him, and began talking to the soldier who was standing beside the wagon. Soon a civilian approached, apparently the sutler, and there began some low animated talk.

Shedd walked up to him, and he noticed how the eyes of the others followed him. "Howdy, Matt!" Bill said. Then low voiced, he added, "You sure are gettin' unpopular all of a sudden! Me, too, for that matter. What's happened? We got the plague, or something?"

"I'm damned if I know. What's the talk around?"

"I don't know. When I come around, they just naturally shut up an' don't say no more. It must be about you or me, or maybe both of us."

Matt glanced around swiftly, impatiently. Since the night before he had been seething inside. He knew what had happened. It was easy enough to bottle up a feeling like that, but once it had been given rein, it was no longer enough. He wanted Jacquine Coyle, and he wanted her now, and the wanting was a fierce urgency that put a drive in every movement and a demanding fire in his eyes and hands.

"To hell with them!" he said impatiently. "I don't know what's got into them and I don't care! Has Pearson given orders for moving out?"

"In the morning, at four o'clock."

"Good! I want to get on with this." Matt turned abruptly. "Shedd, you implied some time back that you were looking for a man who might be with us. Who is he? Why do you want him?"

Shedd's eyes turned away. The big man's face lost its heaviness and suddenly he seemed to harden. "I ain't tellin', Matt. Only I got an idea."

"Shedd," Matt spoke sharply, "if you've anything on your mind, you'd better say it. I want to know just what the score is, all the time."

"I ain't sure." The big man stared toward the sutler's wagon. "I just ain't sure." He stared at his huge, knotted fist. "Matt, I'm a huntin' a man what killed my brother. He wasn't much, that brother of mine. If he'd been killed a few times, by a few men, I'd have shrugged it off an' done nothin'. But he was killed by a skunk, an' I'm skunk huntin' now. On'y, that skunk's got teeth."

"Who?"

Shedd looked up, his eyes bleak and hard. "Sim Boyne."

"Boyne?" Matt stared at Shedd. Everywhere he went he heard that name. A few months ago it was merely a tag to a legend, and now it was running through his life like a red thread.

"You think he's here? With us?"

"I do."

Matt shrugged. "Hell, you can be wrong. There's folks here even say I'm him."

"You ain't. I know that. When I find him, I've got a way of knowin'. But I know you ain't him."

Clive Massey turned away from his conference with the sutler and his eyes crossed Matt's. Suddenly, quick fury flamed in his dark face and he wheeled abruptly and started toward Matt, walking on the balls of his feet. He strode up to him and stopped.

Massey's eyes were hot with rage, a sullen burning rage that seemed to have been smouldering and now had come swiftly to the blazing point.

"Bardoul, I've had about enough of you! You're leaving this wagon train, and leaving it here!"

Matt's eyes widened, and a slow humour grew within him. It was always so, perhaps, he reflected at times, a nervous reaction. Whenever he was faced with such a situation he seemed to grow very quiet and still inside, and words came easily, his mind always found something faintly amusing and preposterous about it all.

"Why, what's on your mind, Clive? Something in particular, or things in general?" Casually, he lifted his hands, rubbing the left palm with his right thumb, chest high. It would make all the difference sometimes, that matter of having your hands in hitting position. "Or is it that you just can't stand me?"

"It's just that I saw what happened last night, and I don't want Jacquine subjected to such indignities." His voice was level and cold.

Something burst suddenly within Matt, but he throttled it back. "We won't mention any names here, Massey!" His voice shook. "And I think the lady has her own ways of handling situations she doesn't like!"

"No doubt." Clive's quick smile flickered suddenly on his lips. "And I have mine!"

Matt saw the movement, and jabbed with his left, but Clive Massey's head shifted and the punch missed, and then Massey hit him with a crossed right.

Matt never saw the punch coming, nor the left hook that followed it. Something slugged him on the jaw like a mule's kick and he hit the ground hard and rolled over, lights and thunder bursting in his brain.

Fighting for consciousness, through the smoky roaring in his skull, he knew he had been hit. He had been hit harder than he had ever been before. He started to push himself up, and a boot crashed into his ribs. He heard shouts and yells, and then another boot, and yet another and another.

Pain stabbed his side, and his head reeled. Through some blank, strange darkness he kept fighting the pain, and pushing against the grass, and then somehow he was on his feet, and he saw the dark viciousness of Clive Massey's face looming toward him, saw those lips curl, and then the stabbing of a punch into his belly and a crashing blow on the jaw. He swung half way around and hit the ground and felt the cool grass against his face, and the dust in his nostrils.

CHAPTER IX

Then he had his hands under him again and he was pushing himself up. How he got to his feet he never knew. Through the roaring in his skull and the taste of blood in his mouth, he knew he had to get up. He seemed to hear Coyle's voice and Buffalo Murphy's, and then a sneering laugh and a blow that jarred him to his heels. Vaguely, he saw Clive Massey set himself, he saw the punch start, but although the will was there, he lacked the strength to pull his head away, and the fist struck his jaw and then the ground hit him hard between the shoulders. He rolled over and something crashed against his skull and a rocket seemed to burst in his brain, but he pushed his hands against the grass and fought his way up.

Massey, his eyes bitter with fury, moved in on him, and Matt shook his head. His face felt stiff and queer, but he was on his feet and he knew he had to fight. He had to fight as he had never fought before. The punch came this time, but he fell inside of it, grabbed Massey with both arms, and tripped him with a backheel. They hit the ground, and he slugged Massey once, then they rolled over.

He was slow getting up, and Massey hit him twice before he could get his hands up. Blood was running into one of his eyes, and his breath was hoarse, but he was on his feet, and moving in. This was an old story to Matt. He had been knocked down before, and he had gotten up. He would keep getting up.

Massey rushed, throwing punches that rocked and smashed, but Matt was no longer worried. He had been hit and hit hard, he had been kicked at least a dozen times, and he was on his feet again. He was no longer punch shy as a man often is before he has been hurt. He moved in, his skill reasserting itself, his strength coming back. The vitality built through many years of hard living on the plains and in the mountains was with him now. He bowed his head and walked in, and suddenly, he began to rip short, wicked punches to Clive Massey's stomach.

Massey was the bigger man, and he was a strong man, and smart in the ways of fighting, but Matt Bardoul kept weaving and smashing and he kept moving in. His face a smear of blood from a cut eye and a smashed lip, battered and swollen, he moved in. He was making a few of them miss now, and through the bloody haze of his sight he could see the moving body of Massey ahead of him.

He feinted suddenly, and lashed out with a right. Massey caught it coming in, and it shook him to his boots. Watching his face, Matt knew the punch hurt, and moreover he knew that it did something to Clive Massey. This man had been down, and down again, he had been punched and booted, but he could still throw a punch like that.

Clive's left lashed out, but Matt's head moved. He uppercut to the chin, slammed both hands in short wicked hooks to the jaw, and then cut Massey's cheek to the bone with an overhand right.

Blood streaming down his handsome face, Clive Massey began to fight like a man in a panic, but he was gone now. Actually, he had lost the fight with that first hard punch Matt had thrown, but he only knew this man must go down and stay down, but he would not. Matt bulled his way in close, hooking those short, wicked punches to the bigger man's stomach, then raking his face with streaking jabs and wicked right crosses. The things Jem Mace had taught him were his now, they were coming back, and they showed in the straight, hard punches, and the blocking.

There was no mercy in Matt. He saw Clive weakening. Coolly, coldly, he set himself and slammed a right to the body. Massey backed up, and Bardoul walked in, deliberately, he slapped Massey open handed across the mouth, and when Clive lunged in a blaze of rage, Matt spread his legs and threw both hands to the body. Clive grunted, and his mouth dropped open, and Matt broke his nose with a short right hook, and then split his other cheek with a left.

Massey went down. Matt stood over him, bloody and maddened with fighting lust. He tried to speak but his swollen lips only muffled the words. He grabbed Clive by the collar and jerked him to his feet. Shoving him back against the wagon he hit him again, twice to the body and again to the face.

Clive Massey's knees sagged, and he crumpled, limp as a rag into the dust.

Turning, his hair hanging over his face, bloody and punch drunk, Matt Bardoul saw through a haze of blood and the fog in his brain, the horror stricken face of Jacquine Coyle.

He tried to straighten up, but there was a stabbing pain in his side, and when he put his hand there, he found his shirt was gone, hanging from his shoulders in a few straggling ribbons.

Somebody put an arm around his shoulders and he walked back to his wagon. He was helped up, and he sprawled in a heap across the piled up goods and his own blankets.

When he opened his eyes again, the wagon was moving. It was hot inside the canvas covered wagon, and he struggled to a sitting position, his head feeling like it weighed a ton. When he moved, a sharp pain stabbed him, and he sat there, staring in blurred half consciousness at the tailboard of the wagon.

He got his canteen which had been put beside him and tried to drink, but his lips were split and swollen and the canteen bumped them painfully, jolted by the moving wagon.

Carefully, as the fog began to leave his brain, he felt all his face. The cut over his eye had been patched, but his cheek bones were swollen until his eyes were almost closed, and his nose and lips were very sore.

He fumbled around and found his gunbelts and

buckled them on. Then he crawled to the rear of the wagon and almost fell into the dust. When he tried to move, he did go to his knees, but managed to get up and get to his horse. It was saddled and bridled, so he crawled into the leather and felt better.

The hot sun felt good, and he rode around toward the front of the wagon. Tolliver was driving. The boy looked up, astonished when he saw him. "You better rest," he suggested, "you took quite a beating."

Matt stared at him. "I won, didn't I?"

"Won?" Tolliver chuckled. "I should smile, you won! You damn' nigh killed him." He shook his head. "Me, I missed it. Shedd said it was the damnedest fight he ever did see."

The sun and the air made him feel better, although his face felt stiff and sore.

"Tolliver," he said suddenly, "what's your connection with that wagon back there? With Joe and Joe's brother?"

Tolliver did not reply while the heavy wheels rumbled over twice, then he said, "I reckon my reason won't interfere none with your wagon train. They are friends of mine, mighty good friends."

"Did you know the law was looking for Rosanna Cole?"

His head came up sharply. "Don't know no such person." Then, inconsistently, he added, "She never done it nohow. She never killed him."

Matt Bardoul shrugged. He stared down at his swollen hands. If Logan Deane elected to make a fight of it now he could never get a gun in those hands fast enough. Not for Deane.

"Personally," he said, "I don't care. They were asking about her at Fort Reno."

He rode in silence for awhile. "They picked a bad outfit to tie to. This wagon train is headed into a sight of trouble. What happened yesterday is just one phase of it. One of these days things will start happening mighty fast."

There was no sign of Jacquine. All day he rode around, keeping his eyes open for her. He wanted to talk to her, to explain . . . but what was there to explain? She had responded to his kisses, she had been with him all the way, and besides, she must know how he felt.

Nor was there any sign of Clive Massey. Matt felt a grim satisfaction in that. No matter what happened now, he had given Massey a taste of his knuckles. The man had been whipped, and very thoroughly. He thought then of the deputy marshal's commission in his pocket.

What should he do about that? In a way, he was glad to have it, but in yet another way it placed him in a difficult situation. He was accustomed to doing things his own way, to answering to no one.

No one came near him. There was no sign of Reutz. Brian Coyle stayed close to the head of his wagons and did not ride up to join Matt or speak to him. Neither Aaron Stark nor Lute Harless looked at him when he rode by. Anger burned in him, a slow, bitter anger. What was wrong with them? Surely they did not believe that ridiculous story about Sim Boyne? Or had something been said about his meeting behind the wagon with Jacquine?

Once, far off on the flank, he glanced back. The light wagon drawn by mules was coming right along. Where it had been when the soldiers looked for it, he had no idea. Probably along the river, hidden in the brush or timber.

It was a good day. The country was dry, but they were making good time and headed almost due north. Off on their left was the towering mass of the Big Horns, and at times a refreshing breeze blew down from them. He was lonely and restless. The pain in his side and the soreness of his lips and face did not prevent him from thinking.

There had been enough of this, enough of loneliness, enough of single life. What he wanted now was Jacquine, and his own ranch in the Big Horn Basin. Had it been left up to him he would have turned off to the west and found his own route through, and let them have the Shell or the Rottengrass, wherever the gold might be. He wanted the grass lands and the long valley, and the green of the thick growth along the Big Horn.

Several times he saw sign of Indians, and once, in the distance, a lone brave. Another time, two warriors and two squaws.

Despite the discomfort of riding, he scouted around. For the first time he saw no drunks in Massey's company. The men were riding in their wagons, every sense alert.

He turned his dun abruptly and rode over to Brian Coyle. The big man's head came up sharply, and there was cold hostility in his eyes. "I've nothing to say to you," he said coldly, "nothing at all."

Anger brought hot blood to Matt's face. "Regardless of that, I'm going to warn you. What you saw happen between Hammer and Sperry was the beginning. There will be more trouble, and a lot of it."

Coyle's face hardened. "If there's any trouble in this wagon train," he said, "it will come from you. We know you now, *Sim Boyne!*"

Matt laughed, but he was angry. "You're a fool, Coyle! Nothing but a damned fool! There's men on this train who have known me for years. Whoever started such a story as that, ought to be horsewhipped!"

There was no backing down in Coyle. "We've got your description, right down to the last notch!"

"May I see it?"

Coyle pulled out a paper from his shirt pocket. "There!" he flared. "Read it! Won't do you any good to tear it up, that's just a copy."

"Over six feet in height, weight two hundred pounds or more, dark hair and eyes . . . ." Matt chuckled. "This could be a description of more than one man. Why, for that matter it could be a description of Clive Massey!"

"Massey?" Astonished anger flared in Coyle's eyes. "Why, that's absurd! It's . . . !"

"Is it?" Matt stared down at his hands. "Is it foolish? Think back a bit. Even your fine Colonel

Pearson knows me. He knew me years ago . . . *is there anyone on this train who knew Massey before he came to Deadwood?"*

The instant he framed the words, he became sure of their truth. It would explain his feeling about Massey, that he was a gunman, a killer. It would explain a lot of things.

Brian Coyle was staring at him, his face wearing a mixed expression of doubt, dismay, and growing realization. "That's absurd." He repeated the words but there was no emphasis in them.

Matt wheeled his horse and raced back to his own company. On the way he reined in suddenly alongside of Reutz. "Listen," he said, "if you're believing the same thing the others are, get it out of your head. Even Pearson will tell you you're wrong. But Massey's our man!"

Dusk was coming by now and the wagons were circling for a halt. Riding swiftly ahead, he swung down and strode into the circle around the fire Jeb Stark was building. Quickly, he explained. He was still talking when a shot rang out.

When they reached the scene of the fight, Elam Brooks lay on his face, blood staining the grass. Only a glance was needed to tell that he was dead.

Bat Hammer stood over him, his eyes ugly. Beside him were Buckskin Johnson and Clive Massey.

Massey's face was horribly swollen and puffed. He glared around. "I saw it all," he said flatly, "it was an even break!"

"Where's Elam's gun?" Ben Sperry demanded. "I don't see no gun."

"It's under him," Massey said. "It fell from his hand." He swung his eyes around at them. "You all go back to your wagons. I will attend to this."

For a second, Matt hesitated. The commission in his pocket could be drawn out. In one instant he could take charge here. Yet actually, he knew nothing. Of course, if Brooks' gun was not under his body, he could arrest Bat Hammer for murder, but that would only put the rest of them on guard. With the others, he turned away. He saw Ben Sperry staring after him, about to speak. Then he turned away and said nothing, so Bardoul walked back to his own wagons.

His head throbbed, and he leaned both hands on the back of the wagon. For a long time he stood there, his head hanging.

"Twenty-eight miles today," Stark was saying, "the best we've done yet."

"What crick is this?" Jeb asked.

"Fork of the Crazy Woman. By tomorrow night we should make Clear Creek if the going is this good."

Lute Harless walked up and joined them, glancing briefly at Matt. He hesitated, staring over at him, worrying about what he should do. The story that Matt Bardoul was Sim Boyne had swept the camp, and many had accepted it as gospel, never questioning the description they had picked up in Fort Reno. Somebody had started the story before they reached Reno, and when the description fitted, they accepted the whole rumour as fact. Lute Harless was troubled. He had liked Matt Bardoul and trusted him, and although he had heard the rumour, he remained uncertain. Finally, he sat down on the ground and waited for the food to be handed around.

He was disturbed in more ways than one. Elam Brooks had been killed, and Lute liked and trusted Elam. He was a staunch man, well known and liked, and his killing seemed to imply that all they had feared was to come about as they had expected.

He was confused and irritated. Thoughtfully, he stole a look at Aaron Stark. Buffalo Murphy walked into the ring of light, not seeing Matt. He stared around belligerently, but nobody made any comment, so he dished up some food and sat down beside Ban Hardy.

Matt's side hurt him and he felt ill. The kicks in the head had given him a mild concussion, and his head throbbed.

He scarcely saw the old Indian move past him and stop at the edge of the firelight.

Murphy was the first to see him. He lifted a hand. "How!" he said, in greeting.

The old Indian looked around. "How," he said

mildly. He gestured. "Many white man come. Too many."

Murphy chuckled. "That's right as rain! This was a good country before it got all cluttered up with white men!"

The Indian looked at him sourly. "No white man need tell me what my eyes can see. The white man came to a land of grass and trees, to a land of clear, cold streams where the buffalo roamed in their thousands and the beaver filled the streams. They came to a land rich and beautiful, and what have they done? They descended upon the land like starving wolves and they have slaughtered the buffalo for their hides and left the meat to rot upon the prairie, they swept the beaver from the streams and ripped the metals from the earth, and where the white man has been, the streams are fouled with mud and the poison from their mines.

"Where there were forests there is now a wilderness of stumps and useless brush, and the rain washes out the soil from around the roots, and the few trees die. Where there was grass, there is desert; where there were buffalo, there are vast and empty plains swept by sun and wind. No longer does the beaver tail slap the water in quick alarm. His people are gone from the clear waters, his dams are broken. So my people are dying also, and you white men will sweep on across the land digging and killing and ripping up the long grass lands until finally you reach the waters in the west, and then you will wash back upon yourselves. You will return upon the land you have raped and looted and fight like snarling, starving dogs filled with hunger and hatred.

"Where you found forests, you leave desolation; where you found plenty, you leave famine; where you found prairies waving with tall grass, you leave a desert. Finally, you will turn back upon yourselves and fight over the scraps until all is gone and you turn and stare about in astonished wonderment at the land you have ravished, and you will say, 'Great Spirit, what have we done?' "

"He's crazy!" Harless said, staring at the old man.

Murphy tugged at his beard. "Maybe. I think the old boy makes sense."

"I have been to your great cities, white men. I went with the great Red Cloud, but what did I see? Only a mad rush for wealth, all fighting and wrangling and hurry, and I found no contentment there, no peace. There is no calm in your people, there is no majesty, you are a people of thieves who sell your daughters for money and barter your souls for gain.

"I shall not live to see the end, nor will you, for the land you have stolen from the Indian is rich, and the looting will take years. The spirit of looting within you will not end, and you will come to call your greed a virtue. You will call it energy and industry, and he who steals the most will gain the praise of his fellow man until finally a day will come when you will look back and see with eyes like mine, and then you will understand.

"You came to our land: a people in search of homes, and homes are good things, but then homes would not content you. There must be more, and more, and MORE! Like beasts you slew my people, like beasts you looted our land, and now you praise yourself for your energy. This you said, is what a white man can do!

"It was not your energy, White Men, it was the wealth you found when you came. Any man can appear rich if he spends all he possesses in a mad orgy! You are like the foolish young brave who found the skins of many animals, and draped himself in these skins, and said 'See! What a great hunter I am! What a great warrior!' but when the skins were sold or given away he had no more. His wealth was gone.

"Some among you have talked of saving the trees, of keeping the grass, but they are a few small voices whispering against the wind. The men you send to speak in your councils speak for the greedy, and for this they are given a part of the spoils, and as they grow old and fat and lose their hair and teeth and the strength of their loins, they grow more rapacious.

"White Man, you have destroyed my people; you are destroying my land; but a day will come when you must face destiny, when you will find the metal you made into cheap trinkets or into objects soon to be worn and tossed away, you will find that metal is the metal you need to survive. War and desolation will sweep over you, and you will be gone. The white man will go. He will die, not slowly like the Indian, but swiftly, suddenly, and then he will be gone.

"The white man is not fitted to survive, for he knows not content. He knows not peace. Wars and more wars and bitter famine and pestilence shall end his pride. He cannot learn. Wherever he goes there is war. The Indian fought, but his battles were short and soon over, and the Indian returned to his hunting and his lodge and his squaw. But the white man lives in violence. Where he goes there is fury, and he will die, tearing at the agony of his wounds, crushed and bloody and wondering because in all his hurry and his doing he has never understood his world nor what he does.

"My people will not be here, but when the fury of the white man is gone, the grass will return, and the forests will grow tall again, for at last, White Man, it is the grass that must always be the victor. It is the grass that made us, the grass built your cities, and the grass fed your flocks. It is the grass that made us, and it is the grass that will come back, sewing up with green thread and winding brown roots the gashes you have ripped in the earth, and the grass will save the water that trees may grow tall, and the flowers bloom again. And the grass will strain the mud from the rain water and the streams will grow clear again, gathering the soil from the desert into bounty once more.

"The white man will be gone. Nothing of him will remain. His cities will fall to ruin, rust will gnaw his steel, and when the years have swallowed him, there will be nothing to mark his passing or the fury with which he looted this green and golden land.

"I shall go, White Man. You have taken my Black Hills from me, the dwelling place of the Great Spirit. You soon will take the Big Horns. My chiefs have died to save their people, and we have fought well, but your ways of war are hard, and my people are not persistent in their hatreds. We have fought well with what little we have, and now we shall go, wrapped in our blankets and sorrowing that this must be an end."

Aaron Stark shifted and looked around. Then he got up suddenly and bent over the coffee pot to fill his cup. "Some of this land ain't much good, nohow," he said, "won't grow nothin. You get a good crop for a few years, an' then its all gone."

Barney Coyle had walked up while the old Indian was talking. He looked up suddenly. "That's right," he agreed, "just like my poke. Spend a few dollars and then there isn't any more." He pushed his hat back on his head and grinned at Ban Hardy. "I guess the idea is to keep putting something in once in awhile."

"Huh!" Stark scoffed. "That sounds mighty good, but how you going to put anything into land? If it ain't there, it just ain't there, that's all!"

Matt straightened and felt the pain in his side sharpen. Holding himself against it, he walked slowly away from the fire. When he was a hundred yards off, he sat down on a stone and stared down at the water of the fork.

It was still and dark, and now there seemed no movement except at intervals when he heard a sudden rippling of the water as though the stream were whispering to him that it was still alive. His head throbbed and he sat still, looking at nothing. At that, he felt better, and he could think better. Carefully, he felt of his hands, working his fingers to loosen them and make them pliable.

Brian Coyle was sitting on his bed under his biggest wagon when Ben Sperry walked up to him. Sperry dropped to his haunches. "Brian, this here setup looks kind of funny to me. My wagon's been gone through."

"Gone through? How do you mean?"

"Somebody searched it. My ammunition's all gone."

Coyle stopped with his boot half off. "Your ammunition? Stolen?"

"Yes, an' I think that's why Elam was killed. I think he found Hammer goin' through his wagon an' found what he was after. He didn't have no gun on him, Brian. Elam Brooks never carried a short gun. He was a rifle man. Carried a Winchester carbine."

Brian Coyle pulled his boot back on and got to his feet. He walked around behind his wagon. "Jacquine? Can I come in?"

"Yes, I'm still dressed."

Coyle clambered in the wagon and began pulling things aside. When he got to the ammunition boxes, they were empty. He stared at them, his eyes hard and his face very serious. Slowly, he got out of the wagon.

"Ben, how much ammunition have you got?"

"Five bullets in my six gun, an' four or five shells in my Winchester. That ain't very much."

"No, it isn't." Coyle stared at the ground. "Ben, you go back to your wagon and keep your eyes open but don't mention this to anyone."

He reached into the wagon for his own gun and belted it on.

"Father . . . ?"

He turned at Jacquine's voice. "Is there going to be trouble? Is something wrong?"

Coyle hesitated. "I'm afraid something is very wrong, Jackie." He spoke softly and gently. "I wish I had left you in Deadwood."

"Father, why don't you go see Matt Bardoul?"

Brian Coyle's face stiffened. "No! I'd never . . . !" His voice died. "Maybe it would be best at that. I'd better talk to Herman first. You stay in the wagon."

Ammunition, of course, was valuable. Coyle started for the Reutz wagons thinking that. It could be a thief. Probably Hammer was a thief. The thing to do was to talk to Herman Reutz, to find out if theirs was an isolated case or if the ammunition had been removed from all the wagons. Of course, nearly all the men were still armed, and their weapons would be loaded. Bardoul's whole idea had been preposterous, and there had to be a solution for this problem.

Brian Coyle was not unaware, however, of the growing strain among the people of the wagon train. He had observed the tightening of discipline in Massey's company with approval, but now he thought of it with misgiving.

If Sperry was right and Elam Brooks had been murdered, the situation was indeed serious. It was characteristic that Coyle did not even consider calling upon Colonel Pearson, for in the days on the march, he had come to recognize the notable inefficiency that characterized Pearson. He was one of those men who mean well but have small intelligence, and no ability to cope with the unexpected. His entire life had been lived to a series of set rules, according to a program, and any deviation upset him severely. He was by no means typical of his profession, yet there were many like him, Coyle knew.

As he walked toward the wagons of C Company, Coyle's footsteps slowed. The first break had been the presence of Abel Bain and his attempted attack on Sarah Stark. The attempted killing of Bardoul had been the natural outcome of that, yet it had a place in the larger scheme, too. The personnel of the law enforcement group, the attempt to collect all the guns in the train, the searching of Sperry's wagon and then the killing of Elam Brooks. All these had been signs of something. Yet, Coyle realized that without Bardoul's suspicions, he might have considered them isolated instances bearing no relation to anything, past or future.

Herman Reutz was sitting on a box near a dying fire. He smiled at Coyle. "Sit down, Brian. I'm helping my fire die." Then he saw Coyle's face. "What's wrong?" he asked quickly.

Brian Coyle sat down and drew out his pipe. Then, in as few words as possible, he explained.

At once, Reutz got up and went to his wagon, then to a second wagon. He walked back and sat down. "Gone!" he said. "Every last bit of it! And I all but emptied my rifle at a herd of antelope today!"

"We've got to do something, Herman. We've got to think fast and act faster."

"We can be wrong about this," Reutz said, "we can be wrong. Bardoul warned us, but this story about him being Boyne upset us all. It threw me off, I know."

Coyle nodded. "Nonsense, of course. I checked with both Phillips and Pearson. He could not have been Sim Boyne. He suggested that Massey was Boyne."

"Well," Reutz said, "the description would fit. They are both big men. We'd best work out a plan of action, but we're going to be handicapped by the fact that we don't know how much time we have."

"You think they would actually try to take over the wagon train? They would have to kill us all!"

Reutz nodded. "The only way for them. If Massey is Sim Boyne we could expect nothing else, anyway. The man is a brute. Worse, he's a fiend. Not just a killer, he's a sadistic murderer. I know something about him."

"We outnumber them, and most of us have some ammunition left. If we moved now, we might swing it."

"Nothing we can do, actually," Reutz protested. "We don't have any evidence, nothing but suspicion and the fact that our ammunition has been stolen. It might be Hammer. That ammunition would sell to the Indians, you know. We're going to have to move carefully. As far as that goes, they probably have spies in our own companies."

"Bardoul was of the opinion, you told me several days ago, that if they struck it would not be until we reached the basin or at least got around the tip of the Big Horns. That would give us some time."

"A little." Reutz knocked out his pipe. "Coyle, we'd better talk to the few men we *know* we can trust. We'd better make a careful check and see that each man has some ammunition, and we had better have a talk with Bardoul."

Matt Bardoul flexed his fingers and palmed his gun. He was fast but not fast enough. He turned and started back to camp. He was almost there when he heard a woman scream and a sudden rattle of shots.

The sounds came from somewhere off in the darkness away from the wagon train, and instantly, he thought of the wagon. He ran for his horse, and swung into the saddle. He glimpsed Tolliver buckling on a gun belt and running for his own horse. From all over the camp, other men gathered. When Bardoul raced out across the prairie toward the sound of the shots, at least twenty mounted men rode after him.

There was a shot . . . another shot, and then silence. The pound of their horses' hooves was the only sound.

Matt was first to reach the small fire by the wagon. If Indians they had been, they were gone now. At first he saw nothing but spilled flour and beans, but then he saw Joe Rucker, sprawled on his face, a bullet through his arm, and another through his head.

Under the wagon, lying on her back, was Joe's brother . . . no longer a brother even in name, for her shirt was torn, and there could be no doubt that Abel Bain had been right. Matt, knelt beside her, and immediately realized that she at least was alive.

Matt glanced around at the crowding men. "Stark, you an' Lute rig up a stretcher, will you? We'll take her back where the girls can lend a hand."

Clive Massey shoved through the crowd. Stahl and Hammer were with him, and the first thing Bardoul saw as he straightened up was a livid scratch across Stahl's cheek. The man was still panting, and his pupils were dilated.

"We'll take her to my company!" Massey said. "One of the girls will come there to care for her."

Bardoul looked at him, the firelight on their faces. This could be it, he thought, and swollen hands or not, he was ready. "No," he said, "the arrangements have already been made. The Stark girls can care for her, and they need not leave their own wagons. That would be much better."

"Who's running this wagon train?" Massey demanded. Matt noticed how his right hand was held and a curious light came into his eyes.

"Pearson, supposedly," Matt said, "but this girl goes to the Stark wagon."

"I think, maybe," Massey said coldly, "we'd better settle this question of authority right now!"

"Sure," Bardoul was relaxed and easy. "Any time

you like. Let's get Coyle and Pearson here first, and Reutz."

"I'm here," Herman Reutz said quickly.

"So am I." Coyle stepped forward and Colonel Pearson was behind him.

Bardoul gave Massey no chance to speak. "This girl," he said quietly, "goes to the Stark wagon. Clive Massey has made it a question of authority." He drew his commission from his pocket and handed it to Colonel Pearson. "Tell them what that says."

Pearson started to read, then he looked up, blank astonishment written on his usually composed features. "Why, this says he is a Deputy United States Marshal!"

"*What?*" Clive Massey leaped forward and ripped the paper from Pearson's hand.

As he read, his face slowly paled and his nostrils dilated. When he looked up, a living hatred blazed in his eyes. "So?" he said. "A deputy marshal? I reckon that authority exceeds mine."

He started to turn away, as all eyes stared at Bardoul, but then he turned and walked back, coming close. "Just what would a deputy marshal be doing on this wagon train?"

Matt Bardoul met his gaze with a taunting smile. "Why, Massey, I'm here to preserve the law, first an' foremost. With a gun if need be. Also, I'm on a special sort of mission. It seems there's a crazy killer loose in the northwest, two of them, in fact, and I'm to find them and bring them in. I'm talkin'," he added, "about Dick Ryder and Sim Boyne!"

He turned suddenly. "Stahl, how did you get that scratch on your cheek?"

All eyes swung to the burly renegade. He started, then glared left and right. "Runnin' through the brush. Didn't I, Hammer?"

Hammer grinned at Bardoul. "He sure did, Marshal. He sure did."

Brian Coyle was looking thoughtfully at Bardoul. The crowd started to break up and drift back toward the wagon train. Coyle walked over to Matt. "Why didn't you tell us you were a marshal?"

"The appointment only reached me at Fort Reno," he said. "It was following me. I didn't even know it was going through."

Coyle started to speak, but Massey was still standing there, watching him, so he turned away. This would change everything. It would simplify things. If they could get together under a marshal, and then . . . he walked to his horse and mounting, started for camp.

Clive Massey looked after him, then followed Stahl and Hammer to their own horses.

Matt Bardoul was the last to go, yet when he reached his horse he saw there were two horses, and beside his stood a big man who waited with his thumbs tucked in his belt. Who waited for him alone and in the darkness.

CHAPTER X

Matt walked up to the horses moving quickly, his hands ready. The dark figure moved and Bardoul's guns were in his hands. Then he relaxed, for the waiting man was Bill Shedd.

"That was fast," Shedd admitted, "but you'll have to be faster. Them swole hands won't help much!"

"What's on your mind, Bill?"

"Plenty." Shedd put a hand on the pommel of his saddle. "Bardoul, I wanted to tell you that you won't have to look any further for Dick Ryder."

"You mean, you . . . ?"

"No," Shedd replied, "I'm not him. Dick Ryder is dead. He was murdered, shot in the back with a shot gun, by Sim Boyne. I'm Dick's half brother.

"He was a bad man, Dick was. He was a mean one. Away from home, that is. My Ma married Dick's old man, an' we growed up alongside one another. Dick, he was always mighty fine around home, done his work, an' treated Ma swell, but he got to trailin' with a bad crowd an' he got meaner an' meaner. Killed folks, robbed them, and done a lot of mighty bad things. Like I said before, he deserved killin', but he didn't deserve gettin' shot in the back by a man worse than him."

"You're looking for Sim Boyne?"

"Yes, I am. I'm killin' him when I find him."

"You said you'd know him?"

"That's right. He's got a couple of bullet scars. One under his belt just over the hip bone, an' one where a bullet went through the muscles of his neck on

164

the right side, just where the neck joins the shoulder."

Matt nodded. "That will help." He swung into the saddle. "Bill, do you think Clive Massey is Sim Boyne?"

Shedd spat. "I don't know," he said thoughtfully, "I don't know. He's a smooth one, that Massey, smooth an' hard to figure."

"Did you know anything about their plans out here?"

"Not much. Only they had an idea of locatin' someplace in the Big Horn country an' raidin' wagon trains and the minin' towns. I can tell you something else, too. They were making a rendezvous with some other men from the bad crowd out here, somewheres. I don't know just where."

Morning found Matt Bardoul riding off on the flank once more. If there had been a rendezvous arranged with other bad men it might well be that within a few days they would come up with this group and the honest men of the wagon train would be outnumbered. As things stood, in a prolonged battle, all the advantage lay with the renegades due to their stealing of ammunition. In a sudden strike, the advantage of numbers might make the need for ammunition almost nil. If they waited, however, until they met this group that waited some place ahead, the doubtful advantage of numbers would be lost.

There could be little time now. Tonight they would bed down on Clear Creek, and the next day would bring them up to the ruins of Fort Kearney, destroyed by Red Cloud's Sioux some years before. They would be entering a wilder and lonelier country where the prospects of a successful attack by the renegades would be vastly improved.

Emerging from some trees along the river, he started back toward the wagon train and saw Jacquine Coyle riding along a ridge. He touched a spur to the dun and raced to catch up with her. She turned as he galloped up, and for an instant he was afraid she was going to ride away.

"Jacquine. . . ."

She interrupted. "Has Father talked to you? He wants to, I'm sure."

He stopped, cut off in what he had started to say. She kept her face averted. "It's something about the wagon train, I don't know what. He talked with Ben Sperry last night."

The wind played lights and shadows with the grass. Matt put a hand on the dun's neck. He knew how imperative it was to talk to Brian Coyle, and to Herman Reutz, but he wanted nothing so much as to talk to Jacquine now, to tell her what he felt, what he really thought. There was something in him that demanded to be said, that needed to come out of him. For a fleeting moment behind the wagon on that other evening, he had felt that she was with him, that she felt as he did, that she responded to him.

Curiously, he was tied up inside. Words did not come easily to him when he felt most deeply, and somehow he always found himself saying the things that meant nothing, and leaving all the things in his heart unsaid and alone there. There was that in him that would not allow him to speak what he felt unless he was sure that this girl felt the same. There were so many words, and all of them futile. Yet women put much faith in words, and the things that were said to them.

He wanted to speak his mind now, but he found himself wordless when he rode beside her. Yet there was something fine about her, some little thing in the way she carried herself, the lift of her chin, her lips. . . .

"Matt," she said suddenly, incongruously, "we know so little about each other although we have talked a good deal. I don't know what you think, what you believe, I know almost nothing about you."

Suddenly, he felt better. He grinned. "Why, what is there to know about any man? And how can a man tell you what he is? Words usually just serve to cover up what a man thinks, or maybe they just antagonize him and make him defend ideas he never gave a thought to.

I reckon it's hard to know what to believe. A man hears so many things, and he reads so many things.

"If there is something, though, if there is . . . well, I believe in the things I love . . . the feel of a good horse under me, the blue along those mountains over yonder, the firm, confident feel of a good gunbutt in my hand, the way the red gold of your hair looks against your throat.

"The creak of a saddle in the hot sun and long riding, the way you feel when you come to the top of a ridge and look down across miles and miles of land you have never seen, or maybe no man has ever seen. I believe in the pleasant sound of running water, the way the leaves turn red in the fall. I believe in the smell of autumn leaves burning, and the crackle of a burning log. Sort of sounds like it was chuckling over the memories of a time when it was a tree.

"I like the sound of rain on a roof, and the look of a fire in a fireplace, and the embers of a campfire and coffee in the morning. I believe in the solid, hearty, healthy feel of a fist landing, the feel of a girl in my arms, warm and close. Those are the things that matter.

"Sure, I'd like to have a place of my own, and some kids. I remember one day I was walking through the streets back in Dodge and a little boy asked me if I was Howard's father.

"Well, now. I hadn't any idea who Howard was, but I looked down at that kid and told him, 'Son, I'm not Howard's father, I'm not anybody's father!' But you know, I felt bad about that all day! It kind of got to me. Maybe I'm too sentimental."

"No, Matt," Jacquine said softly, "I don't think you are."

They rode on, and the dry grass whispered to their horses' hooves, and the tall peaks of the Big Horns gathered cotton blossoms of cloud. The mountains were nearer now, a bold rampart dividing the valley of the Powder from the basin of the Big Horn.

He stared down at his hands, still swollen from the

hammering he had given them. He flexed and unflexed his fingers, trying to work the stiffness out of them and regain the speed and dexterity he might need at any moment. His side still bothered him, but his face felt better. Remembering Massey's broken nose, he smiled grimly. That broken nose would be with him for awhile, and there would be a scar on his cheekbone.

They halted on the crest of a hill and glanced back along the long, winding column of the wagons. Matt studied them thoughtfully. Tomorrow Massey's company would be taking the lead, and his own would be last. An idea was born, and he turned it over thoughtfully, planning ahead.

Whatever was to be done must be done soon. The people of the wagon train could be endangered no longer, and there was a surly aggressiveness showing itself more and more from the renegades that made up Massey's company. He had held off this long because of Jacquine, but he could do so no longer. If there was a rendezvous ahead, as Bill Shedd believed, they might soon be seriously outnumbered.

There was a fort at the junction of the Big Horn and the Little Horn. They might strike out for there and replenish their ammunition, and then go on. It was a question of how much time they had, or how successful a break they could manage.

The difficulty now was that the fort lay due north of them, and the route of the wagon train lay in the same direction for at least three days longer. To break away from the train now would only mean to separate themselves at a distance of a few miles, and to follow a parallel course. The fact that he was a Deputy United States Marshal was of no advantage for the moment. He was aware, however, that if Clive Massey was Sim Boyne, that the man would now be out to kill him as quickly as possible.

Tonight they would bed down on Clear Creek. The following day, with rougher travel, they should make the site of ruined Fort Phil Kearney. A day's travel beyond was Goose Creek, and beyond that, the Tongue. If they were to make a break, the Tongue would be the logical place, for it would be about there that the wagon train would begin to trend further and further west.

Matt scowled at the sunlit plains. If only he knew where the rendezvous with the other outlaws was to be! If it came sooner than the Tongue, it could mean a surprise or a pitched battle. Yet knowing, as Massey now must know, that the honest men of the train were alerted, would he try an attack when there was such great danger of encountering a patrol from the fort? From Fort No. 1?

"Matt," Jacquine asked suddenly, "did you know about the ammunition being stolen?"

He jerked his head around sharply. "What ammunition?"

"From the wagons. Ben Sperry told Father about it, and Father looked and ours had been taken, too. Someone has gone through all or most of the wagons and taken the ammunition. Sperry believed that was why Elam Brooks was killed . . . because he found them in his wagon, or discovered what they were doing. He also said that Elam never carried a short gun."

"No," Matt said, "I didn't know that. If I had known the truth about Brooks, I would have arrested Massey then and there, or tried it."

He rode in silence for a few minutes. "So they have the ammunition? They aren't taking many chances!" His thoughts raced. Something would have to be done about that, and at once.

When they rode back to the wagon train, he checked his own ammunition. Most of it was gone. They had, he found, overlooked a box of .44's . . . enough for quite a battle if need be. Nevertheless, they would need more, and he knew how to get it. The same way Massey's men had gotten it, but at all costs, without an open battle.

They camped that night on the site of the ruined Fort Phil Kearny.

It was a place of memories for Matt Bardoul, and he glanced around thoughtfully. Many of the charred timbers still remained, the timbers of the fort built so painstakingly under the direction of Colonel Carrington, and burned after it was abandoned, burned by the warriors of Red Cloud.

Buffalo Murphy strolled up to where Matt stood looking around, with him was Brian Coyle. "You know this place?" Coyle asked, momentarily forgetful of their own troubles. "I've heard a lot about it."

"Yes, I know it. There was a lot of blood shed over this plot of ground." Matt looked around. "Carrington was a smart man, but no military man, certainly. He picked the worst site in miles for this fort. He put it down here in this space between two rivers, and had no water inside the walls, and too many hills close by. It was a beautiful job of construction for the place and the times, and every bit of work on it done with armed men on constant guard."

"Them Sioux sure hated her!" Murphy commented. "They killed a sight of men along here. The fort was supposed to make the Bozeman Trail safe. Hell! In the first six months after it was built the Sioux killed more than a hundred and fifty men along the trail or at the fort! They ran off a lot of stock, too. Nigh to a thousand head, maybe.

"Right back over yonder," Murphy pointed toward the buttes, "was where Fetterman was killed. Folks say he was a fighter. Maybe so, but he sure wasn't no Indian fighter or he'd never have done like he done.

"Powell was supposed to have taken the wood cutters out, and if he had, it would have been different. He knew the Sioux. Fetterman was one of these here flashy sort of fighters, and he aimed to teach the Sioux a lesson.

"Lesson! He learned his lesson, but it didn't do him much good! Three officers, two civilian scouts and seventy-six soldiers killed, all in a matter of minutes. Only fightin' of any account was done by the civilian scouts."

Coyle glanced at Bardoul. "You were at that Wagon Box fight, weren't you?"

"Uh huh. And hadn't any business there. I was riding up from Reno and risking my scalp to do it and bring some mail through. I spotted some Indians around the fort, so I headed around and ran into Powell and the wood cutters. Powell was smart. He never raised any fuss about things, but he was a good soldier and careful. He dismounted the wagon boxes from fourteen wagons, and used them for a barricade, piling sacks of grain and other stuff on them to stop arrows.

"It must have looked pretty easy to Red Cloud, only thirty-two white men inside, as they had killed four wood cutters before they could get to the wagons. Red Cloud had about fifteen hundred warriors, and Crazy Horse to lead them. Crazy Horse was worth a hundred men, himself. Red Cloud just didn't know Powell. Powell had given the best shots two rifles apiece and had the poorer shots loading for them, and they held their fire until the Sioux were right on top of them, and then opened up.

"It was a lot different than the Fetterman massacre. Powell knew what he was up against and he wasn't a glory hunter, he was a fighting man, pure and simple. It knocked the stuffing out of the Sioux, but they weren't through. They tried it three or four times more, tried it crawling, charging on foot, and another time on horseback. They got right up against the wagons once, but then they broke and ran.

"We lost seven men and three wounded. Nobody knows what the Indians lost, but Powell figured it around a hundred and eighty. It could have been more, maybe as many as two hundred, for Powell was the sort to under-estimate rather than otherwise."

Brian Coyle put his hands on his hips and looked at Bardoul. "I reckon you think I'm a fool," he said, "I remember your warning, but I had never run up against anything like this before. Now I can see what we've run into."

Bardoul shrugged. "I wasn't sure. I was just guessing, then. Now that we're in it we can't do any good by thinking of what we might have done or should have done. We've got to be thinking of what to do. One thing is to keep our own guards on watch, all the time. And keep our weapons handy. I'm thinking they won't try anything before the Tongue, but that's only a guess for I've no way of knowing.

"What we should do is keep right on going when we hit the Tongue and head for the fort on the Little Big Horn. There we can report the whole thing and get an escort if need be; however, if we have ammunition we won't need an escort. Right now we've got to think of the women and children in this outfit and getting as near that fort as possible before the fight. Every mile increases our chance of rescue from the fort even as it increases the danger of attack."

Lute Harless had walked up with Herman Reutz. "I'm for going on as long as we can," Harless said, "I don't like this!"

"All right," Matt agreed, "but all of you stand by tonight. Let your womenfolks stay awake to awaken you, or stay awake yourselves, because there may be trouble."

Coyle looked at Bardoul. "What are you planning?"

Matt swept the group with a glance. "You're all safe men. I'll tell you. I'm going to steal back some ammunition tonight. Just like they stole it from us, only not enough so they'll know, but enough to make all the difference in case of trouble."

"You can count me in on that," Coyle said.

"No," Matt shook his head, "I want only two men with me, and I know who I'm taking. It must be done quietly, and I want men who have woods experience, men who have fought Indians. If we're caught at it, we may have a pitched battle, so my suggestion is that in case of trouble you all center on Reutz' wagons. Assemble there, and it will serve as a rallying point."

The group broke up and Matt walked back to his wagons. Tolliver and Bill Shedd were loitering nearby, smoking. Matt glanced at the young mountain man. "How's your girl?"

He looked up quickly, flushing. "She's some better," he said. "She wants to see you."

"All right." He hesitated. "You two stay by your

wagons tonight and stay together, sleep if you want to, but take turn about, and keep your rifles handy."

Shedd nodded grimly and turning, crawled into his wagon. Matt walked toward the Starks', listening to the rustle of the Pine Creek as he walked. It was coming again, more fighting, more danger, and it was different when there were women. If he knew for sure, they could act without delay, but they did not know, for even the stealing of the ammunition might be the act of one or two of the renegades hoping to peddle it to the Indians. It was all a vast confusion with many indications of a plot, but nothing upon which one could act legally.

When Joe Rucker had been slain, there had been the scratch on Stahl's cheek, and Matt had seen the track of a boot heel near the wagon that looked like Stahl's, but it was indefinite. Elam Brooks had been killed, but the only actual witnesses had been Logan Deane's men. He felt a queer hesitancy to make the actual decision for battle, knowing as he did that the women would be involved. Every day drew them nearer and nearer to the protection of the soldiers.

Sarah Stark was standing beside her wagon, wiping her hands on her apron. She looked up and smiled at him. "She's been asking for you."

He nodded. "Sary, you tell Ban I want to see him at my wagon. Right away, you hear?"

She looked up. "You want Jeb, too?"

Bardoul hesitated. Jeb Stark was a good man. "Yes, send him along. Not with Ban, though. Have him go by himself and get right into my wagon and stay there until I come."

The wounded girl lay on a pallet in the wagon and he could hear her breathing when he climbed through the back end. She looked up at him and her eyes brightened. There was a flush of fever on her cheeks but she put out a hand and caught his sleeve. "You . . . you're a marshal?"

"Yes, Ma'am, I guess I am."

"You . . . you won't blame Tolly for helping us? Please, don't."

Matt shrugged, smiling. "Miss, I sure don't know any reason why he shouldn't help you. There's been some talk about a woman named Rosanna Cole who killed a man in St. Louis, but I haven't seen her."

"Maybe she's guilty, and maybe she's not, that she must settle with her own conscience. This country is big and wide and it's a good country for people to start over in, but as for me, I've got bigger problems and more important ones than hunting up a woman who shot somebody."

She put her hand over his. Her hair was brushed back from her forehead and lay tumbled in dark confusion around her head and face. Her eyes seemed unusually large. She smiled at him, and squeezed his hand tightly. "Thank you. Thank you, very much. That girl . . . I don't think she killed anyone. Someone else did, but the man needed it. He was a brute."

"I wouldn't know about that," Matt said. He ran his fingers through his hair. "Ma'am, I'm going to ranch out west, myself. You and Tolliver would make mighty nice neighbours, so when I start ranching, I hope I have you with me."

A sudden movement from the tailgate of the wagon made him look up. Jacquine Coyle was standing there, staring from one to the other, then without a sound she dropped the canvas and vanished.

Quickly, he scrambled from the wagon. "Jacquine!" he called. "Wait!"

She hesitated, turning toward him, but her face was stiff and white. "Don't let me take you from your lady friend!" she flared.

"My lady friend?" he was astonished.

"Don't try to find excuses, Mr. Bardoul! I heard quite enough. I very distinctly heard you tell her when you started ranching you wanted her with you! That's almost the same thing you told me!"

"But listen!" he protested. "You . . . !"

"Let me alone!" She drew away from him, then turned and fled toward her wagon.

Matt started after her, then halted. For an instant, he hesitated. If anything was to be done tonight it was time he talked with Murphy and Ban. They would be at the wagon, waiting.

Swearing, he wheeled and walked across the camp. Only a few fires still blazed. Most of them had died to glowing coals, and he could see the guards moving out to their posts. In a little while the camp would be asleep, and Pearson had left orders for an early start to make the twenty odd miles to Goose Creek.

Red coals glowed where the fire had been and as he walked toward his wagon a small stick fell into the coals and a tiny blaze leaped up, dancing brightly over the deep red, flickering on the log that lay behind the fire, and dancing on the wagon wheels and sending little ripples of shadow over the dusty white canvas of the wagon.

He turned when he reached the fire, and looked round. All was still. The banjo that had been played earlier was silent. A horse stamped somewhere and blew loudly. Matt seated himself on the log and hitched his gun across his leg. It might be tonight.

Extending his hands over the coals he warmed them and then chafed them gently, his mind working over the problem, working out a plan of action. He would use Murphy and Ban Hardy. Jeb Stark could help by keeping watch. It would have to be done swiftly and silently as possible. If they failed they would have no second chance.

Low clouds lay across the sky, and there was no moon. His mind kept going back to Jacquine and what she had heard. Wrenching his thoughts away from her, he considered the problem again, dropping a small stick into the coals. He got up then, and moved back to his wagon. Buffalo Murphy was leaning against the tailgate.

"Ban here?"

"Inside, with Jeb."

"We'll talk right here then. We've got to get ammunition, and we'd better get it tonight. We want no noise, no trouble."

He pulled off his own boots and dug his moccasins from the pack in the wagon, slipping them on.

"Murphy, you're a good Injun. You come with me. I've got the wagons spotted, I think. Ban, you and Jeb will keep watch. We won't try to get very much, just enough."

Quietly, he outlined his plan of action, Murphy nodding as he made his points. Matt took off his wide brimmed hat and tossed it into the wagon, then watched Murphy drift off into the shadows, and a moment later, Ban Hardy and Jeb Stark. He waited for a moment, then stepped behind his wagon.

While a man might have counted a slow thirty, he did not move, watching what he could see of the open space within the circle of wagons. The fires were all dying, but vaguely the scene was visible, and nothing stirred. If anyone was spying upon them, he did not show himself.

Carefully then, Matt Bardoul circled among the wagons, moving ghostlike in the space between the twin circles until he neared the Massey wagons.

He counted a dozen men sprawled under their blankets, sleeping near the wagons. One by one he studied them, aware that the slightest noise might awaken them. A few had been drinking, and they would be comparatively safe, but others among them were woodsmen, and they would be the ones to watch. Like a shadow, he moved to the rear of the nearest wagon.

Something moved in the darkness, and he saw the huge form of Buff Murphy. Big as the man was, he moved as silently as the wind moves through the grass.

There was a chance that someone would be sleeping within the wagons. Earlier, he had spotted the wagons that carried the ammunition, for most of the Massey wagons were lightly loaded, and now a couple of them began to leave deeper tracks, and offer more resistance to the pull of the oxen.

Matt slipped a hand under the canvas at the rear of the wagon. Carefully, he explored the darkness. Then lifting the canvas, he climbed in.

It was the work of a minute to find the ammunition boxes. He lifted two of them out of the pile and placed them near the tailgate, then he heaped up sacks and old clothing in the space they had occupied. Looking out, he spied Jeb Stark in the shadows, and motioned to him. The hillman moved up, and Matt passed a box to him, and then a second.

Jeb had placed the first on the ground, the second he kept and moved off into the shadows. Matt picked up the first box and followed him, and then waited for Murphy and Hardy. "Any more?" Ban breathed in his ear.

He shook his head, and they moved carefully away. Matt grinned and shook their hands as they broke up and each returned to his wagon. They had done it, and now there would be enough ammunition unless the fight was prolonged.

With the gray of dawn, they moved out. Matt rode near Reutz. "Ride by Murphy's wagon," he said, "and load up. Get some shells for your men, too!"

All day, under a lowering gray sky, the wagons moved north. Warily, Matt kept an eye on the Massey crew, but saw no indication that they had discovered the theft. For the time then, they were safe. When they bedded down that night on the Goose, they had made twenty-one miles. He walked by Jacquine's wagon, but she was not around. Disconsolate, he returned to his own.

Barney was waiting for him. It was the first time he had seen him in days, but he knew that owing to the illness of one of Coyle's drivers, Barney had been handling a team.

"Matt," he said excitedly, "a few minutes ago one of Massey's men got on a horse and rode away! From the way he looked and from what was said, I have an idea he was going to meet someone. Dad told me you'd heard there was a rendezvous arranged up ahead, somewhere."

"Thanks, Barney. You're exactly right. You keep a gun handy, and be sure it's loaded and ready. Something may break and it may not."

"Can't we do something now? To stop them I mean?"

"That's what I'd like to do, but after all, what do

we know, Barney? All of it is a lot of suspicion with a few disconnected things that seem to tie in with those suspicions. You can't arrest a man or shoot him for what you think he's going to do, and we haven't a shred of evidence against anybody that would hold in court. Moreover, we've got to think of the women and children, for if a battle starts some of them are going to get hurt."

Barney nodded soberly. "Everybody looks worried this evening, even some of the women who don't know anything may be wrong. It's like the whole wagon train was suddenly touched with some sort of blight. Nobody is singing this evening like they usually do, and nobody was riding out from the wagons today. Even Jacquine acts different."

Matt started to speak, then thought the better of it. What he had to say should be said to Jacquine.

What Barney had said was true. Silence seemed to have fallen over the wagon train. The groups around the fires talked in low tones and the men moved about restlessly. Buffalo Murphy leaned his back against a wagon wheel and his eyes seemed never to stop moving. Ban Hardy kept nervously hitching his gun belts, and Jeb Stark moved from time to time out of the circle of light and vanished into the darkness beyond the wagons. Once a branch cracked loudly in the fire and Ban's gun was half out of his holster before he realized.

The tension lay upon all of them, and upon Massey's men as well. From that part of the great circle there came no shouts as usual, nor laughter. It was silent, as the camp waited with queer expectancy for something to happen, and nothing did.

The night passed without incident and the morning broke gray and dull with lowering clouds and a faint spattering of rain began to fall as the wagon train began to rumble out upon the trail toward the Tongue. Matt glanced down at Tolliver beside whose wagon he was riding. "If we had a way through those mountains, we could make the Shell easy. It ought to be just due west of us."

"We've changed our course, haven't we? Looks like we're bearing more west."

"That's right. Northwest now."

By mid morning Matt dug his slicker from behind his saddle and got into it. The light spatter of rain turned into a crashing downpour. The wagons continued, moving slower and slower, and scattering out to find firmer going away from the ruts of the other wagons which filled with water as rapidly as they were made.

Matt bowed his head into the storm and kept the dun moving up and down the line of his wagons, a line that grew more and more extended as the morning drew on. Where a wagon was stuck or having difficulties, he was beside it, putting a shoulder to the wheel, or moving obstructions.

Through the gray rain the Big Horns loomed like a monstrous wall, close on their left. Time and again he found his eyes straying toward them, remembering the green depths of their forests, the free running streams, the leaping fish, and the deer. This was a man's country, if one had ever been built, and beyond the mountains was the basin. He was eager to be back, eager to have a place of his own and be working again at something he could build, something to last.

The rain drove against his face and rattled like hail upon his poncho. There was no time now for talk, for it was work to keep moving. Luckily, it could be no more than a dozen miles to the Tongue by the route they were following, and the day should be short unless too many wagons became stuck.

Squinting his eyes against the battering rain, he drew up and stared ahead. His own wagons were scattered over at least a mile of trail. Those of Coyle were some place further ahead, and Reutz must be behind. Yet both were lost in the rain. He bowed his head to let his hat brim shield his face and rode on.

There was no sign of a let up. He laid a hand on the dun's wet shoulder and spoke to him. "Rough going, isn't it boy?"

The horse cocked an ear at him and shook his head with disgust. Had it been left to him he would have turned his back on the rain and wind and cropped some of this good grass. Wet it might be, but it was grass and good. There was no sense in driving on into a rain, but then, when did men have horse sense? The dun plodded patiently ahead like a husband with a nagging wife, letting the storm blow by his ears.

Raising his head, Matt saw one of his wagons stopped, the oxen straining. He rode rapidly over the soggy prairie to lend a hand. It was Aaron Stark.

When the wagon was rolling again, he put his head in over the tailgate. "How are you, Ma'am?"

The girl lifted a hand, and then he heard her say, "All right, thank you."

Matt walked back to his horse which he had left to one side and wiped off the saddle. He put a foot in the stirrup and swung up. His stirrup was twisted, and he bent to pull it around in place, feeling with his toe for it. He got it straightened, and looked up. A body of horsemen were riding toward him, and even as he straightened up, a gun flared and something struck him a wicked blow on the head, even as he felt himself falling, he grabbed for his gun, struggling to get at it under the poncho.

At the first shot, his horse had leaped frantically, and his precarious hold on the stirrup was lost. Another shot rang out, and he felt himself falling. Down . . . down . . . the ground hit him with terrific force and he saw a wave of blackness rolling toward him and fought desperately to stave it off, his hand fighting for a gun, and then he felt his hold on consciousness slipping, and as the blackness rolled over him, he knew he had failed.

Clive Massey had struck under cover of the rain when the wagons were scattered and without unity, and when everyone was busy fighting to keep moving. He had struck and struck swiftly, and there was no chance for concerted defense, no chance to use the ammunition they had recovered, no chance for anything but to fall and die, each man alone, each man fighting.

Rain spattered on his face as he lay sprawled in the mud and dimly, through the veil of the rain and his failing awareness he heard Stahl's voice, grim with satisfaction. "Got him!"

"Who is it?" That would be Hammer.

"Bardoul! Matt Bardoul, By God! Drilled him right through the head, first shot!"

The rain pounded down upon the prairie, and the wagons rolled on as if nothing had happened, and the dun horse dashed off through the rain, stirrups flopping loosely. Behind it, face down in the mud, Matt Bardoul lay sprawled, and under him a darker stain began to mingle with the rain and stain the mud a deep crimson.

Then the sound of the wagons was gone, and the prairie was silent again but for the rushing, driving rain, battering at the soil and bending the grass before it, and through the gray curtain the dark loom of the Big Horns lifted high, strong, formidable.

Almost two miles away Ban Hardy lay on his back under the rain, face up to the clouds, riddled with bullets. He had been alone when he saw them coming, and he had reached for his gun, but he had no chance. Four men had opened fire on him at once and he tumbled from the wagon seat to the mud. Riding past him, Bat Hammer had let drive with two more shots.

It had been amazingly quick, amazingly simple. Nine of the honest men were killed, and only one of the renegades. Clive Massey, his dark face hard, turned to Logan Deane. "See? I told you it would be easy."

"Where's Bardoul?"

"Stahl killed him, damn the luck! I wanted that job for myself."

"You might not have done it. He was fast, that one."

Massey's eyes glinted as he looked at Deane, and then his lips smiled. "I suppose he was," he agreed, his eyes calculating, "I suppose he was."

Massey turned to ride away. "What about the women?" Deane demanded.

"What about them?" Massey looked around.

"I wouldn't be no party to bad treatment of them.

We've got the wagons, and that was what we wanted."

"The women," Clive Massey said carefully, "are my concern. For the time being they will be left alone, but only for the time being."

Massey rode on through the rain, and Logan Deane stared after him, and after a minute, he followed.

CHAPTER XI

Night crept down the austere flanks of the Big Horns and stretched tentative shadows toward the trees along the river. The rain did not moderate, driving relentlessly into the lank grass and beating it into a thick carpet tight against the earth. Rain pounded against the black, glistening poncho of Matt Bardoul, stretched flat upon the grass, one arm outflung.

The rain slapped and whipped at his face, worried by the driving wind, yet as darkness came on the wind dropped to a few scattered gusts, and the drive left the rain and it began to fall lightly, easily, almost caressingly upon the wounded man.

The light touch of the rain did what the earlier, driving rain could not do . . . it brought him out of it.

Matt's eyes fluttered open upon a world of damp and darkness. Nor did he move, just lying there, tight against the earth, his mind an utter blank. A drop hit his eyeball, and the lid blinked shut. The action seemed to arouse his thoughts, and they stirred.

At first, they came slowly. Where was he? What had happened? *He had been shot by Spinner Johns! He was lying in the street! He . . . !* But no, that was weeks ago. Yet where was he? Why was he wet? What had happened?

Then he remembered . . . there was something he had to tell Jacquine. Something she had misunderstood. Jacquine . . . Coyle . . . the wagon train . . . Clive Massey. . . .

He had been shot.

He was wounded.

What had happened? And where was he? He drew
his extended arm back, got the palm under his chest,
and pushed up. He rolled on his side and the rain fell
upon his face. He opened his mouth and let it wash
down his throat, but there was not enough to satisfy
his great thirst.

Carefully, he lifted his right hand and moved it toward his head. Something was wrong there. He had
been shot in the head. His fingers found a bulge there,
and his hand came away sticky with mud and blood.
He got his hands both under him, and pushed himself
up to his knees, making his brain spin with the effort.

Waiting, while the dizzy spell passed, he took
stock. He had been shot, but although wounded, he was
alive. The wagon train had gone on. Had they taken
it? Or had they just shot him down?

He saw his hat lying there and picked it up, but it
would not go down on his head, so he let it rest where
it was. Automatically, his hands reached for his pistols.
They were gone. They had been stripped from his
body.

That told him something. They had believed him
dead, then. What happened to his horse? He stared
around in the rain soaked darkness but could see nothing but the vagueness where he was. He got to his feet
then, and stood swaying, trying to assemble his
thoughts. He was weak, too weak to go far. Yet there
was no sense in moving an inch until he knew where
to move.

Methodically, he recalled his memory of the day.
They had left Goose Creek, and they had crossed a
small stream that emptied into the Goose. Hence, somewhere, not too far ahead, would be Wolf Creek. Beyond that was the Tongue. It could be no more than six
miles away, or perhaps seven. Facing in what his mind
told him was the northwest, he started to walk.

A long time later he opened his eyes to find himself lying on his face again. How far he had come, or
if he had moved at all, he did not know. Yet he must
move. Somewhere ahead of him was the wagon train

and Jacquine, helpless in the hands of Clive Massey, or Sim Boyne, or whoever he was. He forced himself to his feet and carefully put his left foot forward, then his right.

That time he must have taken fully twenty steps before he fell. It was weakness, he knew, yet he had to keep going. He rested, then started again. He made six steps, twelve, twenty again, and then eight. Sometimes he only stumbled and did not fall from sheer weakness. Yet it took him a long time to get to the Wolf.

When he got there, he crawled to the rushing waters and took a drink. Heavy rains had swollen them, and the waters were muddy, but it tasted good. He drank, then drank again.

Crawling back near a huge tree, he cowered close to the trunk. There was some loose brush around, and he pulled himself up and wove some of the brush into the thick, low hanging branches. He fumbled with them for a long time, and contrived a partial shelter. Then he hunched the poncho around his ears and with his back against the bole he fell asleep.

When he awakened again the rain had ceased and the sky was gray. He was suddenly wide awake, yet when he moved he found he was very weak, and it was nothing less than a miracle that he was alive at all, to say nothing of the distance he had covered the night before.

Keeping his seat, he took careful stock of the situation. He must not even think of the wagon train nor of Jacquine. If he was their only hope, then he must regain his strength before attempting to face Massey or Deane. To do that he would need rest and food. There was no shelter anywhere nearby, and no food that he could get without effort on his own part. Yet despite the need for food, the less he moved for awhile, the better.

There were berries on some of the undergrowth, and he picked at them off and on for over an hour. Despite their smallness, they made him feel better. The sun lifted, and pointed an accusing finger at him through a rift in the clouds, yet the rift became wider, and the warmth began to dry his clothes. Steam lifted from them, and he leaned his head back, soaking up the growing warmth.

Somehow he fell asleep, and when he awakened it was almost noon. He picked more berries, then crawled to the stream for a drink. All through the day he rested there, alternately sleeping, eating berries and drinking. Finally, night came again, and he slept.

When Matt Bardoul opened his eyes in the morning he was very weak. In moving, he noticed that his clothing on the right side felt stiff. It was only then that he discovered his second wound. He recalled hearing the shot fired, but had felt no pain, and no shock.

Pulling off the poncho, he rolled it up, and then he examined his wound. It had closed up and although slightly inflamed, did not look bad. The bullet had gone through his side just above the hip bone. Searching his pockets, he found a heavy clasp knife he always carried, and with this he cut himself a good sized stick for a cane. Then tucking the poncho over his belt in behind, he got to his feet.

Then he started to walk. When he had made what he believed was a half mile, he rested and took stock. He did not feel badly, although very weak, and he needed food. Yet his best bet was to continue on to the Tongue. The closer he got to the fort, the better his chance was of finding help. Also, the closer he would be to the wagon train.

Once, about mid morning, he found a bit of biscuit dropped by someone in the wagons, and ate that. He fell asleep then close to a bush, and was awakened sometime later by a bawling mingled with angry snarls. Rolling to his knees, knife in hand, he saw four timber wolves attacking a buffalo calf. Nearby, several others were harrying the cow. Getting a firm grip on his club, he lay beside the bush until the wolves had pulled down the calf, and then he got to his feet and yelled.

Instantly, the wolves wheeled to face him. He started toward them, waving his stick. Three of them made off at once, but the fourth stood his ground, only backing a little and snarling. Matt continued toward the wolf, walking steadily, and the animal glanced left and right to reassure itself of an easy retreat. When no more than twenty feet away, Matt lifted the club once more and shouted. The wolf fled.

The calf was already dead, and he knelt over it, cutting up as much of the meat as he could carry. Then he moved back to the stream, and leaving his meat, returned for more. When he reached the stream after his second trip, he collected sticks and built a fire.

While he was broiling the meat, he studied the situation. For all his effort, he had made no more than two miles, yet once he had eaten, he should be able to do better. As he sat over the fire, his eyes kept noticing some dark object lying out toward the ruts of the wagontrain, and finally he decided it was a man.

Thinking of that, he let his eyes wander over the trail, and after a bit, he picked out another. His lips tightened and he felt something well up within him that was between rage and hatred. He ate, his eyes averted. When he had eaten what he could, he rolled the rest of the meat in a haversack made of the poncho, and got to his feet.

He walked slowly, but directly toward the body lying upon the trail. It was Ban Hardy, and he was literally riddled with bullets. Matt knelt over him and went through his pockets. He found his wallet, containing a picture of Sarah Stark and a few faded letters. Matt stowed it away in his pocket, then got to his feet. It took time he needed, but he gathered a few stones and covered the body, then he went on.

The second body was that of Will Stark, one of Aaron's sons. Will was only sixteen. He had been shot twice through the chest.

"There must be some back behind me," Matt told himself, "but not many. I think I was pretty far back."

He found two more bodies before reaching the Tongue. One was a man from Coyle's company, and the other was Bill Shedd.

Shedd, too, had failed. He had set out to get Sim Boyne, and he had failed. How many more would he find at the Tongue?

By now, an idea of the situation was beginning to fit itself together in Matt's brain. The attack had been premature because they had known something of the plans made by Bardoul and the rest. Massey had not waited for the Tongue, but had struck at once, taking advantage of the scattered wagon train when there was no chance of unified defense, and when due to the terrain and the travel as well as the driving rain, it was impossible for them to be together. It had been a neat piece of generalship, there was no question of that.

Yet it left Massey with a problem. He had still to get the wagons to a place where they could be hidden or disposed of, and he did not have drivers enough. For that reason if for no other, few of the wagon train personnel would be shot if they did not offer any resistance. There was a chance no women would be annoyed for the same reason, as peace must be kept as long as possible to get the wagons out of reach of appeal to the fort.

That left the only chance the prisoners had for survival, to lie with an accidental meeting with an Army patrol, or Matt.

Of course, nobody on the wagons knew he was alive. In that lay his greatest chance of success, yet it gave the people of the wagons very little to hope for.

When he had crossed the Tongue, he was on the edge of what had been their camp for the night. He sat down and cooked more of the meat, and drank thirstily. After resting, he got up and made a careful survey of the campsite.

He found where a number of the men and women had been herded together for better guarding, and where they had been fed. A few scraps of food and many tracks in a close area, and very few tracks elsewhere aside from other, more scattered signs, proved this was the correct conclusion.

Bathing his head for the first time, Matt found that mud and blood had caked together to stop the bleeding. The bullet had curved around his head under the scalp, and was still under the skin on the back of his head. Taking a chance, he cut a slit in the scalp and forced the bullet out. Then he bathed the wound again and rested.

He was weak from loss of blood and shock, but despite the walking, he felt better. Yet he knew he had come but a short distance and the wagons, hurried by Massey, would have covered at least forty miles in the two days of travel. Without a horse he would fall farther and farther behind. Had he his full strength, he could have overtaken them on foot, but there was no chance in his present condition.

The course the wagon train was taking would lead them to the Little Big Horn, and from there they might strike across toward the Big Horn itself, or follow a route that would take them south between the river and the mountains. Yet he had no way of guessing their actual destination without following the trail.

Darkness came swiftly, and Matt rolled up in his poncho, but despite his weariness and the throb in his head and side, he lay awake for a long time. Finally his mind a confusion of dreams, he slept.

He awakened with a start, long before daylight. Rolling out, he built a fire and then went to the stream where he bathed his face and head, then cooked the best of the remaining buffalo meat and ate all he could manage. He had no way of carrying water, but with the recent rain there was a chance he could make it. The Little Big Horn lay some twenty miles to the westward.

His head throbbing, his face dark with beard, he started out. Somewhere ahead of him was the wagon train, and when he found it, he would know what to do. Head down he started plodding along the ruts the wagons had left.

The grass was high now, high as the wheels on the wagons that had rolled across this prairie, and had he possessed a rifle there would have been no need to worry about food, for there was all the game a man could want. Prairie chickens and rabbits darted away as he approached, and once, late in the afternoon, he saw off in the distance a pair of antelope, but this time there were no wolves to make his kill for him.

Three times during the morning he stopped to rest, once for all of an hour. Yet despite his weakness, he kept going, content only when he was moving. Once, in midafternoon, he stumbled from weakness and fell headlong, and that time he lay long before moving again, and when he started once more, rested every little way. He must keep going, but at all costs, he must not stop or be stopped.

His years along the frontier and the hard, rough life he had lived had built stamina that did not fail him now. When he started again, he moved along for a mile, then rested and started once more. He was determined to make the river before he stopped, no matter how many hours it took him, and the distance was between eighteen and twenty miles. Once, sighting a band of horsemen, he took to the brush. Even at that distance he recognized them for Indians, for their manner of riding was distinctive. Concealed in the brush, he waited, and after only a few minutes, saw six Indians riding along the wagon trail.

Clutching his knife, he waited. They were Sioux, and young warriors, which was all he needed to know, for if they found him they would not hesitate to kill him and take his scalp, and he was without any weapon but the knife. Once, they reined in, and he saw a tall young warrior on a spotted pony staring down at the trail. Once, he half turned his pony as if to ride toward the brush, but the others shouted something at him, and rode along. Twice, he turned in his saddle to glance back.

Obviously, the warrior had seen his trail, and probably was undecided whether it was made at the time the wagons passed or not. Yet when they had gone on, Matt did not at once emerge from cover, but kept to the shallow place between the hills, utilizing every bit of cover. It slowed his pace, but after a few minutes, he saw the Indian on the spotted pony returning.

Evidently he had noticed the tracks he had seen did not continue, and saying nothing, had decided to count coup on the straggler by himself. Matt eyed the

Indian with care. He was a young warrior, agile and strong. He possessed no rifle, and no doubt was hoping to get one when he found his man. It was the paint pony that interested Matt . . . if he could get that horse . . . he crouched in the brush, waiting.

The Sioux had turned aside from the trail and was following his path through the grass toward his first hiding place. Carefully, Matt slid backwards through the brush, rearranging the grass and branches as he moved, trying with all his skill to cover his trail. In his present weakened condition, an attack upon the Indian would be sheer suicide unless he was at once successful.

When he reached a dense section of brush he went into it, and after passing through, concealed himself in the grass near his trail. He lay very still, gripping the knife.

The afternoon was warm and very still. The sun lay upon his back, and the dew-heavy grass smelled fragrant to his nostrils. Flat as he could lie, pressed tight to the earth but with one leg drawn up and his toe dug in for a quick move, he lay waiting.

A fly droned lazily in the warm summer sun. It sat upon a leaf and walked about curiously, then flew to Matt Bardoul's hand, where it prowled without apparent purpose, then took off. The sun warmed his back, and his muscles soaked up the heat. His hand upon the haft of the knife grew sticky and he drew the hand away, wiping it on his left sleeve.

No sound came from the brush, but suddenly the Indian was there, lean and powerful with tan, lithe muscles. He was led among the leaves at the edge of the brush, his eyes studying carefully the open valley before him, dotted with clumps of brush. He carried a bow in his hand, and an arrow ready for shooting.

Matt needed no one to tell him how quickly that arrow could be let go. He had seen the Sioux in action before this. He lay very still, breathing carefully, his eyes riveted upon the warrior. There could be no escape now, for the Indian was too close, and he would trail Matt and find where he had doubled back. There was only one chance, and that was Matt's ambush. When the Indian came abreast of him, he must be killed.

The whole action must take no more than a split second, and there must be no sound. The knife must win on the first stroke. In ordinary condition, without his wounds, Matt could have bested the Indian in a hand to hand fight, but now there was no room for a gamble. None at all.

The Sioux was careful. Young he might be, but he had seen war. You knew that in the way he moved, and there was confidence in him, too, the confidence of victories past. Matt's grip tightened on the knife, and he waited, tense and ready.

The warrior moved from the brush and crouched, staring down at the trail, then he straightened and looked all around him. There was something in that trail he did not like, and Matt almost grinned to see the Indian's face, so close now that every change of expression could be noted. From the trail the Sioux knew the man he was following was not trying to get away, he knew the man understood how to leave or conceal a trail.

Now, the Indian moved. Matt was aware of the faint, earthy smell, of the slight movement of the tall grass as the Indian came forward, and of the fly that buzzed mournfully about. In the far distance, above the low hills, a bit of lonely cloud drifted across a pale blue sky.

The eyes of the Sioux were black, his skin dark and his hair black and greasy. When he moved there was only the whisper of the grass. He wore only a breech clout, and carried beside the bow and quiver of arrows, only a scalping knife.

Matt's tongue touched his dry lips. The Indian was abreast of him, but looking ahead, searching the brush and the hillside. He hesitated there, and Matt Bardoul held his breath, and then the Indian took a step, then another.

In a long, soundless leap, Matt shot himself from the earth. The Sioux, warned by some small sound or a premonition of danger, wheeled like a cat, but Matt was too close for the bow and arrow, and the Indian dropped them, wasting time in a futile grab at his knife. Matt struck with his own knife, and the Indian caught the blade on his arm.

Blood whipped from it in a crimson curtain that covered his arm like a sleeve. Matt struck with his left fist and caught the Sioux in the mouth, staggering him. He struck again with the knife, blade held low, stabbing for the soft parts of the Sioux's body. Again the Indian warded it off, getting only a thin red scratch across his stomach, but now he had his own knife out.

Matt struck with his left for the Indian's wind as they went down into the tall grass and thrust again with the knife. That time it struck home, and the Indian gasped, his black eyes ugly with hatred and battle lust. Matt got the knife out, and they rolled over. He felt a flash of pain across his shoulder and then he got the Indian's wrist and forced it back, fighting desperately to hold the blade away from his body.

Wild with fear, for he knew his strength was going fast, he lunged and threw the Indian off. The Sioux was on his feet like a cat, and sprang for Matt, and Bardoul dropped on his back as the Indian leaped for him, and stabbed upward with the knife. Too late, the Sioux saw his mistake and tried to twist away from the blade, but it sank into his body just below the ribs and went in to the hilt.

For a moment then there was a bitter, soundless struggle. Matt shoved on the blade, twisting and gouging to point it upward toward the Sioux's heart, his breath coming in great, agonizing gasps. He finally jerked the knife free, and in a last desperate effort, thrust again.

The body tightened under him, then relaxed. For a long time, Matt lay still, then he withdrew his knife and wiped it on the grass. Gathering up the bow and arrows, he crawled, gasping for breath and faint with weakness, for the brush. In a haze of pain and sickness, he knew he could not remain where he was. The other warriors would be returning, looking for the missing

Indian. He had to get that horse and get away, and quickly as possible.

Despite his weakness, he managed to get to his feet. He looked around before he moved. The grass where they had fought was bloody and crushed as though wolves had made a kill. He moved into the brush, then hesitated. The paint pony was tied to a tree not twenty feet away!

He moved toward it, but the pony smelled the blood and jerked his head back, rolling his eyes. Matt spoke softly to him, but the paint wanted no part of him. The strange smell of a white man as well as the blood made the pony snort and jerk his head wildly, yet Matt moved toward him, and finally got a hand on the rawhide with which the pony was tied.

This was a battle that had to be won here, for he was in no shape to ride a pitching horse. He spoke softly again, talking to the pony with low voice and soothing tones, then tentatively he put out a hand and after some effort, got it on the pony's neck. He caressed it gently and talked softly. On a sudden inspiration, he moved the quiver of arrows closer to the pony's nose, and the familiar smell seemed to quiet the animal. Matt unfastened the rawhide and swung to the blanket that did duty for a saddle. Then he guided the pony back down the trail, and when he saw a draw running north and away from the route followed by the Indians, he took it, letting the pony run, which he seemed eager to do.

When he was at least three miles from where he had killed the Sioux, Matt turned the pony back toward the Little Big Horn and rode on. He felt sick in his stomach and his head throbbed painfully. He had been cut slightly on the shoulder and the wound had bled, but the bleeding had stopped and now his buckskin shirt was stuck to the wound with dried blood.

Sick, he reeled in his seat, and the pony shied violently, so violently that he lost his seat and fell headlong. With a startled leap, the pony was gone, racing off into the late afternoon.

Wearily, Matt got to his knees, then to his feet.

The pony was gone, but the ride had helped. There ahead of him was the dark line of trees, of which he could see only the tops, of the valley of the Little Big Horn. Moving on, Matt kept going doggedly, fighting against weariness and sickness until he reached the dense growth of willows along the bank. With his last remaining strength he crawled into them, and concealing his route as well as possible, crawled until he found a low hollow under some wild berry bushes, a place made by a wolf or some large animal. Crawling in, he put his head on his arm.

A long time later, he opened his eyes. It was dark, and his mouth felt dry and his head throbbed. Every muscle in his body seemed to be stiff and sore and when he moved it was all he could do to repress a groan. Crawling out of his cover he got to the river bank and drank long and deeply, and then he bathed his face and head with the cold water.

The night was clear, and glancing at the stars, he could see that it was well past midnight. Crawling back to his cover, he was soon asleep.

Sunlight through the brambles awakened him and he lay very still for a few minutes. The last of his meat had been lost when he was thrown from the horse, but he had retained his poncho. He bathed in the Little Big Horn, then crossed the stream. He was no hand with a bow, although some Crows had once instructed him in its use and he believed there was a chance he might find some game that he could kill. Matt found a few berries and then kept on until he came to the place where the wagon train had stopped.

He was standing beside a huge tree studying the scene when he heard a slight movement in the brush. Fading back, his heart pounding, he waited. Then he heard it again.

It was a horse, walking through the brush. Now it had come to an open place, and apparently it hesitated there. Listening, he heard another movement, and then saw three Indians, Brules by the look of them. Obviously they were trailing the unsuspecting horseman. The horse started on again at a slow walk, following a course that would bring him close by where Matt Bardoul was standing!

His hand reached for the bow, and he notched an arrow, waiting. Then the brush near him parted and the horse came through. Instantly, his face broke into a grin. It was the dun! His own horse!

Carefully, he lifted a hand. The dun's head came up with a jerk, and he moved toward it, whispering.

The dun hesitated, rolling his eyes, then something familiar must have arrested his attention, for he stretched an inquiring nose toward Matt. And then Matt was beside him, slipping the Winchester from its scabbard. "Stand, boy!" he whispered. "We've work to do!"

An Indian came through the brush, and evidently they had seen the horse and believed it riderless, for he stepped right out in the open, and then he glimpsed Matt and gave a startled grunt and whipped up his own rifle. Matt fired from the hip at no more than thirty yards, then whipped the rifle to his shoulder and nailed the second Indian. The third vanished into the tall grass, and Matt swung into the saddle.

Quickly, he searched his saddlebags. There was food here, and ammunition. It was easy to see what had happened. When he had been shot from the dun's back, the horse had dashed away, frightened. When it recovered from the fright, it began to follow the wagon train, seeking the company of the horses it knew.

A few minutes ride proved that the wagons were headed for the Big Horn, and Matt hesitated over what course to adopt. A day's good riding would take him to the vicinity of Fort No. 1 and the Army, where he might get help to recover the wagon train. On the other hand, matters must be reaching a crisis with the train. If they had not met the reinforcements they expected, most of the men of the train would be needed as drivers, and there was small chance Massey would allow the women to be molested and risk an out and out revolt by the men, so there was a chance.

Matt wheeled the dun and headed down the Little Big Horn. He was in very bad shape, but just being in the saddle and having a rifle again made him feel much better.

It was a beautiful country through which he travelled, with some fine strands of timber along the Little Big Horn, and grass that grew three feet tall, while there were wild cherries, currants, wild strawberries, gooseberries and grapes in profusion. The dun seemed glad to have him in the saddle again, and kept a good pace.

Matt was riding at a lope through the broken and precipitous hills along the east bank of the river when suddenly he noticed a rusted field kitchen. He slowed his pace, and then in the space of the next two miles he saw weathered saddles, tin pails, canteens and tin plates with here and there an overcoat or cap.

This was the Custer battlefield where the might of the Sioux had fought their last battle. In a short distance, Matt Bardoul counted sixty-nine graves, most of them merely a thin film of earth thrown over the body. Here and there wolves had dug into the graves, and under one tree he saw a skull in an Army cap.

Matt did not stop, riding over the field and heading back closer to the river. At night, he was still riding north, but there was no time for delay, he watered and rested the horse, then remounted and continued. Dawn was graying the sky when he glimpsed the fort.

Several headquarters and barracks buildings were nearing completion, and already carpenters were moving out to their work. Below, in a long hollow, numbers of tents were pitched in regular rows, and soldiers were moving about, washing mess gear. Matt touched a spur to the weary dun and cantered down into the camp.

A sentry challenged him, and then seeing he was a white man, looked at him curiously. Matt's beard was days old, and the wound on his head was still matted with blood where he had not dared wash too much of it away. His shoulder and side were dark with the stain of it, and he carried his rifle across his saddle bows. "Where's your commanding officer?"

The soldier indicated a tent, his eyes curious. Matt rode on, hoping the officer would turn out to be the same they had met earlier. He swung down in front of the tent, and walked up to the flap, that was drawn back.

A tall young man with blond hair and a mustache was writing over a camp desk. He looked up when Matt spoke, his eyes sweeping him with obvious irritation at the interruption. Quickly, Matt explained, but even as he talked he could see the rising scepticism in the officer's eyes.

"You want me to let you have a patrol?" he said. "My orders wouldn't allow it even if I felt it essential. From what you say yourself, the trouble is among the personnel of the wagon train, not with Indians. I have no orders to interfere in anything of the sort."

"But, Man!" Matt protested. "Those men are outlaws! One of them is Sim Boyne, the Natchez murderer!"

"Sorry!" the officer shook his head, "I can do nothing for you. My orders are to build this fort and to avoid trouble with the Indians. That is all. I have received no information about any wagon train, nor about any such person as Sim Boyne. Certainly, I can't be ordering troops out on the whim of every would be settler, who believes he is in trouble."

"Listen!" Matt protested, rage rising within him. "I'm a Deputy United States Marshal!"

"You are? You have your papers, I suppose?"

Bardoul clapped a hand to his coat. They were gone! Of course, he might have known they would take them. "No, I don't," he said, "they were stolen from me."

The officer shrugged. "I can't do anything for you. As a matter of fact, I am only acting in command. The officer commanding should be back at the post by Monday, at the latest. He might help you."

"Monday!" Bardoul's jaw stiffened. "That's three days. It will be too late!"

He wheeled and walked from the tent, catching

the reins of his horse as he left. Walking rapidly, he went down to a camp kitchen that still smoked lazily. The cook looked up. "Anything to eat?" Matt asked wearily.

"Sure thing!" The cook glanced at him curiously. "You look like you could use it. What's the matter?"

Over a cup of coffee, Matt explained. The cook nodded, then jerked his head at the tent from which Matt had come. "What you might expect of him. He's a stickler. Never makes a move unless he's told to or it is covered by regulations."

"How about making me up a pack of grub?"

The cook looked at him. "You going out again? The way you look?"

"You're damned right I am! I'm riding out to-night."

"Better get some rest. That horse of yours could use it, too. I'll fix you a bit of grub, though. And say, there's a carpenter over there, third building down. He's got him a pair of Colt pistols, brand, spankin' new. If you've got the money, you might buy 'em."

At daylight, the Colts slung about his hips and plenty of ammunition bought or borrowed from the carpenter in his saddle bags, Matt Bardoul rode out of camp on the zebra dun. He had no plan, only to come within striking distance of the wagon train, and to reach, if possible, some communication with Murphy or Stark. If he could get guns in the hands of a few of the honest men, there would be little to worry about. They would at least have a fighting chance.

All that day he rode, and the following morning he picked up the trail of the wagons once more. Washed, shaved and refreshed from his brief stay in camp, he was feeling ready for anything. The doctor who dressed his wounds had just looked at them grimly, and told him he was a fool for luck. Then added that he should have rest and quiet. "From the look of you," he went on to say, "I doubt if you'll get it. And you'll probably live!"

They had grinned at each other, and the doctor,

to whom he had told his story, added, "I wish I was going with you. It would be worth it."

The dun took to the trail like he had reasons of his own for catching the wagon train, and as he rode, Matt tried the Colts. They were better balanced than his own guns, a beautiful pair of guns. He tried them on a couple of rabbits, then fed shells into the empty chambers and returned them to their places.

He rode and rested, then rode and rested again. When he rested he made coffee or soup, but for the most part he ate in the saddle. He rode into the ruins of old Fort C. F. Smith, near the foot of the mountains, and the first thing he saw was the body of a man, partly covered by brush. It was Ben Sperry. He had been shot three times after being brutally beaten.

Matt's face was hard when he swung back into the saddle and headed south, riding swiftly. The trail turned up a creek toward a deep canyon that cut into the hills, and Matt slowed his horse to a walk. There could be no outlet in this direction for they were driving right back into the mountains, heading southeast. Then he was close, very close.

He had stopped to drink at the stream when he heard a groan, and wheeled, gun in hand. He was looking right into the eyes of Logan Deane.

The gunfighter lay on his stomach on the bank of the stream, a few feet above it, and his face was gray with pain. Matt caught him by the shoulder. "Logan! What happened? What's the matter?"

Deane's eyes focused. "Bardoul . . . kill him. Kill that . . . Massey." His voice faded and Matt got up on the bank and knelt beside him, but only a glance was needed. How Logan Deane was even able to speak was beyond him. The man had been shot, not once, but at least five times through the stomach, and left to die.

"You . . . were right . . . he pulled . . ." Deane seemed to gather himself for an effort, "sneak gun on me. Get there . . . quick."

Holding a canteen to the man's lips, Matt gave him a drink, but Deane pushed him away. "Get . . . Massey!"

Suddenly, he heard a new sound. He straightened, listening. He heard it again . . . the ring of an axe!

Then he was close, very close. Matt loosened his guns in their holsters and waited, standing there, letting his nerves grow quiet and his senses poised.

CHAPTER XII

What was taking place with the wagon train, Matt did not know. He knew that at last he had reached the end of the trail in more ways than one. Now, at last, there would be a showdown and he would face Massey as he had long wished to face him . . . with a gun. Yet there would be a difference between this and any other fight, for now the lives and happiness of others were at stake.

Because of that he must plan shrewdly and with care. Victory, if it was to be had at all, would have to come with a sudden strike, giving the renegades no chance to organize or get set for a battle. He must approach shrewdly, study the situation, and find some way of getting guns into the hands of the honest men.

First then, he must locate Buffalo Murphy, if he was alive, and after him, the Starks and the Coyles, and those whom he knew would be most resolute in the face of danger and gunfire. Then and only then could he risk a break, and then he must find and kill Clive Massey.

There was no other choice. Looked at calmly, it was Massey who must be destroyed. He was the brain and the hand, the brain that conceived and planned, the hand that enforced, and once he was destroyed the whole outlaw force might come apart at the seams.

The manner of the death of Logan Deane convinced him anew that Massey was a ruthless, sadistic killer. To gut shoot a man in that manner meant to leave him hours of torture, hours of suffering when time would drag on and there could be no hope of life, only the cruelty of endless agony. Massey had known this when he killed Deane.

Matt turned away from the fallen man knowing there was nothing he could do, and walking into the brush, he concealed his horse, tying it where the grass was good in a small glade surrounded with brush and trees. He took his guns then, checking the twinbelts to assure himself that every loop was full. Only then did he turn and start through the woods. He moved carefully, uncertain as to how the camp might be guarded, or how soon he would come up with the wagon train.

The lodgepoles towered above him in slim, erect columns, all of a size, and the forest beneath them carpeted with the fallen pine needles of many years. He walked steadily, his mind reaching ahead to plan for what he might find.

Suddenly, he had come to the edge of a cliff. Below him, no more than sixty feet, was a rock walled valley floored with green. At the upper end a waterfall fell from a gap in the cliff into a pool. Nearby, a number of men were building log structures, at least two of which were already completed. Around them Matt could see the outlaws on guard.

This then was why they were alive. Massey was using their labour until the very last. There was no evidence of the women.

Matt stretched out behind some manzanita and studied the layout with careful eyes. There was only one approach he could use, for aside from the entrance, undoubtedly guarded with care, the only way into the valley was at a place where the wall was broken by a long pine clad slope that let an arm of the forest reach into the valley. Even as he watched he saw several men, shouldering axes, start for that hill. Two guards accompanied them, and Matt decided this must be where they were cutting the timber for the cabins.

There was no other evidence of timber falling around, and he believed he could see where the logs had been snaked along the ground by oxen.

Getting to his feet he moved back into the timber

and worked his way along the mountainside in that direction. It was no more than a mile, yet it required all of an hour to cover the ground without risking detection.

He heard the ring of axes before he reached the spot, but got into a good position in a thick growth of brush where he could watch the men at work, and see their guards.

Six men made up the group, and two guards, both of whom carried shotguns. Matt's lips went dry when he saw them. It was no wonder the captives had made no effort to escape. No man gambles with a shotgun. A rifle or a pistol if one is desperate enough, but a shotgun? No.

Matt studied the group with care, and saw that one of the wood cutters was Jeb Stark. Even as he watched, two more men came through the trees from camp accompanied by a third guard. One of these men was Buffalo Murphy.

Lifting his head slightly, Matt gave out the lonely call of a loon.

His eyes were on Murphy, and he saw the big man straighten and mop a hand across his brow. Murphy had heard him . . . *he knew!*

Suddenly, Matt's head jerked around and his Winchester lifted. A man with a rifle had moved out of the woods opposite him and behind the woodsmen. It was Phillips!

Bardoul waited, his mouth dry and his heart pounding. If Murphy had heard his call, then Phillips had also, and Phillips was armed, which implied that he was riding with the renegades. Any old Indian fighter would know that call. Yet the scout made no move, and gave no indication of awareness.

Murphy turned and attacked his tree from another angle, a move that brought him face to face with Bardoul's position. He swung his axe, then straightened and brushed his hand across his brow, eager to let Matt know he was ready for anything.

Matt's eyes shifted to Phillips, and he jumped when he saw the Indian fighter was gone!

Bardoul faded back into the brush and slid his knife from its scabbard. He moved stealthily from tree to tree, then crouched behind the earth matted roots of a huge deadfall. He had only to wait a minute or so when he saw Phillips.

The Portugee moved purposefully through the brush, but making no effort at concealment. When he drew near the place from which the loon call might have come, he paused and leaned his rifle against a tree. Turning then, he walked away some twenty feet and seated himself against a tree trunk. Taking out his pipe, he lit it.

His meaning was obvious enough. He was perfectly aware that Matt Bardoul or someone was in the woods near him, and he wanted them to feel there was nothing to fear from him. Matt waited, uncertain. After a moment had passed, Phillips took his pipe from his mouth and said, "If it's you, Bardoul, ye can talk. That call sounded like yours."

Matt spoke only loud enough for the Portugee to hear him. "You have been a good man, Phillips, but go against me now, and I'll kill you."

"I've a short gun under my shirt," Phillips replied, "but you could beat me, and unless I'm some mistook you'll have a knife handy that you could kill me with by throwin' before I could get my gun into action. Come out, or stay where you are, but listen:

"The women are all right, but today is the last of their free time. I've spoken for them, arguin' that the men would work better and make no trouble if their women were unmolested, but Massey's restless and some irritated at that wildcat of a Coyle gal. She's not been so easy as he'd expected.

"I'm with you, all the way. Murphy knows that, for we've talked it over some, and so does Stark, and we've a plan, but it is not such a good one."

Bardoul moved out of the brush and Phillips grinned at him. "You look to have been through some grief your ownself," he said, "and you're right in trustin' no man. In the past I've been a hard man at times, but once you've a taste of being' a hero, it makes things different somehow. It gives a man something to live up to."

Matt set on his heels. "Phillips, if you're right there is no time to waste. We had better get down there and take over this minute. We've got to get rifles and those shotguns in the hands of our own men, and this lot of timber fallers are as good as any we could find."

"With luck we'll do it all right. The rest of the guns are in the smaller of the two finished buildings. That's where Massey is. The women are in the other building. He's got thirty men down there altogether, and a rough lot they are, the ragtag an' bobtail of the mountain country. He thinks I'm with him, and I've been hunting for the lot of them, getting them fresh meat.

"The man's mad, Bardoul. He's a crazy killer, that one. Safe for no man, and quick to kill. The way he killed Deane . . . I didn't see the first of it. When I came up, Logan was already down and Massey over him, standing there cold blooded and shooting into him, slow, timed shots, picking his places.

"He's mean to get along with as a ruttin' moose, and he'll kill anything or anybody that crosses him.

"Oh, he's Sim Boyne, all right! He's bragged of it! Talks of the killings along the Trace when he was a boy. There's blood on his hands, and a sight of it."

Swiftly, Bardoul outlined the plan he had worked out and Phillips nodded. Finally, he took his pipe from his mouth and scratched his cheek with the stem. "Maybe she'll work, anyway, we've got to try. We've no choice, for Massey will be wild tonight. The Coyle gal got away from him last night and he finally gave up and went back to his own quarters, but he was as mean as a she grizzly with cubs.

"Bat Hammer, Stahl, and the rest of them are almighty worked up about Massey not givin' them the Stark girls and that gal of Tolliver's."

Portugee Phillips got to his feet and started back toward the clearing and at a safe distance, Matt followed. Phillips went right into the clearing and crossed to Murphy and although Matt could not see the exchange of looks, Phillips must have given Murphy an almost imperceptible nod as he strolled by and engaged his guard in conversation. On cat feet, Bardoul worked through the trees and brush behind the guard.

Once, the man started to turn as though his ears had detected some subtle sound, but Phillips touched his arm and the guard looked back. Matt raised up behind him and put the point of his knife against the man's left side. "Move," he whispered, "and you'll get this knife between your ribs!"

The guard stiffened as if struck, and Phillips reached up and took the shotgun from his hands, tossing it to Murphy. Then shielding the guard from observation with his own square built body, Phillips stripped off the man's gun belts. Holding the knife with his left hand, Matt slipped his six gun from its holster and slapped the man over the head. Coolly then, he dragged the man back into the brush and tied him.

The action had been swift and silent, occupying a few seconds only and nobody seemed to have noticed a thing but the ever wary Jeb Stark. He straightened from his work, and his eyes went from Murphy to Bardoul, and then he walked toward his own guard. Then he pointed, and said to the guard, "How would that tree over there be?"

As the guard's head turned away, Matt and Murphy closed in on the remaining guard. The man gave a stifled gasp, and Jeb's guard started to turn. The distance was too great for a blow, but Jeb held his axe with a grip close to the head. He threw it, butt foremost, hurling it with all his strength. It caught the guard on the temple and he went down in a heap. Swiftly, Stark bent over him, getting his guns.

The ring of axes stopped, but Buff whirled. "Work, damn you!" he said hoarsely. "Keep those axes going. There must be no warning now!"

Swiftly, as the axes rang, Matt distributed the guns among the men. The first four he ordered to hide their guns under their shirts, while oxen were hooked to the nearest logs. "Haul that load down where Barney Coyle and Stark are working," Matt told them. "You walk alongside with Phillips acting as your guard."

The whip cracked and the logs started to move, one man driving, the others trooping along behind. Matt waited, his Winchester ready, in case there was a sudden alarm, but there was none and all the men continued to work quietly.

Moving from tree to tree, Matt went down into the valley and circled the log house where Massey made headquarters. At any moment the battle would open, and he must get as close to Massey as possible when the showdown came. As he rounded the cabin he saw the logs stop near Barney and Stark, and their guard turned to look into a drawn pistol.

Clive Massey appeared suddenly in the doorway of his cabin, and stepped out, walking rapidly toward the building where the women were kept. He walked like a man who had made up his mind. As he got to the door of the other building, he turned and shouted: "Bat! Stahl! Come on, you two! You've been belly aching about the women, now . . ." Whatever else was said was lost to Matt's ears as the two men drew nearer, and then all three went into the house.

Matt darted across the hard packed earth toward the wall in time to hear a cry of protest.

An outlaw walked around from behind the wagon where he had slept, all unaware of what was happening. He was a big man with his powerfully muscled shoulders bulging the inadequate cloth of his shirt. His face was a stubble of beard, and he looked irritable and mean.

He stepped out, rubbing his eyes, and then one hand stopped moving and his eyes flared wide. With an oath, his hand swept down for his gun. Bardoul was standing facing him one instant, and the next instant Matt's gun was bucking.

His first bullet caught the big renegade in midstride and the man seemed to stumble, his gun half drawn, and then he took three, stumbling, halting steps

forward before his knees buckled under him and he
went to the ground. He turned as he fell, and uttered
no sound.

With that shot the camp exploded into confusion.
A man in a blue shirt charged around a building and
was almost torn in half by a shotgun blast, smashing
him back as if suddenly jerked from behind. With the
roar of the gun echoing against the canyon walls, the
man went to the ground, screaming in his death
throes.

Hammer and Stahl lunged from the doorway of the
cabin and Stahl ducked around the corner, but Hammer
halted in the doorway, grabbing the jam with his left
hand while he dropped his right in a sweeping draw.
The draw was fast, but never completed, for Aaron
Stark, bowie knife in his fist, hit him like a charging
bull. Hammer cried out, and then they both flopped
from the door to the earth, fighting like madmen. Hammer was the younger man, but the old man's rage
turned him into a fury, and Matt saw Hammer twist as
the knife struck down again, and as Bat squirmed to
free himself, the knife of the old mountaineer rose and
fell again and again. Aaron Stark had seen his youngest
son shot down brutally by this man, and he had waited
for the moment.

Bardoul ran for the door just as Massey appeared
in it, dragging Jacquine. Massey stopped there, his face
scratched, his hair tumbled, and stared wildly about,
seeming to see in one frantic moment the end of everything. With an angry cry he sprang back into the door,
shoving the girl ahead of him, slamming it shut behind
him even as Bardoul's shoulder hit the heavy planks.
The door held.

A bullet struck over his head, and Matt wheeled
in a crouch, a gun clenched in his fist.

Not ten feet away was Stahl. He had fired his first
shot while skidding to a halt from a run, but when Matt
turned and the renegade recognized him, his fury vanished into blank astonishment, then blind panic. He
swung his gun up, but Matt squeezed off a shot that

jerked Stahl back on his tiptoes, his body bent at the waist. Matt's second shot went right through the top of his skull.

Then, dead silence fell on the camp. Everywhere Matt saw the bodies of outlaws or honest men carrying guns.

He turned then. Clive Massey was inside. A sadistic killer, crazy with injured vanity and desperate with the crashing of all his schemes, but inside with him were the wives and daughters of the men from the wagons.

Somehow, Massey had to be gotten out of that building, at whatever the cost. It would be like him in his insane rage to turn his gun on them all, but he would kill Jacquine first. Matt Bardoul looked up at the plank door, and his mouth dry, he called out: "Come on out, Massey! You're through! Come out and give yourself up!"

The sun was warm on his shoulders, and he stood there, tired of fighting, yet knowing that death still waited in the guns of Clive Massey.

"Come out?" Massey's laugh seemed to hold genuine humour and triumph. "Don't be a fool! I'm here, but so are your women. Do anything to hurt me, and they all suffer. You let me go free or they all die, one at a time!"

Aaron Stark had come up, and Matt saw Murphy, Tolliver, Lute Harless, Kline and Reutz. And then the Coyles and Pearson.

"What about it, Bardoul? Do I come, or do I start shooting?"

Only an instant did Matt hesitate. "Come on, damn you! Come on out! You get a horse and ten minutes start. After that, I'm on your trail!"

"Leave your friends behind," Massey shouted, "and I'd like nothing better."

The door swung open, and Jacquine Coyle was framed in it, her eyes wide and angry. Massey was behind her, gun in hand. "I'm taking her for a hostage to assure my getting out of camp."

Matt stood flat footed, staring at Massey. All the

hatred he felt toward the man came welling up within him, but he stifled it. If Massey took Jacquine, he knew what would happen. At the edge of camp he would kill her. It was like him to destroy what he could not have. Yet there was a chance, a chance that lay in Massey's vanity.

"Hiding behind a woman's skirts?" He thickened the sneer in his voice. "Why don't you meet me man to man? Are you yellow, too?"

"You think I'm such a fool? You would be easy for me, but what of your friends? I wouldn't trust a man of them!"

Massey was backing toward the horses as he spoke. "What a fool you are, Bardoul! You and that Logan Deane! Gunmen! Bah! You two are a couple of milksops, not worthy of the name of men! I killed him Bardoul! Beat him to the draw!"

Matt started to speak, to tell him how he had beaten Deane, but then he realized that knowing Massey's secret was his ace in the hole, for if the man used the trick against Deane, he would also use it against him.

"You're afraid, Massey! You wouldn't meet any man on even terms. You aren't a gunfighter, you're just a killer! A murderer! You couldn't equal Deane the best day you ever saw!"

Clive Massey was near the horses now, but he stopped. The innate arrogance and viciousness of the man would not allow him to leave the field without at least one triumph, and coupled with this was his hatred of Matt Bardoul.

Across the level ground and over Jacquine's shoulder, their eyes met. It was no hatred of Bardoul's that drove him now, it was the knowledge that he was fighting for the life of the girl he loved. The knowledge that Massey would never leave her for him, or for anyone else. The name of Sim Boyne had become a synonym for brutal murder, and he would not stop now.

"If it weren't for your friends," Massey shouted furiously, "I'd kill you now!"

Matt Bardoul smiled slowly, putting all the contempt and doubt he could into his smile and his voice when he spoke. "They will stand aside, and if you kill me, you can go free. You agree to that, Buff? Coyle?"

Both agreed. Murphy at once, Brian Coyle with doubt. Aaron Stark was about to speak up in angry dissent, but Murphy caught his arm warningly.

Matt could see Jacquine looking at him, her eyes large and beautiful, her face white and strained with fear and doubt.

"All right, then!" With a quick, angry gesture Massey threw the girl from him. "You've marked me, Bardoul, with this broken nose, but By God, I'll kill you!"

With his right hand at his coat lapel he faced Matt, taking three quick steps to draw nearer, his eyes ugly with the hatred in them.

Matt stood with his hands hip high, crouched a little, watching Massey. "All right," he said quietly, "whenever you're ready!"

Half crouched, his hair blowing a little about his brow, he waited, watching that deadly right hand. Aside from Massey and himself, none knew on what a slender thread his life hung, for they alone knew where Massey's gun was kept, and with what speed it could get into action.

From the beginning Matt had believed he could taunt Massey into a fight, for the man's fierce arrogance and vanity would not allow him to refuse. Yet he knew well enough how deadly such a gun could be, and what a hole a .41 would tear in a man's vitals at their present range of ten feet. He had seen the holes blown into Logan Deane, a man almost as fast, if not faster, than he himself. Matt's only advantage was that he knew what to expect, and Deane had not.

Bardoul waited, and his lips were stiff, and a slow trickle of sweat started from the roots of his hair and trickled down his brow. His mouth was dry, for they stood close, so close neither man could very well miss, and he knew he must score with his first shot.

The hand at the lapel relaxed its grip, ever so

slightly. "It will be a real pleasure to kill you, Bardoul! A pleasure I have denied myself too long!"

The fingers were no longer gripping the lapel, although they remained in the same position, his right hand held high. The fingers were relaxed now, and ready.

"Then if you aren't yellow," Matt taunted, *"go for your gun!"*

The hand of Clive Massey dropped no more than four inches and Matt saw the derringer shoot from his cuff into his fingers, but even as the hand moved, Matt had drawn in a sweeping, half circle movement that brought his gun up, blasting flame.

Massey's gun seemed to explode with flame, but his own bullet must have hit the renegade one hair's breadth sooner, for the shot went high, and he felt the angry *whip* of the bullet past his ear. But Matt had stepped a little to the side and fired again as his foot came down.

Clive Massey's body jerked sharply, and sobbing with fury, he tried to bring his gun to bear, but Matt stepped again, and again as his foot planted his gun boomed. Massey's gun coughed sharply again, but the shot went wild, and he dropped the derringer into the dust and clawed for the gun at his hip. Matt fired his fourth shot, lifting the six gun carefully and firing right at the man's heart.

The renegade went down to his knees, his face contorted with a fury that was glazing over with a gray ugliness that presaged death. He stared at Matt, his hand clutching at the gun, and in the last breath he drew, he lifted the gun and twisted to get a shot at Jacquine. Matt sprang forward and kicked the gun from Massey's hand and it flew high, then fell into the dust. Massey struck out at the foot, slapping at it like a petulant child, and the effort toppled him into the dust where one foot straightened slowly, and his jaws worked spasmodically, as with unspoken words.

Jacquine rushed to Matt. "Are you hurt? Are you shot?"

He slid his arm around her waist, his lungs feeling tight and his pulse pounding with suddenly released tension. "No, honey, I'm all right."

"A sleeve draw!" Murphy exclaimed. "I've heard about them. Never did see one before."

"It's a gambler's trick, and sometime ago, that night of the killing of Joe Rucker, I noticed his hand go to his lapel when it looked like a showdown. That started me thinking. He had the gun hanging down his sleeve and all he needed to do was drop his hand to shoot the gun right into his palm. They say when you've practiced it, it is the fastest draw there is. That's how he killed Deane."

Matt Bardoul kept his arm around Jacquine's waist. "Let's get away from here," he said. "Let's go down by the pool until they get things straightened up."

Suddenly, he happened to see Pearson, and the former Army officer stood at one side of the group as if lost. For a moment, Matt looked at him, realizing that in a sense the man had always been lost. By some mischance he had made the Army a career, and he had become a colonel when he should have been teaching in a grade school or the floor walker in a department store.

Captain Sharp's message came to his mind. "Colonel," he said, "at Fort Reno Captain Sharp wished me to tell you that Arch Schandler was dead . . . in the confusion I've been unable to tell you until now."

"Schandler? . . . Dead?" Orvis Pearson uttered the words with a queer, shocked unbelief that held Matt Bardoul where he stood, with Jacquine at his side.

"He was someone near to you?" Matt asked gently.

Pearson looked up at him, a sort of dazed misery in his eyes. "Why, yes," he said, "he was my son." He let his eyes wander off over the camp. "He was a soldier, sir. A very good soldier. He was with us . . . down there. He was one of them, one of the soldiers the day I . . . failed."

Pearson's hand trembled as he lifted it to his chin. "He changed his name, after that. But he was a fine soldier, Bardoul. A very fine soldier. A better man than his father."

"I'm sure he was a good soldier," Matt said gently, "why, if he was the Schandler I recall, a corporal, he was one of the best men that day."

"Yes, he was a corporal." Pearson turned away, his face still and white.

"Sir . . . ?"

Pearson turned back to Matt, waiting.

"What are you going to do now, if you don't mind my asking?"

"Why . . . no. Not at all." The Colonel looked suddenly old, tired. "Why, as a matter of fact, I don't know. I guess . . ." he seemed shocked, dazed.

"Listen," Matt suggested, "why not try ranching? Down here where I'm going, in the basin? There's good grass there, and water. I know there's room enough for both of us."

"You'd have me, Bardoul? There's nothing left at all unless I'm honest. I wouldn't admit it down there, but . . . well, I've failed at most things. Maybe this time . . . ?"

"Sure. There will be room for us both. We can probably help each other a good deal."

"Thank you, sir. Thank you, Bardoul." His face flushed a little. "I've been a proud man. A very proud man, and I am afraid it cost me a lot. Bardoul, you were fine that day. I wish my son could have seen me . . . like that. That was the worst of it, you know, him being there."

Matt put his hand on Pearson's shoulder, feeling oddly choked up. "He probably understood. It was a bloody mess that day. I'd forget it, if I were you."

As they moved off. Jacquine tightened her hold on his arm. "Why, Matt, he seemed so different!"

"I know, honey. He's like all of us, probably. Each man has his illusion of himself, only most of us are never called to face the truth as he was that day. Had he been in battle before he won a command he would probably have been all right."

"Matt . . . all that time you were gone, Buff Murphy would never let me believe you were dead. Always he told me not to believe it, he said you would be a hard man to kill."

Bardoul looked down at her as they stopped by the pool. "This looks like some sort of an end . . . or is it a beginning?"

She leaned back against the clasp of his hands on her elbows, looking up at him, her face flushed, her eyes very bright. "Matt, do you think I would make a good rancher's wife?"

"Why not?" he said seriously. "You can learn to herd cattle, cut hay, split wood . . ."

"Mathieu Bardoul!" Jacquine protested. "If you think I'm going to do all that, why you're sadly mistaken!"

"All right! All right! Anyway, with all those kids you'd be busy enough without that."

Jacquine's expression grew ominous. "All what kids? How many?"

"Oh," he shrugged carelessly, "maybe fifteen or so. Fifteen seems like a good number!"

"Fifteen?" She was horrified. *"Fifteen?* If you think . . .'!"

He drew her close, laughing at her, turning her chin up with his fingers, and bending his own head lower. Her lips trembled as his met them, and then slowly they relaxed and lost their fright and became warm and soft and yielding.

After awhile with her head against his chest, she said softly half pleading. "Matt? Would it have to be fifteen? Couldn't we sort of compromise?"

"Well," his expression was judicious, "we might! Now maybe we should go back. We have wagons to unload, and the rest of a town to build."

ABOUT THE AUTHOR

LOUIS L'AMOUR, born Louis Dearborn L'Amour, is of French-Irish descent. Although Mr. L'Amour claims his writing began as a "spur-of-the-moment thing," prompted by friends who relished his verbal tales of the West, he comes by his talent honestly. A frontiersman by heritage (his grandfather was scalped by the Sioux), and a universal man by experience, Louis L'Amour lives the life of his fictional heroes. Since leaving his native Jamestown, North Dakota, at the age of fifteen, he's been a longshoreman, lumberjack, elephant handler, hay shocker, flume builder, fruit picker, and an officer on tank destroyers during World War II. And he's written four hundred short stories and over fifty books (including a volume of poetry).

Mr. L'Amour has lectured widely, traveled the West thoroughly, studied archaeology, compiled biographies of over one thousand Western gunfighters, and read prodigiously (his library holds more than two thousand volumes). And he's watched thirty-one of his westerns as movies. He's circled the world on a freighter, mined in the West, sailed a dhow on the Red Sea, been shipwrecked in the West Indies, stranded in the Mojave Desert. He's won fifty-one of fifty-nine fights as a professional boxer and pinch-hit for Dorothy Kilgallen when she was on vacation from her column. Since 1816, thirty-three members of his family have been writers. And, he says, "I could sit in the middle of Sunset Boulevard and write with my typewriter on my knees; temperamental I am not."

Mr. L'Amour is re-creating an 1865 Western town, christened Shalako, where the borders of Utah, Arizona, New Mexico, and Colorado meet. Historically authentic from whistle to well, it will be a live, operating town, as well as a movie location and tourist attraction.

Mr. L'Amour now lives in Los Angeles with his wife Kathy, who helps with the enormous amount of research he does for his books. Soon, Mr. L'Amour hopes, the children (Beau and Angelique) will be helping too.

BANTAM'S #1
ALL-TIME BESTSELLING AUTHOR
AMERICA'S FAVORITE WESTERN WRITER

☐	20257	HIGH LONESOME	$2.25
☐	14883	BORDEN CHANTRY	$2.25
☐	13606	BRIONNE	$1.95
☐	14328	THE FERGUSON RIFLE	$1.95
☐	13622	KILLOE	$1.95
☐	13602	CONAGHER	$1.95
☐	14829	NORTH TO THE RAILS	$2.25
☐	13879	THE MAN FROM SKIBBEREEN	$1.95
☐	14763	SILVER CANYON	$2.25
☐	14530	CATLOW	$2.25
☐	13611	GUNS OF THE TIMBERLANDS	$1.95
☐	13605	HANGING WOMAN CREEK	$1.95
☐	14534	FALLON	$2.25
☐	13779	UNDER THE SWEETWATER RIM	$1.95
☐	14234	MATAGORDA	$1.95
☐	14119	DARK CANYON	$1.95
☐	14882	THE CALIFORNIOS	$2.25
☐	13969	FLINT	$1.95

**Buy them at your local bookstore or use this
handy coupon for ordering:**

LOUIS L'AMOUR 1

BANTAM'S #1
ALL-TIME BESTSELLING AUTHOR
AMERICA'S FAVORITE WESTERN WRITER

☐	14931	THE STRONG SHALL LIVE	$2.25
☐	14977	BENDIGO SHAFTER	$2.50
☐	13881	THE KEY-LOCK MAN	$1.95
☐	13719	RADIGAN	$1.95
☐	13609	WAR PARTY	$1.95
☐	13882	KIOWA TRAIL	$1.95
☐	13683	THE BURNING HILLS	$1.95
☐	14762	SHALAKO	$2.25
☐	14881	KILRONE	$2.25
☐	20139	THE RIDER OF LOST CREEK	$2.25
☐	13798	CALLAGHEN	$1.95
☐	20180	THE QUICK AND THE DEAD	$2.25
☐	14219	OVER ON THE DRY SIDE	$1.95
☐	13722	DOWN THE LONG HILLS	$1.95
☐	20219	WESTWARD THE TIDE	$2.25
☐	14227	KID RODELO	$1.95
☐	14104	BROKEN GUN	$1.95
☐	13898	WHERE THE LONG GRASS BLOWS	$1.95
☐	14411	HOW THE WEST WAS WON	$1.95

Buy them at your local bookstore or use this handy coupon for ordering:

Now Available!
The Complete Sackett Family Saga in a Boxed Set

THE SACKETT NOVELS
OF LOUIS L'AMOUR

$29.95   (01300-9)

Now, for the first time, the 15 novels of the Sackett family have been collected in four handsome large-size volumes with a beautifully designed gift box. Each volume has a special introduction by L'Amour.

These best-selling L'Amour novels tell the story of the American frontier as seen through the eyes of one bold family, the Sacketts. From generation to generation, the Sacketts conquered the frontier from the wild forests of the East to the dust cattle trails of the Great Plains to the far mountains of the West. Tough and proud, the Sacketts explored the wilderness, settled the towns, established the laws, building a mighty Western tradition of strength and courage.

You can enjoy all these exciting frontier stories of the Sacketts by ordering your boxed set today. And remember, this boxed set is the perfect gift for a L'Amour fan.

Use this handy coupon for ordering: